ILLUSIONS OF LOVE

"Do you think Kristina Brown is dead?" Skye began, savoring the warmth the drink produced.

Creed shrugged. "I'd rather not talk about Kristina. Let's talk about you and me."

"What's there to talk about?"

Creed pierced her with those brooding dark eyes of his. "Let's not play games. Before Rick interrupted, we were going at it pretty hot and heavy."

"And you brought me back to continue where we left off?"

He rose and went to stand by the fireplace. "Not necessarily. Although I wouldn't be opposed, if that's what you want."

Talk about laying your cards on the table! Skye got up, moving closer to him. The back of Creed's hand brushed her cheek as he lowered his lips to hers. She put caution aside, ignoring the voice in the back of her mind warning her to proceed carefully. This man could be dangerous, and not just to her physical well-being. He had the power to flip her heart inside out and wreak havoc with her emotions.

BOOK YOUR PLACE ON OUR WEBSITE AND MAKE THE ARABESQUE ROMANCE CONNECTION!

We've created a customized website just for our very special Arabesque readers, where you can get the inside scoop on everything that's going on with Arabesque romance novels.

When you come online, you'll have the exciting opportunity to:

- View covers of upcoming books

- Learn about our future publishing schedule (listed by publication month and author)

- Find out when your favorite authors will be visiting a city near you

- Search for and order backlist books

- Check out author bios and background information

- Send e-mail to your favorite authors

- Join us in weekly chats with authors, readers and other guests

- Get writing guidelines

- AND MUCH MORE!

Visit our website at
http://www.arabesquebooks.com

ILLUSIONS OF LOVE

Marcia King-Gamble

BET Publications, LLC
www.msbet.com
www.arabesquebooks.com

ARABESQUE BOOKS are published by

BET Publications, LLC
c/o BET BOOKS
One BET Plaza
1900 W Place NE
Washington, D.C. 20018-1211

First Printing: May, 2000
10 9 8 7 6 5 4 3 2 1

Printed in the United States of America

Acknowledgments

This book is dedicated to all of the high-school misfits: the Skyes and Creeds of the world, yesterday's failures, today's successes. A special thanks to my parents, Charles and Cynthia, for realizing I was different. To Dominic Froio who graciously lent his expertise and guidance, sharing with me his experiences as an undercover cop. To Alison Davis, an old school friend, for giving me great insight into the world of the exotic dancer. My gratitude to my critique partners and supportive friends: fellow authors, Linda Anderson, Debbie St. Amand, Marilyn Jordan and Margaret Fraser. May you all find real love and not just the illusion.

One

Abracadabra. He Gonna Reach Out And Grab Ya.

Skyla Walker rolled her eyes and snapped the newspaper shut. "Captions like this make the whole profession look bad," she muttered, struggling into a sitting position.

Skye picked her way across the room, side-stepping the newspaper clippings scattered on the floor of the rented chalet. She pinched the bridge of her nose, thinking of how best to approach this interview with Creed Bennett. Would he remember her?

For months now the media had touted Creed Bennett's return to Mills Creek. He was the local boy who had made good, the prodigal son returning home after a long absence. As far as Skye was concerned, he was scum. Most definitely, Creed Bennett was responsible for the disappearance of at least five women, if not their deaths.

After graduating from high school, the Mighty Creed, as he called himself, had left the little Pocono town of Mills Creek to pursue higher education. Somewhere along the way he'd achieved international fame. Now he was an even better known illusionist than David Copperfield.

Skye snorted at the pretentiousness of the word. "Illusionist! Try magician." For the most part, Creed's following consisted of desperate women of a certain age. Her cousin, Kris, had been one of his victims.

Even at the tender age of sixteen, Creed had shown promise of being a spectacularly good-looking man. He had skin the color of butterscotch and eyes so black they were almost midnight blue. That killer smile had charmed the pants off most of the female population of Mills Creek High. Some would gladly have laid down and died for him. Skye shuddered. Is that what had happened to Kris? Had she lain down and died for Creed?

The phone rang, startling Skye from her reverie. She fumbled through the piles of newspapers, frantically searching for the cordless. She found the instrument just beats before the answering machine picked up.

"Hello."

"Hey, gal. Glad I caught you at home."

Skye smiled, picturing her boss, Peter Martini, on the other end, a lit cigarette clutched between his nubby fingers.

"What's up, Pete?"

Skye's editor cleared his throat, a deep rumbling sound, resonant with the tobacco he regularly inhaled.

"Set for your interview with Creed Bennett?"

"I am."

"This could make front-page news, gal. Be sure to play up the bachelor angle and focus on the fundraiser. What our readers want to know is why he's decided to come home. And uh . . . Skyla . . ."

"Skye."

"Whatever you do . . . don't bring up Kristina Brown. Creed Bennett's not a suspect. No way. No how. This is a human interest story. We want the boy to feel right at home. After all, he's Mills Creek's biggest claim to fame."

"Not to worry. I know what I'm doing."

"Good. You be careful, you hear?"

Now what was that supposed to mean? Skye clicked the off button, disconnecting the phone. It was useless reminding Pete, a man old enough to be her father, and equally as rigid, that she was a veteran reporter. Granted, her previous assignments tended to revolve around the glitzy world of art and entertainment, but five years as staff writer for Le Monde had served her well. As one of the few foreigners, she'd been forced to prove herself time and time again.

A communications and language major, Skye had participated in an exchange program her junior year in college. She'd gone to Paris, fallen for an avant-garde painter, and decided to stay on. While the love affair with Jacques was long over, the one with Paris had never run its course.

She'd been lured back to Pennsylvania by the offer of a senior staff writer's position if she proved herself. To sweeten the pot, the *Pocono Record,* desperately in need of new blood, had agreed to pay her living expenses for six months. Excited about the possibility of doing some feature writing and getting away from fluff, Skye had jumped at the opportunity. Citing a family emergency, she'd taken an extended leave from Le Monde. Unfortunately, Kris's disappearance had provided the perfect excuse.

Skye's entire family had assumed Kris had run off with Creed. The two had supposedly grown close over the years. On several occasions, Creed had flown Kris down to Fort Lauderdale. This last time she hadn't returned. Now there was a nationwide search for her.

Skye's reporter instincts told her something wasn't right. Kris had never been the impulsive type. Nor was she the type to abandon friends and family on a whim. Hoping to find some mention of Kris, Skye had started reading everything she could about Creed. What she'd learned had made her instantly wary. Kris hadn't been the only one to succumb to Creed Bennett's charms. At least five women linked to the Mighty Creed had disappeared. Most recently a decayed body had surfaced in the Everglades. That body had turned out to be Marla St. James. Thank God it hadn't been Kris.

Skye put that thought firmly out of her mind. She glanced at her watch. "Drat!" Fifteen minutes to navigate the treacherous mountain roads and confront the Mighty Creed.

"Lydia, I've been back in town exactly—" Creed propped the receiver between ear and shoulder and glanced at his watch—"three days, four hours, and fifteen minutes. Couldn't this interview have waited?"

In an effort to get his temper under control, Creed inhaled and counted to ten, while Lydia, his publicist, continued to talk non-stop. Finally, he'd had enough.

"Lydia, I don't give a rat's carcass about damage

control. I have nothing to hide. I'm no longer a suspect. I came home for a little r&r, to enjoy the house I built five years ago. I'm exhausted; can't you understand that? The last thing I want to do is answer a bunch of asinine questions some pesky reporter throws my way."

"Listen to me. This is your hometown. Here you're admired and loved. Kids view you as a role model. If you could get out of Mills Creek and hit it big, so can they."

Creed gritted his teeth as Lydia continued rationalizing why this interview was so important.

"Look, Lydia," Creed interrupted. "I haven't a clue who Skyla Walker is. Nor do I care whether she's some hot-shot transplant from Paris. I hate reporters. I just want to be left alone."

He hung up before Lydia could get another word in.

As Creed strolled the length of his solarium, pulling at the neck of his nubby wool sweater, he felt, rather than saw, a pair of eyes on him. Creed nodded in the direction of the hovering man. "Might as well come in, Rick."

His man-Friday didn't need to be told twice. He bounded into the room, narrowly missing the abundance of foliage artfully arranged to look like a tropical jungle. Rick radiated the type of energy Creed wished he had. He flung his lanky body onto the cream-colored sofa and placed Bass Weejuns on the adjacent ottoman. "Your reporter's here," he announced. "And, man, is she fine. Mind if I sit through the interview?"

"I most certainly do." The last thing Creed needed was Rick hanging around talking and making the woman feel welcome. "Where is she now?" Creed asked, not even trying to hide his annoyance.

"Vilma left her cooling her heels in the living room. Man, oh man, she's got a pair of legs on her . . . and a butt . . . wait until you . . ."

Creed quelled him with a look. "Might as well get this over with. Have Vilma bring her in. If we're not done in fifteen minutes, I want you at that door rapping. You're to announce that my other appointment is here."

"Aye, aye, sir." Reluctantly, Rick got up. "Sure I can't stay?"

"No. If you want to hit on the woman, catch her on the way out."

Cutting his eyes at Creed, Rick loped out of the room.

Skye's left eye ticked, a sure sign she was furious. Creed Bennett had some nerve, leaving her here, waiting for what seemed hours. One toe of an expensive leather pump tapped out an erratic rhythm. To pass the time, Skye surveyed the room, grimacing at the opulent surroundings. She was forced to admit the designer had taken understated elegance to the next level. Champagne walls, plush beige carpeting, and a butter-soft wrap around sofa cocooned her in warmth. Huge copper pots filled with ficus plants gave the impression of comfort and coziness. Floor to ceiling windows let in lots of light, creating airiness and providing an unobstructed view of the mountains.

Skye pressed her nose against the glass pane, relishing the coolness. She loved Pennsylvania. She loved her mountains and, in Paris, missed looking out her window and seeing the beautiful reds and golds of the changing leaves. Later, she'd missed the snow-capped peaks and felt a certain emptiness knowing that ski slopes weren't just around the corner. Paris, with all of its upscale sophistication, was nothing like home.

Even so, she'd made a conscious decision to stay away, hoping that with time, painful memories would fade. In Paris she'd metamorphosed from the chunky self-conscious girl with the mouthful of braces, to an acceptable woman. No one would ever call her beautiful, but she'd learned to make the best of herself.

"Harrumph."

Someone cleared his throat behind her. Skye realized she'd been a million miles away. She turned to see a tall, elegant brother eyeing her curiously. A middle-aged woman, wearing an apron, hovered a step behind.

"Skyla Walker?" The dark-skinned man arched an eyebrow.

"Skye," she automatically corrected, hating the formal version of her name. It always reminded her of a prim school teacher.

The man's golden eyes scrutinized her. He stroked a well-trimmed beard and extended a hand. "Rick Morales, at your service. I'm Creed's personal assistant, otherwise known as all-around gopher. He'll see you in the solarium."

"Mrs. Walker, can I get you coffee, tea, water?" Creed's housekeeper asked.

"Ms. Walker. Nothing, thanks." Skye surreptitiously wiped her sweaty palms on the tailored beige skirt that stopped a discreet two inches above the knee. She'd wanted to wear her boots, but it was still too warm.

"Follow me," Creed's housekeeper said.

Rick Morales stepped aside, ushering her ahead with a flourish. Skye smiled her gratitude. She could have sworn he winked at her.

They entered a glass enclosed room that appeared to be perched on the edge of a cliff. From the abundance of potted plants, Skye got the distinct impression she was in the tropics. Her eyes were drawn to the panoramic view unfolding in the valley below. She inhaled deeply, overwhelmed by the kaleidoscope of autumn colors: vivid burgundies, golds, and pinks, tinges of plum, mocha, and beige, all against a background of green carpet made up of the surrounding hills and valleys.

The restless movements of someone to her left attracted her attention. She heard the swish of clothing. Skye's eyes snapped in the direction of the sounds. The housekeeper had somehow noiselessly disappeared and she faced the magician. Creed Bennett was nothing like she remembered. He stared into her face, making no attempt to rise. Managing a smile, Skye forced herself to move toward him.

"Skye Walker," she said, extending her hand and forcing him to get up. He towered over her. She didn't remember him being this tall, his shoulders that broad. He clasped the hand she offered. There wasn't even a hint of a smile.

"I believe you know who I am," Creed Bennett said, in a voice that could only be described as surly.

Skye noticed the expensively cut fawn-colored slacks, the hand-knit sweater that must have cost a

fortune, the loafers that screamed Gucci. This hometown boy had come a long, long way. Creed's father
had been the local drunk, barely able to hold onto
his job at the shoe store. After school and on weekends, Creed had worked at the hardware store to
earn money for a car, or as some said, to help keep
food on the table.

Despite all that, Creed had been one of the most
popular boys at Mills Creek High. That, of course,
had everything to do with his looks and his ability
to keep everyone in stitches. He'd had a quick wit,
and even at that age could lighten the tensest of moments by drawing a nickel out of the dour French
teacher's ear, or an egg from the physics teacher's
toupee. Creed had definitely been the class clown.
The man standing before her now wasn't laughing.
He was nothing like the jovial boy she remembered.

That boy had called her up and asked her to go
to the junior prom with him. He'd stood her up,
choosing instead to go with that year's homecoming
queen. She'd sat at home crying, drowning her sor-
rows in Boone's Farm. He'd never apologized.

"Ms. Walker?" Creed's gritty voice drew her back
to the present. They stood facing each other. "Would
you like to sit?" he asked, reluctantly.

Skye lowered herself into a leather club chair opposite him, using that time to gather her composure.
She felt Creed Bennett's gaze on her face and flushed.
He still had the most beautiful eyes. She busied herself
removing a notepad, pen, and recorder from the
roomy pocketbook she'd set on the floor before her.

"Do we know each other?" Creed asked, surprising
her.

Skye was tempted to lie. The fact that he'd even

had to ask indicated that she wasn't the faintest memory. But Mills Creek was a small town and eventually it would get out.

"We went to school together," she offered.

"We did?"

"Ummm hmmm."

"I would have remembered," he murmured.

She wasn't sure she'd heard him right. "Excuse me?"

"Nothing. Shall we carry on with this . . . uh, interview?"

Skye watched him pace the length of the room, skillfully navigating around the profusion of greenery. He flexed his shoulders and made sweeping circles with his head. Creed Bennett was tense—very tense. Skye crossed one leg over the other, adjusted her skirt, and set the recorder in motion. "Ready when you are," she said.

Creed's black eyes fixed on her. "What is it you'd like to know?"

Skye forced a bright smile and worked on making her voice sound normal. "The ladies would like to know why you're back in Mills Creek."

Creed ran a finger through short cropped curls. He took a long time answering. "Ladies?" he chuckled, mirthlessly. "Mills Creek's my home."

"They know that," Skye said evenly. "But you haven't made it home in . . . what is it? . . . ten . . . twelve years? Why now?"

Creed sighed and tugged at the neck of his sweater. "Ms. Walker, I built a rather expensive home here five years ago, which I've never used." He gestured to his surroundings. "I've been so busy working, I've never had the time to use it. What is it they say? All work and no play makes Creed a dull boy . . ."

"That's right. You've been in demand," Skye said, somewhat impatiently. "You've been touring—worshiped by the international jetset."

Creed had the grace to blush.

"Tell me, how come in all these years," Skye pressed, "you've never found time for marriage . . . relationships?" She knew she was pushing the envelope.

"I've been involved," Creed growled. "I just never found anyone I wanted to marry. Must we get personal?"

"Ah, but it's a question our readers would like to have answered."

Creed glared at her. Skye decided to back off. She asked a few more questions and dutifully recorded his answers.

"It's good of you to perform at the benefit," she said, winding down. "All the proceeds go to sickle cell anemia and breast cancer research. Certainly worthy causes."

Creed nodded. His pacing had taken him steps from her. She could smell a whiff of expensive cologne, something woodsy and masculine.

"Were you in my homeroom?" Creed said, out of the blue.

She'd sat next to Kris, right behind him. It was the perfect opening, too good to pass up. "Yes. Me and Kristina Brown—the woman who's missing."

Skye heard Creed's sharp intake of breath, felt his gaze on her face. She scribbled busily, refusing to look at him. A sharp knock on the door created a welcome diversion. The same lanky man with the beard appeared, the one who'd introduced himself as Rick Morales, all around gopher.

"Creed," the man said, flopping onto the arm of Skye's chair. "Your afternoon appointment is here." He turned to Skye. "Did you get everything you needed?"

"She did," Creed said, already retreating. "Except for information on Kristina Brown—the real reason she's here." Creed turned to give her a searing look. "Let's save that topic for another day."

Flashing his killer smile, he closed the door firmly behind him.

Two

"That Skye Walker is an interesting piece of work," Rick said, between bites of salmon.

"That she is. Pass the rolls, please." Creed pointed to the covered wicker basket holding Vilma's freshly baked bread.

Rick shoved the basket containing cornbread and crispy rolls in Creed's direction while Vilma, their housekeeper, stood holding silent vigil in the background.

"A rare combination of beauty and intelligence wrapped into one," Rick added, darting a look at Creed.

"She's a reporter."

"Yes, a very attractive one."

"Hmmm."

"Is hmmm a yes or a no?"

"Neither." Creed glowered and shoved a forkful of fish into his mouth. He chased it with an expensive Bordeaux, then set the glass down. "Rick, I don't want to talk about the Walker woman, or any reporter for that matter. The entire breed irritates me. Let's discuss my schedule."

Rick shrugged. His grin was irrepressible. "I

wouldn't judge every woman by Chantal. She was bad judgment on your part, Creed. Even I could tell she was a barracuda."

"Rick!"

"Okay. Okay. Back to business." Rick bit into a piece of golden cornbread. "Hugh called. One of Oprah's gopher's wants to know if you'll do the show."

"When's this?"

"In a couple of months."

"I don't know about that."

"Come on, Creed. You love Oprah. You support everything she stands for. And it's a terrific opportunity to plug *The Magic In You* and mention the scholarship fund you've set up."

"I'd rather not commit."

Rick had a good point, though. The new book needed the publicity and he hated to turn Oprah down. She'd been supportive of him from the very beginning. Now he'd become a regular on her show. Still, for sanity's sake he needed to be out of the limelight.

Speculation and not-so-subtle questions from strangers were beginning to wear him down. He was finally getting used to being home again and was looking forward to unwinding in his Pocono haven. In Mills Creek, schoolmates remembered him as the class clown, and older folk considered him Jed's boy. They weren't at all in awe of him.

"Oh, come on, Creed. Don't tell me you're planning on vegging in this God-forsaken place for long."

"That's exactly what I intend to do," Creed said, rising and tossing his napkin on the table. "I'm here

to de-stress. And I'm going to start off by finding
Tikka and taking her for a walk."

"If we're stuck here for months," Rick called after
him, "I'm going to make a play for that Walker
woman."

"Suit yourself."

Creed headed in the direction of the den, confident the German shepherd languished on the new
sofa.

Creed threw the Jag into park. Tikka, seated in the
passenger seat, panted loudly, drooling all over the
black leather interior. Creed had decided to take the
shepherd to the old schoolyard, where she could
roam free and where there were fewer opportunities
for her to run into squirrels. He'd heard the old
high school had been closed down and boarded
up—abandoned, actually. A newer, more modern
version, had been built up the street a bit.

"Come on, girl," Creed said, opening the passenger door.

Salivating, the remnants of her slime all over his
dashboard, Tikka bounded out.

Mills Creek High's grounds were the perfect spot
for the dog to get some much needed exercise.
There were numerous hills and dales and a small
copse, where Tikka would have fun exploring. Creed
remembered the thicket of trees had been the
school's much used lovers' lane. He'd had his first
sexual experience there.

Creed unhooked Tikka's leash. The dog raced off,
immediately making a beeline for the wooded area.
He shoved his hands in his pockets and headed in

the opposite direction, where he knew the track fields were.

It was a glorious autumn evening and Creed inhaled the crisp air, pushed the sleeves of the cable-knit sweater to his elbows, and looked up into the rickety bleachers. There he'd been cheered on to victory more times than he could count.

Immediately he was transported to another time, another place. He'd loved Mills Creek High. School had been a sanctuary; a place to retreat, where only he was the focus of attention. Adults didn't shout or scream threats at each other there, nor was he subjected to the back of anyone's hand. At school he'd come into his own and found peace.

Growing up the son of the local drunk hadn't been easy. An only child, Creed had shouldered responsibility at an early age. He'd acted as both son and surrogate husband to his abused mother. Teenage Creed had been responsible for keeping food on the table and giving his mother the affection she so desperately craved. What little money Jed made got drunk up.

Enough of this maudlin stuff, Creed thought. He focused on the interview he'd given earlier that day. Skye Walker had said she'd been in his class. Funny that he couldn't place her. Of course he'd never admit it to Rick, but there was something about the woman he found attractive.

She had skin the color of burnished amber and a set of legs destined to stop men in their tracks. She had impossibly high cheekbones and a full pair of lips that reminded him of an exotic super model. It was her eyes that drew him, though. Long, long lashes, opened wide to reveal a pair of round hazel eyes. Despite her obvious control, those eyes had flashed animosity at him. Why? he wondered. What was her relationship to Kristina Brown?

A high pitched yelping got Creed's attention, followed by the more familiar woofing that was Tikka's. Creed loped off in the direction of the woods, hoping that Tikka had not cornered some tiny animal and gotten herself into a fight. Luckily, it was still light enough to see, and he picked up his pace as the intensity of the barking increased.

As he drew closer, a woman's shrill voice shouted orders. "Back off, you big bully. Leave Hogan alone. Come, baby. Come to Mommy."

Breaking into a run, Creed pushed his way through the brambles and flew up an overgrown path. He stifled a grin at the scene in front of him. A Jack Russell terrier, a sixth of the size of Tikka, had his shepherd by the throat. The animal's back legs swung back and forth precariously. Tikka, not one to lose her temper easily, made low growling sounds, warning the animal that she could easily be dessert.

The attacking dog's owner's back was toward Creed. She brandished a stick. "Get back here, Hogan," the woman shouted, "before that brute makes you his dinner."

"Tikka," Creed shouted. "Heel."

The shepherd appeared to shrug her shoulders, easily dislodging the smaller animal. The Jack Russell landed in a little heap about a foot from its owner. Whimpering, Tikka raced over to Creed. The terrier followed, teeth bared.

"Call your crazy dog off," Creed commanded.

Skye Walker turned blazing eyes on him. "Don't you know better than to let that beast run around unsupervised?" She scooped the Jack Russell up in her arms.

The ferocity of her words stopped Creed dead in his tracks, that and the loathing flashing from those beautiful hazel eyes. "And your dog was on its leash, of course?" Creed eyed the bright red lead Skye dangled from one hand.

She at least had the grace to blush. "Hogan and I have been coming here for months . . . ," Skye sputtered. "Ever since we got back to town. We've never encountered another living soul, up until now."

Tikka remained obediently at heel, making high-pitched whining sounds. The terrier, sheltered in its owner's arms, yelped piteously, acting very much the aggrieved. Creed crossed his arms and surveyed Skye Walker's flushed face. She wore a stylish, spiked haircut, in slight disarray from attempting to keep the dogs at bay. She reminded him of a pixie.

"Back in town from where?" Creed quizzed, although he knew the answer. Lydia, his publicist, had already filled him in.

Skye narrowed her eyes. "Paris," she said stonily.

Creed smiled and arched an eyebrow. "Parlez-vous Francais?"

"Fluently. Do you?"

Creed made a motion with his hand. "I get by."

He suddenly had a memory of an overweight teen-ager with a mouthful of braces whom the guys had picked on mercilessly. She'd had a weird name. What was it they'd called her? Skywalker. No, Luke—the hero of the "Star Wars" movie. But the way they'd taunted her had been cruel. He also remembered the sick joke they'd played. He'd found out about it years after, too late to rectify it. Kareem Davis, one of the jocks, pretending to be Creed, had telephoned the girl, inviting her to the prom. She'd been stood up and everyone knew it. The junior class laughed about the prank for weeks.

As much as Creed disliked reporters, he felt the need to right an ancient wrong. He hoped Skye had forgotten the unpleasant incident. Although reluctant to bring if up after all these years, he could at least offer an olive branch. The sky overhead was growing rapidly darker and the air more crisp. It was now or never.

"Truce," Creed said, extending a hand. "What say we head for Eve's diner? I'll buy you a cup of coffee and anything else your heart desires."

Skye scowled at him as if she couldn't believe her ears. "And what are we to do with the dogs?"

"Take them home."

She seemed to contemplate his offer and eventually came to a decision. "I'll meet you at Eve's in twenty minutes. If you get there first, order me a hot chocolate and a slice of Eve's apple pie. And, Mr. Bennett, this time, don't stand me up!"

Skye sat in one of the red vinyl booths at the rear of the diner, drumming her fingers against the Formica table. She'd been there ten minutes and still no Creed. He'd better show up.

Skye remembered the other time he hadn't shown. She'd sat for hours in the white chiffon dress with the pink sweetheart roses on her wrists, waiting. Her expectations had been so high that night. Too high. A dreamboat like Creed Bennett had asked her out.

When it dawned on Skye she'd been stood up, she'd downed a bottle of Boone's Farm and taken a pair of scissors to the dress. Lucky for her, she'd passed out before she could do damage to herself.

The tinkle of laughter and the buzz of conversation ebbed and flowed over the music of the old juke box. Eve's diner hadn't changed much since high school. Decorated in sixties chrome and vinyl, it was a place where rich and poor celebrated the passages of life. Even the waitresses were an institution. Skye recognized the ageing brunette with the padded bra, hovering. What was it they'd called her? Torpedo Tits; T.T. for short.

"How about a cuppa coffee, hon?" T.T. squinted at Skye, snapped her gum, and fumbled for a pad in her stained apron pocket.

"Bring the lady a cup of hot chocolate and a big slice of Eve's apple pie. I'll have my coffee black." Creed's deep voice came from someplace behind her.

The waitress's hand flew to her ample chest. Turning, she spotted Creed. "Why, Creed Bennett, you're a sight for sore eyes. I was just saying to Jed I haven't seen you around in awhile." She preened and patted her poodle cut.

"How are you, Daisy?" Creed kissed the woman's highly rouged cheeks. From out of the air, he produced a long-stemmed red rose and presented it to T.T.

The waitress reddened. "Oh, Creed," she gushed, "you're such a tease." Obviously pleased, she sniffed the bloom and turned away.

Creed placed a hand on Skye's shoulder and squeezed. "Have you been waiting long?"

Despite her resolve not to let him get to her, the timbre of his voice and the gentleness of his touch set her heart aflutter. She hoped he didn't notice her hands trembling. Skye reminded herself she was on a mission. She was here to find out as much about Kristina as she could. She couldn't let herself drown in those blue-black eyes.

"You're fifteen minutes late," Skye snapped.

Creed slid into the seat across from her. "Sorry. Had to return a phone call."

T.T. returned, bearing a coffee pot and a tray holding Skye's hot chocolate and pie.

"Cocoa and pie, hon." Both were unceremoniously set down before Skye. Creed's coffee was poured with a lot more finesse.

Skye wrapped her hands around the warm mug. "You must know the entire town is looking forward to you performing at the benefit. You're quite the draw. Certainly the biggest name this small town has ever attracted."

Creed smiled. "I wanted to give something back to the community. Sickle cell and breast cancer are both worthy causes."

Skye remembered hearing something about Creed's mother dying from breast cancer. Now wasn't the time to bring that up.

"Will you be there?" Creed asked, abruptly.

"Wouldn't miss it for the world." Skye sipped on her chocolate, savoring one of the minuscule marshmallows floating on the top.

Looking her full in the face, Creed set his mug down. "You said you were back from Paris. How long were you there?"

"Seven years."

"What brought you home?"

"This job."

"You packed up and left Europe to work as a reporter for the Pocono Record?" His voice sounded incredulous. His tone irked her.

"What's so bad about working for the Pocono Record? Reporting is an honest living."

"Is it?" Creed's voice remained even, but the temperature around them dropped several degrees.

Skye popped another marshmallow in her mouth and refused to be baited. "Do you have a problem with reporters, or just me?"

Unexpectedly, he chuckled, and she was amazed at how much his face softened. The laugh lines around his eyes fanned out, and the tips of his fingers brushed her hand lightly. She couldn't let those picture perfect features get to her.

"I did say truce, didn't I?" he said, almost absentmindedly. "Why the interest in Kristina Brown?"

Skye blinked and thought quickly. "She was a classmate. Now she's disappeared and her parents are worried sick."

"And, naturally, you've assumed I had something to do with her disappearance." Creed's face remained expressionless.

Skye took a long sip of chocolate and a tiny bite of pie. "Last I heard, you were dating her."

"You heard wrong."

Skye wondered how to phrase this delicately. "The few times you came home you were seen around town together. From what I've heard, she spent more time at your place than hers. Kristina was a bank teller, hardly in a position to fly first class. Yet it's common knowledge you paid for her airline tickets.

Her parents tell me when she visited Fort Lauderdale she stayed with you."

"You've been talking with the Browns?"

"I'm a reporter. What do you think?"

Creed's eyes narrowed. A muscle at his jaw worked overtime. "You don't want to know what I think. So that's the real reason you agreed to meet me here. You need information." His eyes flashed dangerously. "What is it you'd like to know about Kristina?"

"More coffee, hon?" T. T. returned, brandishing a pot. She ignored Skye.

He placed his palm over the top of the mug. "No, thanks, Daisy." Reluctantly, the waitress skittered away.

Skye noticed Creed's long, slender fingers, and the way the tips wrapped around the base of the mug. He had hands like an artist. Had those fingers wrapped themselves around Kris's neck and choked the life out of her?

"I'd like to find Kristina," Skye persisted.

"Why?" Creed's blue-black eyes scanned her face, issuing a silent challenge.

She'd never met anyone this direct.

"Like I said, she was a classmate and a friend. The last anyone heard, she left Mills Creek to be with you."

He knocked back what remained of his drink. "Would you believe me if I told you I haven't seen Kristina in months?"

He had to be lying. From everything she'd learned, Kris knew no one else in Fort Lauderdale except for Creed. There would be no other reason she'd get on a plane and fly south.

"If that's so," Skye said, "then you must know of

others in Fort Lauderdale she might have visited. People I can speak with."

He shrugged. "Kristina was a private person and very much a loner. You should know that. She told you what she chose to tell you."

Skye wasn't buying his story one bit. Her reporter's instincts told her he was being evasive. He knew more than he was saying. She smiled and dug into her pie, hoping to distract him. "How long will you be in Mills Creek?" she asked.

"As long as it takes to unwind."

"Stressed out? I thought an international performer's life was a pampered one. You've got people to wait on you hand and foot, and a watch dog to handle the mundane details most artists don't want to be bothered with."

His eyebrows rose. He squinted at her. "I take it you're referring to Rick?"

"Ummm hmmm."

This conversation had gone on long enough. They were going around in circles. She'd agreed to meet him partially out of curiosity and partially because she'd hoped that he'd say something that might give her a clue as to Kris's whereabouts. She'd also had this insatiable need to see him up close and personal again—to convince herself that she was immune to the polished sophisticated man that he'd become.

But as Skye sat, refusing to squirm under his glare, all the hurt of prom night came flooding back. Even back then, Creed Bennett had been heartless. He'd had a love-them-and-leave-them attitude. Why, at this late date, would he develop a conscience?

Three

"No! No! No! Don't smile."

Betsy, Creed's makeup artist, placed plump hands on her hips and pretended to glare at him. She circled, wielding sponges and brushes, squinting to repair the damage he'd done. Makeup was Creed's least favorite part of getting ready for any performance. But thinking of the ridiculous scene with Skye and her ferocious Jack Russell terrier had made him smile.

"Okay, all done. You can get up now." Betsy playfully tickled the tip of Creed's nose with one of her brushes. He snarled at the redhead as she pranced away. In the spirit of Halloween she'd dressed as a corpulent black cat.

Creed had hired Betsy after watching her do an incredible make-over on a customer at a Fort Lauderdale department store. Betsy had been an employee of Burdine's. Sensing that her talent was being wasted, Creed had made her an offer on the spot. Since then, she'd become a valued part of his entourage.

Creed rose, buttoned the gold button on his cherry-red jacket, and brushed a fleck of lint off his black

wool pants. He smoothed the collar of the turtleneck
sweater until it felt right.

"Why didn't you wear a costume?" Betsy groused.

Creed arched an eyebrow and scowled at her.
"This is my costume, woman. I wear it to do shows;
otherwise I wouldn't be caught dead in red and
black."

Betsy snorted. "My point exactly. I've seen that outfit so many times I actually have nightmares about
it. It's Halloween; couldn't you have gotten wild and
crazy, and dressed the part of a wizard or sorcerer?
You could have done the hat and cape thing, complete with moons and stars."

Creed shook his head and swallowed his laughter.
"You're suggesting I dress the illusionist part." He
wiggled his eyebrows and made a face. Everyone
knew his chubby makeup artist was one card short
of a full deck. Still, crazy or not, he loved her zan-
iness. She never took him too seriously. Creed
tweaked Betsy's tail. "Sorry, what you see is what
you get."

"Pl-ee-eeze! That's so old." Betsy preened, arching
her back like the cat she was dressed as. "What was
so funny earlier?"

How could he explain that he'd been thinking of
Skye Walker and that snippy little dog of hers? The
way her hazel eyes had flashed dangerously at him.
The way she'd taken him on, not backing down one
bit. If he mentioned her name, he'd only open himself up to questions, and he wasn't prepared to discuss Skye Walker yet. Especially with one of his
employees.

Creed wondered if Skye was in the audience. He
felt a rush of adrenaline just thinking about her. A

strange reaction, given the woman had a tendency to get on his last nerve. She'd said she planned on attending the benefit, but he hadn't seen her since that evening at Eve's. Her plans could easily have changed.

Rick burst into the dressing room, rubbing his hands gleefully. He circled Creed. Betsy put on her mittens, waved a paw at them, and padded by. "Got to do Felicity," she said, closing the door behind her.

"You've got a packed house," Rick said, flinging himself onto an old sofa. "There's a line outside that's a good city block long. They've started turning people away."

"Good. The proceeds should be bountiful then. When am I on?"

"After the Whitney Houston impersonator."

"Oh, Lord!"

Creed recalled how hokey these small-town productions tended to be. He reminded himself, not for the first time, that all the money would benefit his two favorite charities. It wasn't as if he'd planned an extravagant performance. The old playhouse's stage simply couldn't accommodate the type of elaborate production he was used to putting on. He'd keep his illusions simple and the whole thing would run about twenty minutes.

"Some old guy's looking for you," Rick said, sailing a note in Creed's direction. "Said to give you this."

Creed palmed the paper then pocketed it. He already knew who it was from. He would save it to read later.

"How are Felicity's stage jitters?"

"The usual. Says she feels like throwing up. Never

mind the woman's assisted you in front of audiences twenty times bigger than we'll see tonight."

Creed poured himself a glass of water. "Give her a break; she'll calm down. She's been doing this . . ."

"Two months and two days," Rick filled in. "Guess who I bumped into?"

"You know I hate guessing games."

Rick sat up and crossed one long leg over the other. "Skye Walker's out front interviewing your audience. She looks particularly fetching tonight in her Cleopatra costume. I told her you might do a quick interview. That's all she needs to complete her article."

"You did what?"

Rick held up both hands, stilling Creed's protest. "Hey, I said maybe. And I said after the show, when you're more relaxed." Rick smiled slyly. "Thought you didn't mind me making a play for her."

"I don't."

There was a soft rap at the door. Rick bounded to his feet and threw the door wide open. "Yes?"

A petite champagne-skinned beauty smiled shyly at him. "Esther says it's twenty minutes before show-time. She wants to know if you need anything. Water? Coffee, maybe?"

Esther Hesseman headed up the local breast can-cer awareness group. She, along with a dedicated bunch of volunteers from the sickle cell foundation, had been the one to come up with the idea of a joint fund raiser.

Rick deferred the question to Creed, again flop-ping down on the sagging couch. "Creed?"

Approaching the door, Creed smiled at the timid young woman. He snapped his fingers and a trio of doves descended to perch on his visitor's shoulders. They cooed softly before flying back to him.

"Oh, my!" The woman's hands flew to her chest.

Creed ruffled the birds' feathers. "Tell Esther not to worry. Everything's just fine."

Skye sat in the cramped theater, mentally going over the day's happenings. Her mind wasn't on the duet on stage singing a syrupy romantic ballad. Earlier, her sources at the Miami Herald had called to say Marla St. James had been sexually molested before she was killed. The coroner had likened the murder to an old newsworthy case where rough sex had been the defense used. Marla's body had been found with a red silk scarf tied around her neck.

Skye had discovered that Marla St. James once worked for Creed. She'd been his makeup artist. The press claimed the two had had a relationship. But for some unknown reason, Marla had been terminated. When she disappeared, it had been assumed she'd left town. Now, three months later, her rotting body had surfaced in an Everglades swamp.

Another performer took the stage and Skye ticked off the names of the women who were missing. Tamara Linley had, at one time, been Creed's administrative assistant and Gal Friday. Barbara Conway had been an intern who'd worked as Creed's stage assistant one summer. Ona Di Santis had cleaned his house. Add to that Marla and now Kristina. The list of women kept growing.

True, only one had turned up dead, but how could you explain five missing women—the common link being Creed? Skye focused her attention on the stage. A comedian delivered pat one-liners with a certain aplomb. The audience tittered and clapped. She shifted in her seat, restless now. How much longer until Creed?

Skye browsed through the program. Four more acts and he would be on. He would be the grand finale. Could she handle a juggler, another comedian, and a Whitney Houston impersonator in between? Nah. She needed fresh air.

The press were all seated in prime fifth-row seats, close enough to see the action without having to tilt their heads back. Skye saw the competition busily scribbling: a reporter from the Daily News, another from the Post, and her arch-rival from the Scranton Times. She was the only one with the exclusive interview with Creed. If they went to press tomorrow, she would scoop them all. She owed Rick Morales.

"Excuse me," Skye whispered, stepping over the toes of the local anchorman seated beside her. In the dim theater, Russ Jackson, her photographer, dressed like Mark Antony, shot her a curious look. Skye shook her head, signaling he wasn't needed.

When Skye arrived in the lobby, angry people milled about demanding non-existent seating. She shoved her way out front, looking forward to the cool night air and less crowded conditions. Outside, a fairly large group still gathered. Skye found a quiet spot, removed a cell phone from her bag, and dialed.

"Pocono Record," Peter Martini's gravelly voice answered, on the fourth ring.

"Hi, it's Skye."

"Why are you calling? The performance should have started by now."

"It did. I expected voice mail to pick up, not you. Planned on leaving a message."

Pete chuckled. "That boring, huh? Creed Bennett hasn't been on yet or you wouldn't be calling."

Skye sighed. "What makes you say that?"

"You're obsessed with the man. No way would you be talking to me if the Mighty Creed were on."

"Nonsense." Even as she protested, she felt herself flushing. Treacherous hormones were getting the better of her. "I've arranged another interview with him after the show."

Pete chortled. "That's my gal. Think we can go to press tomorrow?"

"Plan on it. After the performance, I'll stop by the Halloween party then head back to the office."

Nearby, a grizzled, elderly man had attracted the crowd's attention. He appeared drunk, and his wobbling voice floated on the evening breeze.

"That's my son in there. My boy. Big time magician." The man tilted a silver flask and swallowed greedily. "Salud, Mighty Creed, now that you're famous you don't know your own father." He wiped his mouth on the back of his coat sleeve.

That disreputable drunk couldn't be Jed. After Creed's mother's death, she'd heard his drinking had increased and he'd been hospitalized more often than not. She'd assumed he was dead.

"Got to go, Pete. Looks like I have an opportunity to interview Creed's father," Skye said, disconnecting the call.

She approached the old man, who was being heckled by the crowd. The young people milling about didn't seem to believe his claim. They challenged him.

"Sure you are. Creed Bennett's a big-time star. What's his father doing out on the street and not in there?" A punk type, with his eyebrow and lip pierced, pointed to the theater.

"Creed Bennett don't have no broken down drunk for a father," a teenager in baggy jeans and over-sized platform boots sneered, lips clamped around a smoldering cigarette.

"Who you calling a broken-down drunk?" Jed staggered in the direction of the girl, shaking his fist at her.

"Stay away from me," the teenager shrieked. "I'll call the police."

Skye planted herself firmly between the two. Even from that distance she could smell the booze on Jed. "Mr. Bennett, I'm Skye Walker from the Pocono Record. Would you have time for a quick interview?" she asked.

"See!" Jed swaggered, puffing up his chest. "Cleopatra knows who I am. She knows I'm somebody."

Someone tossed the core of an apple at him. It narrowly missed Skye but bounced off Jed's shoulder. He swung a fist in the general direction of where it came from.

"Mr. Bennett," Skye said, tugging on his tattered coat, "it will only take a few minutes." Even as she said it, she felt like a heel. In Jed's current state, what kind of coherent interview could he give? Nothing that reflected well on Creed. She ignored her feelings of guilt and pressed on. She was a reporter, and a good one at that. This was her job. She couldn't let her emotions get in the way.

" 'Course I can make a few minutes for the press," Jed hiccupped. He appeared barely able to stand up straight. "Creed's my boy," he bragged to the crowd, ignoring their derision.

Skye pushed the play button on her recorder and shoved it under Jed's nose. Nearby a strobe light flashed. Russ, her photographer, had followed her out. Skye squelched her conscience and began questioning Jed.

Creed stood backstage, Felicity at his side.

"You're on next," a volunteer whispered.

"Ready?" Creed squeezed Felicity's hand, hoping to reassure his quivering assistant.

"Ready."

On stage, the Whitney Houston impersonator concluded her song and the Master of Ceremonies took over. "Let's have a big hand for Whitney," the overly enthusiastic announcer boomed.

The audience, in a good mood, complied. The curtain descended and the playhouse plunged into darkness, giving the stagehands time to put the few props Creed had requested in place. Creed had chosen a Temptations song. The music started up softly then soared. The audience sang along and swayed to "Just My Imagination." Fingers snapped. The hissing sound of the smoke machine signaled it was time to take their positions on stage. Holding Felicity's hand, Creed parted the curtains and stepped out. After a minute or two, a lone spotlight illuminated them. The crowd went wild, their deafening applause forcing the announcer to shout.

"Put your hands together for Mills Creek's own world-famous illusionist, Creed Bennett."

A roar came from the audience as Creed and Fe-

licity, levitated a good four feet off the floor, smiled
and waved.

Skye slipped back into her seat just as Creed asked
for a volunteer from the audience. She'd had a devil
of a time getting away from Jed. Once he'd started
talking, he didn't want to stop.

Russ elbowed her. "Come on, girl, go." She hesitated too long, and a shapely young woman with a
head full of braids raised her hand and was chosen
instead.

Skye found herself mesmerized by Creed. On
stage, he appeared larger than life, a dynamic force,
and an extremely handsome one. His stage assistant,
a tall willowy type, who looked like she should be on
a runway, sat on a chair. Making a great production
of it, Creed threw a shimmering cloth over his assistant's head, then began an intricate dance around
her. The crowd was beside itself. Skye could see why.
All that undulating hip movement had set a number
of female hormones into high gear. Reluctantly, she
admitted to herself that the man had a nice tush.

The volunteer from the audience joined Creed in
his sensual dance. He gestured to her to remove the
cloth. The audience gasped, spotting the empty
chair. A loud burst of applause threatened to bring
the house down. Seconds later, Creed's assistant
came dancing down the aisle. The audience was on
its feet, shouting cat calls and whistling so loudly that
Skye's ears rang. The standing ovation continued for
several minutes, even after the theater was blanketed
in darkness and the curtain descended.

No doubt about it, Creed Bennett was good. Given

the little theater's limitations, it had been a tremendous performance. Skye suddenly couldn't wait to see him. She convinced herself the reason for her excitement was the promised backstage interview. That, and the one just completed with Jed, would certainly make for scintillating reading and add more ummph to her article.

Who was she kidding? She, like the rest of Mills Creek's females, had been sucked in by his charisma and good looks. She was star struck. No, she'd been star struck since the day she'd first laid eyes on Creed Bennett—what was it, twelve years ago? Even now, old, well-concealed feelings were beginning to surface. It was nothing she wanted to act on—nothing she would even consider. She couldn't betray Kris.

Rick slapped Creed on the back. "Superb performance, as usual."

Ignoring his assistant, Creed continued to cream make up off his face.

"You know that old guy who wanted to see you?"

Creed grunted. "Yeah."

"He got carted off by the police. There was some kind of altercation and they took him away for being drunk and disorderly."

Creed shrugged. Typical Jed. He remembered the unread note in his pocket. He had no particular desire to see his father. He blamed him for his mother's death. Even if he hadn't directly caused it, stress had triggered his mother's cancer. Married to an alcoholic, Nina's life had not been easy. She'd waited too long to seek medical help and the disease had spread to other parts of her body.

Creed remembered how angry he'd been after her death. Angry and bitter. Even so, he'd tried to reach out to his father, especially when he'd learned he'd lost his job at the shoe store. But Jed hadn't seemed to want his help. Creed wasn't a big name then. Jed always considered a magician to be right up there with a loser and told him so in no uncertain terms. Still, Creed sent money every month, increasing the amount when the bank threatened to foreclose on the family home. Jed drank up every last bit of that money and they'd lost the house anyway. Creed finally decided not to be an enabler.

Rick's voice intruded on his thoughts. "Think you'll have time to see Skye Walker? She wants to ask a few wrap-up questions and snap some behind-the-scene shots."

Creed groaned and wiped his face on a towel. "Okay. She can have five minutes."

Rick rubbed his palms together and winked at Creed. "Shouldn't be such a hardship talking to that babe. I'll gladly switch places if you'd like." Creed glowered at him. Undeterred, Rick continued, "Incidentally, you need to put in an appearance at the Halloween party."

"What Halloween party?"

"The one at the town hall."

"You're pushing it." He was bone weary and feeling every one of his twenty-eight years. He wanted to go to bed. Attending a noisy party meant being pleasant and constantly on. "What time does this thing start?" Creed asked.

"Nine-thirty. Kareem's meeting you there, remember?"

Kareem Davis, his old friend, was back in town because of a sick mother. "An hour, Rick. That's it. Then I'm out of there."

A knock on the door heralded Skye's arrival. Rick threw the door open. "Hey, right on time."

Creed groaned, "Hope this doesn't take up my night." He tossed the damp towel at Rick. "Let's get this over with," he grumbled, just as Skye was ushered in.

"It won't," Skye said, casting a cursory look around the dressing room. She had a coat draped over her arm. A young man dressed in a ridiculous Roman costume trailed her. He carried a camera.

"Russ is my photographer," Skye introduced.

Creed's eyes roamed her bare midriff. Skye Walker had chosen the perfect costume to showcase her figure. She could easily put Cleopatra to shame. He made himself remember why she was there.

"Sit. What is it you want to know?"

Rick patted a spot on the couch next to him, but Skye declined the seat. She motioned to the photographer to start snapping pictures. Creed flashed his practiced smile at the camera, as dozens of strobe lights went off.

Why was he letting this pushy reporter get to him? After Chantal he should have learned.

Four

"Looking good, Mama."

Skye ignored the biker's comments and followed the line of costumed revelers into the town hall. It seemed that all of Mills Creek had come out. Flanked by Russ, as Mark Antony in an imperial purple tunic, and two Hershey kisses in silver and gold foil, Skye found she was anxious to get this over with. She longed to return to the office.

She was jostled by partiers in creative costumes. Ahead of her a giant condom wobbled. The man, elevated by stilts, carried a huge brunette blow-up doll. He waved a garish sign: "Safe Sex Practiced." Others weren't so outlandish. They stuck to the more traditional, and the abundance of French maids and witches was truly awesome.

Skye recognized some of the women she'd gone to high school with. They clutched the hands of young children and spouses. If she had stayed in Mills Creek, she too might have married. She squelched the thought as soon as it had surfaced. No regrets; she'd chosen career over family. She focused on how worn down and tired the women looked. At twenty-seven, they seemed twice their age.

Skye stopped to chat with a couple dressed as the King and Queen of Spades. She recognized them as being in her senior class but couldn't remember their names.

"Did you attend the benefit?" she asked the man.

"Sure did, Skye."

"So what did you think?"

Russ snapped a picture as the female chimed in. Her cheeks were flame red. "That Creed Bennett is awesome. He always has been. I was captivated."

Skye moved on to another couple and their kids. The husband was dressed as bug repellant and his family, ants. By the time she was through interviewing them and others, she was sick to death of hearing about how wonderful Creed Bennett was. Everyone made it sound like Creed was the best thing since sliced bread.

Inside, the town hall had been decorated to represent an autumn harvest. Scarecrows stood guard at every corner, and bales of hay provided additional seating. Colorful leaves were strung like garlands, and sheaves of corn hung off the ceilings. Already, kegs of beer had been tapped and people gulped from oversized glasses. Against the walls, huge buffet tables held platters of cold cuts and salads, and on the dance floor, a handful of younger people gyrated spasmodically. Skye was tempted to clap both hands over her ears to shut out the noise of an awful rap tune.

"I'm getting a beer. Want anything?" Russ asked, heading off toward one of the makeshift bars at the back of the room.

"No, thanks. I'll find us a good spot to take pictures and watch the festivities."

After Russ left, Skye looked around for a place where they could view the party without being obvious. She found a vacant table in a remote part of the room and removed her coat. Simultaneously, she spotted Rick Morales and Creed inundated by fans. Creed was at his most charming, flashing his devastating smile. The women practically swooned. Rick must have sensed her looking at them. He waved, smiled, and beckoned her over. Creed, looking bored, merely nodded in her direction. He'd been that same way when she'd interviewed him after the performance—bored, sullen, providing one-syllable answers to her questions.

Rick Morales whispered something to Creed then headed her way. *What did he want?* Skye wondered. Self-consciously, she smoothed the long skirt and adjusted the midriff blouse of the Cleopatra costume. Sensing Creed looking at her, she refused to make eye contact.

"Hey, good-looking, how about some champagne?" Rick waved a bottle of Moet at her.

"No, thanks."

"Come on, don't be a party pooper; live a little." He handed her a glass.

Skye could tell by Rick's too-bright eyes that he must have had several hits of the stuff.

"Want to dance?" he asked, indicating the crowded dance floor.

Skye smiled at him. He, after all, had been the reason she'd gotten the interviews with Creed.

"Okay," she found herself saying, thankful that the rap tune had been replaced with an R & B song. She took a sip then set her champagne down.

Rick held her hand and led her to the floor. He

was a good-looking man and certainly charming—nothing like his temperamental boss. Tonight he was impeccably dressed in grey wool slacks and a herringbone blazer with felt patches at the elbows. Underneath, he wore a black cotton shirt, with a red silk cravat at the neck. Something about his neckerchief reminded her of Marla St. James. Hadn't Creed's old makeup artist been found with a red silk scarf wrapped around her neck? Skye squelched the gruesome thought and focused on what Rick was saying.

"What does one do in Mills Creek for entertainment?" Rick asked.

Skye smiled and shouted over the music. "There are wonderful restaurants nearby. If you're the outdoors type, in winter you ski and skate, and in summer you canoe and attend the festivals. There are also several upscale resorts close by. Believe it or not, we do get quality entertainment up here."

"Perhaps some day soon you'll show me the sights," Rick murmured, twirling her around.

"Perhaps she won't have time." Creed's deep voice interrupted. "Look, Rick, sorry to break up this touching moment. I need you to find Esther Hesseman and give her these autographed copies."

Creed waved a couple of books at Rick. Even as he spoke, his eyes remained riveted on Skye. What did he find so fascinating? she wondered.

Rick, obviously used to being hunted down, didn't seem too put out. "Sure thing. But a gentleman never leaves a lady stranded on the floor. Why don't you finish the dance with Skye?" He handed her over.

Creed's eyes flashed dangerously and his mouth

tightened. He didn't say a word, but simply looped his hands around Skye's waist and drew her close. She could smell his spicy cologne; it was a scent that made her think of pine trees and the upcoming holiday season.

Skye felt the old excitement beginning to bubble. Creed's touch, brief as it was in high school, always made her feel giddy. She put aside her good sense, closed her eyes, and followed his expert lead. For the few moments it would take for the song to wind down, she could forget what a bastard Creed Bennett was.

"Check out the paper. Skye Walker did a terrific job with your article. You even made front-page news." Rick slapped a folded copy of the Pocono Record in front of Creed before slipping into his seat at the table. "I'm starving. What's for breakfast?"

Vilma, hovering in the background, whipped the covers off platters of scrambled eggs, french toast, and fruit.

"Coffee?" she asked, waving a china pot at Rick.

"You know it, darlin'."

Creed still hadn't said a word. He was too busy reading. First, he examined the photo of himself that took up half a page. The photographer had done a pretty decent job of capturing his best features, even minimizing his nose. Next, he read the caption: *Creed Bennett, Illusion or Reality?* What was Skye Walker up to?

"I think Skye was pretty objective," Rick said, through a mouthful of eggs.

Creed held up a hand, silencing his assistant. He continued to peruse the article. Pushy or not, Skye

Walker was a good writer. So far he'd give her an A for accuracy. She'd obviously done her research and followed his career from its onset. And she most definitely had a way with words. She made him sound like he was the second coming of the Messiah. Creed flipped the page and saw a photo of disreputable Jed. No doubt, his father had been drunk and disorderly. He always was. Creed felt the blood rush to his head and the air whoosh out of his lungs as he read on. Damn Skye Walker!

This reporter had the opportunity to interview the Mighty Creed's father. Jed Bennett, a native of Mills Creek, had this to say about his famous son. "Now that Creed's a big star, he forgets I exist. I love that boy more than life itself but fame's gone to his head and he's forgotten about me . . ."

"Blast that woman and the horse she rode into town on," Creed shouted, slamming his fist on the table. The plates on the table rattled and Vilma hurried to steady them. "Typical reporter," Creed groused, "sticking her nose into other people's business."

"Something wrong?" Rick arched an eyebrow.

"How much of this article did you read?"

"The whole thing."

"And you didn't find it offensive? The woman is completely out of line."

"Actually, I thought Skye brought a lot of sensitivity to the piece. She even handled the part about your association with the disappearance of those women rather well. How come you didn't tell me your father was still alive? I would have given you that note a whole lot quicker."

"As far as I'm concerned, Jed Bennett doesn't exist."

"Why don't you read the piece in its entirety?" Rick continued to wolf his meal down.

What Rick said made good sense. Still, the idea of the Walker woman mentioning he'd been considered suspect infuriated him. What was she trying to do—ruin him? Admittedly his friend, Kareem Davis, had played a cruel trick, pretending to be him and inviting her to the prom, but would she nurse an old grudge all these years?

Creed continued to read.

> *Mr. Bennett's name has surfaced in the press more and more lately. He's been associated with five missing women. Most recently, the body of Marla St. James, his former makeup artist, surfaced in an Everglades swamp. Although the police have questioned Mr. Bennett, he is not considered a suspect at this time.*

"That does it," Creed snarled, leaping up and flinging his napkin across the table. "I'm finding that woman and wringing her neck. Rick, get me Skye Walker on the phone." He brushed by a startled Vilma and headed for the den.

Several minutes elapsed before Rick joined him, carrying the cordless. "Skye's not at work. They said she wouldn't be in until later this afternoon."

"Is she listed?"

Rick's eyebrows rose. "You're going to call the woman at home?"

"You bet. Find her number in the directory, or, better yet, call the operator and get her address as well."

Rick seemed about to protest, then changed his mind. "You're the boss," he said, dialing.

Skye rolled over and placed the pillows over her head. Even that didn't block out the rumbling thunder. She'd heard of storms, but this was a doozie. The noise sounded like it came from inside the house. Hogan's high pitched yelping eventually penetrated her fog. He probably needed to be let out. His wet nose nuzzled her cheek and a mewling sound now came from the back of his throat.

"Hold on, boy. I'm getting up."

Skye sat up and placed trembling fingers on her aching temples. She shouldn't have had that third glass of champagne or stayed up so late putting the finishing touches on her article. Her mouth was an arid wasteland and tasted as if someone had stuffed cotton in it. Her head felt as if it had hosted last night's Halloween bash.

No sign of Hogan now; where had he disappeared to? She heard low whining coming from the outer regions. The little dog's nails scratched the wooden floor as he circled. If he could, he would dig himself a hole under the door. Skye placed both feet on the floor. A banging at her door startled her. No mistaking the noise this time, someone was pounding at her front door—pounding and screaming her name. What could be so urgent?

Not caring what she looked like, Skye raced to answer. It would have to be an emergency from the sound of things. Rubbing the grit from her eyes, she threw the door open. A cool autumn breeze blew into the chalet as Hogan pushed past, practically knocking her over. He snarled at the visitor and lunged for the cuffs of his pants.

"Restrain your dog," Skye heard a deep male voice say.

Creed Bennett! What was he doing here?

"Hogan!" Skye shouted, squelching the urge not to laugh. The dog had a firm grip on Creed's pant leg and showed no sign of letting go. "Hogan! Down, boy. Get into the house this minute!"

Creed hopped from one leg to another in a desperate attempt to dislodge the Jack Russell terrier. He swatted the air with a newspaper, to no avail. Skye felt her eyes watering and her shoulders begin to shake. Creed Bennett practically foamed at the mouth. Well over six feet tall, he was being kept at bay by a puny twelve-pound terrier. He appeared ready to kill something or someone. Skye found the scenario hilarious. She gave in to the laughter, actually roaring.

Her reaction seemed to enrage Creed further.

"This isn't funny," he snarled. "That beast should be muzzled. First he attacks my dog, now me."

The expression on his face made Skye roar even more.

"Come on, Hogan, darling," she got out, between fits of laughter. "Down, boy. This man lacks a sense of humor."

"I lack what?" Creed sputtered. "What's humorous about having a vicious, untrained animal attack you?"

Who was he calling vicious or untrained? Not her

Hogan. But now wasn't the time to argue that point. "Hogan, heel!"

Reluctantly, the dog relinquished his hold on Creed's pant leg. Where his teeth had made contact, there were now several distinct puncture marks. Creed spotted them at the same time Skye did.

"Now, see what your dog did?"

"I'm sorry," Skye said, deciding it was wiser to eat crow. "I'll replace your pants, of course. I'm sure they're terribly expensive."

"Price isn't the issue." Creed glared at her. "Never mind my clothing. I'm here to talk to you about this." He slapped the folded newspaper into her hand, at the same time his eyes raked her body. She found herself blushing. "Do you always answer the door like this?"

Hogan, deciding he disliked Creed's tone of voice, growled softly. Skye was immediately conscious of her state of undress. The oversized T-shirt that came down to her knees suddenly seemed inadequate. She didn't have a stitch of clothing under it. Hopefully, that wasn't obvious. She must be quite a sight, with her knee-high socks and hair pointing north, south, east, and west. She made a futile attempt to smooth the spikes down.

"How did you find out where I lived? And how did you get by the guard at the gate?" she challenged.

"I have my ways. This is a small town. It's brisk out here; I'd like to come in."

Skye was tempted to leave him out in the cold. The nerve of the man, showing up on her doorstep bristling with attitude. "Suit yourself," she heard herself say. "I'll be back in a minute." She flung the newspaper on the kitchen counter and closed the chalet's door behind him.

Creed's entry brought with it cold air and the woodsy smell of pine. Skye left the room quickly. She reappeared after a few minutes, wearing an ankle-length robe. By then, Creed had taken a seat on her rented sectional couch. Hogan stood guard not far away.

"What was so important that you needed to come here?" Skye demanded, flicking the switch on the coffee pot.

Creed followed her to the kitchen. He jabbed a finger at the still-folded paper on the counter. Although she was five foot eight, he towered above her. "Where do you get off writing this stuff?"

"That piece was extremely well researched and held nothing libelous. Now, suppose you tell me why your boxers are in a twist?" Skye asked.

"I don't wear boxers," Creed said softly, too softly, the hint of a smile making his lips twitch.

Skye decided not to even go there. Better to stick to business. "Obviously your back's up about something or you wouldn't have driven out here."

"I don't appreciate you interviewing my father."

"Why? He's an adult and this is a free country."

"You coerced him into that interview."

Skye chuckled. "Au contraire. He wanted to talk. Jed's never been known to hold his tongue."

"Don't give me this 'au contraire' business. Save that for your friends in Paris."

"My, we're testy." Needing to maintain a safe distance from this man who'd practically muscled his way into her house, she walked away and poured herself a cup of coffee.

Creed moved in. "Am I making you nervous?" he asked, placing a finger under her chin.

"You flatter yourself," Skye said.

Hogan growled. Skye shushed him, and, turning, opened the door to let the dog out. But even as she'd ground out the words, her heart pounded and her palms were sweaty. Filled with the scent of pine and man, the small chalet had now become claustrophobic. Skye put her fluttering stomach down to being alone with Creed—a man linked to five women's disappearances, if not their deaths. But she wasn't afraid of him. She never had been. More likely she was afraid for herself and this inexplicable attraction that still lingered.

Turning abruptly, she ran smack into Creed. His chest was as hard as granite. With one hand, he reached out to steady her. The other caressed the side of her face.

"Stop it," Skye choked out.

"Why?"

"Because . . ."

"Because you want to kiss me as badly as I want to kiss you."

"I don't . . ."

He silenced her by placing his finger against her lips. "You're a thorn in my side, Skye Walker. I haven't a clue why I'm attracted to you. I don't even particularly like you." The last was murmured.

With that, Creed bent over and pressed his lips to hers.

Skye stiffened, resisting the urge to slap his handsome face. The thing she'd wanted to happen twelve years ago had finally happened. She'd dreamed of this—dreamed of him kissing her good night after the prom. She knew she should pull away, send the arrogant man packing. She did neither.

Creed drew her closer and deepened the kiss. Standing on tip-toe, Skye wound her arms around his neck, savoring the feel of his exploring tongue. The warm, clean smell of him made her lightheaded. Creed's kiss was everything she'd expected and more. She could tell he'd had lots of practice. Even so, they matched each other move for move, as if they'd done this a million times before.

A scratching at the front door brought Skye back to her senses. She pushed out of Creed's arms, and threw the door open. "This should not have happened. You had better leave."

Creed wore a dazed expression on his face. He collected his paper and edged by her. "Gladly." His eyes turned cold and hostile. "If you found my kiss that repulsive, you shouldn't have been so accommodating. I understand the word no."

The door banged behind him.

Five

Three days later, Creed sat at a table at the Woodlands Country Club across from his agent. Hugh had driven up from New York to meet with him.

"When do you think you'll be ready to tour again?" Hugh Lancaster asked, sipping on his second Campari and soda. "I've been inundated with calls, and an incredible offer from the Saudis just came in. A spokesperson for Prince Hassan wants to know if you'd entertain for some birthday bash he's throwing for his son."

Creed sighed heavily. "Hugh, I . . ."

His agent ran thick fingers through bright red curls. "Now, before you say no—the money's good. Very good." He named an incredible sum.

Creed whistled. He gazed out of the window and onto the green, where two retirees teed off. While the offer was substantial, he sure didn't need the money. Besides, Saudi Arabia wasn't one of his favorite places. He could never get used to a country where women were shrouded from head to foot in black and considered chattel, where booze was forbidden—though plenty could be found on the black market, and where owning a magazine such as Cosmopolitan or Playboy could land you in jail. He sipped his wine and set the glass down.

"Although the publicity's died down quite a bit, this business with Marla's really gotten to you," Hugh said, breaking into his thoughts.

"How could it not? Marla was my makeup artist for over three years. It broke my heart to see her get mixed up with the wrong crowd. Now she turns up dead."

"Wasn't she an addict?"

Creed nodded. "Yeah, dabbled in some pretty dangerous stuff. Heroin to be exact."

"Ay yi yi."

"Are you gentlemen ready to order?" The waitress, who'd served them their drinks earlier, hovered.

"Hugh?"

Hugh ordered the sushi, Creed the Caesar salad. After the waitress left, the men continued to talk.

They'd just received their entrees when Skye Walker, and a man Creed did not recognize, walked in. They were seated at a table across the room in front of the fireplace. Was this a date or business?

Creed found himself eyeing the man's olive complexion and straight black hair. So, Skye Walker liked Italian stallions. This one looked twice her age. Creed lost track of what Hugh was saying; his eyes were glued on Skye in her elegant copper pants suit, a silk scarf casually draped over one shoulder. She laughed at something the man said, removed a black beret, and ran a hand through her tousled hair.

Creed remembered the way she'd kissed him back. There had been a lot of promise in that kiss—promise and barely concealed passion. He'd liked the way their tongues had intertwined, liked the feel of her slim body in his arms. Even after he'd been abruptly thrown out of her house, her scent had lingered in his nostrils.

He knew it was madness to even consider cultivating more than a casual relationship with the woman. She was a reporter, after all, a breed not to be trusted. In hindsight he acknowledged he'd overreacted to Skye's article, but he'd been burnt once, badly. Three years ago, he'd let his guard down, allowing a pretty face and winsome personality to get in the way of good sense. Chantal, the reporter he'd been involved with, had used him. She had taken everything he'd told her and shared it with the world. She'd created a name for herself by betraying him. She'd even won an award for her exclusive on Creed. To this day, he still couldn't bring himself to watch *World Entertainment Tonight*.

"Creed, are you with me?" Hugh waved a hand in front of his face. He followed Creed's gaze. "Attractive woman," he said. "Then again, you do know how to pick them."

The man seated across from Skye must have sensed they were being scrutinized. He said something to her, rose, and pushed his chair back. Skye's eyes locked with Creed's. Creed choked on a bite of lettuce and reached for his water.

By then the stallion was almost on top of them. He hesitated a discreet distance from their table. Up close, he looked street-wise and not in the shape Creed had initially thought. A distinct paunch made his sweater appear overly tight.

"Don't mean to disturb your lunch. I'm Peter Martini, Skye's editor," the man said, in a gritty voice that was pure Brooklyn. Coming closer, he shook

Creed's hand, then Hugh's. "I wondered what you thought of Skye's article."

"I'm Hugh Lancaster, Creed's agent," Hugh interjected, before Creed could open his mouth. "Rick Morales faxed me a copy of Ms. Walker's article. Frankly, I was impressed. She's got a unique way of telling a story. Not too many reporters stick to the facts."

Pete slapped Hugh's back. "Our Skye's one hell of a gal. Straightforward and honest as the day is long. Why don't you meet her and convey your sentiments in person? Skye," he bellowed, raising more than one eyebrow in the room. "Skye, get over here and join us."

Peter Martini took the seat Hugh held out, leaving the vacant one next to Creed open. Skye hesitated for a moment before rising. The only outward sign of her irritation was the manner in which she threw her napkin down. Slowly, she crossed the room, leaving a trail of gaping males behind her.

The men stood as Skye approached their table.

"Hello, gentlemen," she said, easing herself into the seat next to Creed, studiously avoiding eye contact with him. Creed nodded his greeting, keeping his face expressionless. He sipped his Campari, feigning interest in the red liquid.

Pete made the introduction. "Skye Walker meet Hugh Lancaster. Creed you already know."

"Have a drink with us," Hugh said, crooking his finger to call their waitress over.

Mentally, Creed groaned. It would be agony sitting next to Skye Walker, her elbow accidentally brushing his, the scent of her perfume tickling his nostrils. He alternated between wanting to kiss and throttle the woman. Skye threw Pete a furious look. With an almost imperceptible shake of her head, she challenged her boss to turn down Hugh's offer.

"We'd be delighted," Pete Martini said, settling in. "Skye, what will you have?"

"Cappuccino."

"Cappuccino for the lady and an ice cold Bud for me. You can skip the glass." Pete waved his hands expansively as the waitress moved off. "You guys heard the latest?"

Hugh shook his head. "What's happening?"

"One of our local girls disappeared. The family waited the usual twenty-four hours before filing a police report. Skye and I are off to interview the parents."

It was happening again, Creed thought, women disappearing around him. He couldn't seem to get away from it.

"Who?" Creed asked. It was the first word he'd uttered since Skye sat down.

"Old man Washington's granddaughter," Peter Martini said. "The family's owned the car wash since I've been in Mills Creek. Jamie's several years younger than you and Skye, a college senior. Felix, her father, is beside himself. She'd come home for the weekend to see you perform, and when she didn't return to the house, they assumed she spent the night with a girlfriend.

"When she didn't show up the following day either, the parents got nervous. Tried calling the school. No one's heard from her and she hasn't returned to college. They're hoping publicity and a substantial reward might bring them information."

"That makes two women from Mills Creek who've

disappeared into thin air," Skye said, finally deigning to look at Creed. "First Kristina, now Jamie. This used to be a sleepy little town, but no more."

From Skye's tone of voice, the implication was clear. Pete coughed and shot her a warning look. Skye examined manicured nails painted the same color as the outfit she wore, an intriguing copper that complemented the honey of her skin.

Their waitress returned, setting down their drinks. "You guys seem to have relocated," she said, to no one in particular. "Best I go ahead and take your lunch order."

Pete guzzled his beer straight from the bottle. "Sounds like a capital plan," he said, smothering a burp between splayed fingers.

What a character Skye's editor was. Creed's lips twitched in amusement. He sensed Skye's scrutiny and darted a quick look her way. Her sultry hazel gaze swept his face. Creed felt as if he'd been zapped by an electric prod. He gulped his Campari and focused his attention on Peter Martini.

Later that afternoon, Skye and Pete sat on a big, comfortable couch in the Washingtons' living room. The ride up the mountain had taken well over an hour, but since there was no snow, the drive had been relatively easy.

The main residence, a rustic old farm house with beamed ceilings and wraparound porches, sat on eighteen acres of land, complete with a trout pond and babbling brook. Leslie, the missing woman's mother, reclined in a wing-back chair, sniffling loudly, and twisting a damp handkerchief between her palms. Felix, the father, held out a picture of his daughter.

"Jamie's a beautiful girl," he said, struggling to keep his voice emotionless, "and a smart one. She wouldn't wander off with strangers."

"She's my life," his wife sniffled. "If something happened to her I don't know what . . ."

Skye accepted the photo Felix proffered. An attractive, dark-skinned beauty with a full head of braids smiled winsomely at the camera. Skye scrutinized the picture thinking something about the young woman looked familiar. The thought niggled the back of her mind.

"Good-looking gal," Pete interjected, peering over Skye's shoulder. "Could she have visited a friend?"

"Not without telling us." Leslie Washington's voice wobbled. "Jamie was so excited when she heard Creed Bennett was in town and performing at the benefit." Another outburst of tears threatened. "She's several years younger than Creed, but our older son, Don, went to high school with him. None of us dreamed he would turn out to be a big name. We sent her the plane tickets. Knew she would kill to see him in person."

Skye remembered Don as something of a bully; a loud, boisterous teen with a tendency to shove people around. He'd been hard to miss in a high school where blacks could be counted on both hands. She'd made a point of staying away from him.

"When exactly was the last time you saw Jamie?" Skye asked, removing a notepad from her bag. She was distracted, unfocused, and certainly not up to form. She had Creed Bennett to thank for that. Drat the man, showing up in the most unlikely places.

Who would have thought he'd be lunching at the country club? Who would have thought, thanks to Pete, she would be forced to lunch with him?

Felix screwed his face up. "Let's see, the benefit was Saturday night; it started at seven. Jamie dressed and left here around 6:00 P.M. That was the last Leslie and I saw of her. Don said she was at the Halloween party talking to that Morales guy, Creed Bennett's assistant."

So that's where Skye had seen her. She'd been amongst the groupies mobbing Rick and Creed. Come to think of it, the woman who'd volunteered to go on stage had braids—could that have been Jamie?

Leslie sobbed softly, managing to get out, "The police officer who took our statement says she's the second young woman from the Mills Creek area that's gone missing."

"Did the officer say who was the first?" Skye probed.

Leslie nodded. "Yes. The first was a woman who worked at the bank. Grover said she was a friend of Creed's."

"Kristina Brown."

"That's the one. Felix and I found out that our Jamie's the sixth woman coming in contact with Creed to have disappeared."

"What else did the police say?" Pete asked.

"He said wherever Bennett shows up, women go missing."

"A chatty sort of fellow."

Felix shrugged. "We've known Grover all his life. He's more a friend than a police officer."

Though visions of a lean caramel-colored face and

blue-black eyes kept her off kilter, Skye continued to question the Washingtons. She scribbled their responses and eventually rose. "Okay," she said, "I think we have enough. This piece should make tomorrow's paper. The ten-thousand-dollar reward is a big incentive; you're bound to get lots of calls. Just be mindful that there're bound to be cranks amongst them."

That Saturday morning, Creed swung the Jaguar off Route 209, following the colorful signs for the Fire Brigade's Fall FoodFest. In the passenger seat, Tikka panted noisily.

As a boy, Creed had enjoyed this annual event. Being outdoors, with a crisp autumn breeze ruffling his clothing and reddening his cheeks, invigorated him. He'd loved the smell of candied apples, roasted chestnuts, and corn on the cob. He'd loved hearing the barber shop quartets roaming the aisles, and especially enjoyed seeing the artisans at work. The round-eyed children, trailing balloons, he'd found absolutely fascinating.

God knew he'd needed to get out of the house. His five-thousand-square-foot home had suddenly become claustrophobic. He was sick to death of working out in his gym, T.V. bored him, and none of the books in his library held his interest. Rick had headed off for Manhattan, claiming to have a date, leaving Creed flipping through the paper, perusing the movie schedules. Thankfully, the ad for the festival had caught his eye.

Creed circled the huge lot, sliding into a space a good quarter of a mile down the road. He parked

the car and turned off the ignition. Tikka's nails
made a scratching sound against the door panels.

"No, Tikka!" Creed admonished, grabbing the
shepherd's leash. With the other hand, he reached
for his baseball cap in the back seat. He slid from behind the wheel, bringing the animal with him. As they
set off at a brisk pace, the deep bass of an oom-pa-pa
band drifted their way.

Creed reached into the pocket of his open leather
jacket, removing a pair of dark glasses. He perched
them on the bridge of his nose, clamped the cap on,
and settled the bill low on his forehead. What he
wouldn't do for a few precious hours of anonymity,
just to be allowed to wander the fair undetected.

As he got closer he was caught up in the throng,
carried along by the crowd there to enjoy the festivities. Around him, vendors hawked their wares noisily.
The smell of food hung heavily in the air.

"Check out booth 4 for the best bargains," a young
man shouted, clanging a brass bell.

"Jams, jellies. The kind your grandma made," another screamed, vying to be heard.

"Pickled herrings that way."

"Apple dunking. Bring your kiddies."

Tikka sniffed noisily at the heels of the people
ahead, occasionally stopping to nuzzle another ca-
nine. So far, so good. No one recognized him, or if
they did, they were far too intimidated to offer more
than a vague smile before moving on.

Creed stopped in front of one of the food stalls,
debating whether to purchase cider or hot chocolate.
He heard a commotion behind him and turned to
see a good sized group of men gathered at a booth.
Beer was being dispensed by the yard, and a contest

to see how fast each yard could be guzzled was well underway. A man's loud and somewhat slurred voice got his attention.

Creed would recognize that voice anywhere. Even now, the timbre gave him the willies. As a child he'd shivered every time he heard it, knowing that a sharp blow or offensive comment was bound to follow. In his nightmares, he still heard that voice and his mother's pleas not to hit him. In a trance, he remained rooted to the spot, unable to put one foot in front of the other and move off. In morbid fascination, Creed watched Jed down one yard of beer and reach for another. His father had aged badly. Creed wondered where he lived.

Sensing he was being scrutinized, Jed's bleary eyes swung in his direction. Their gazes locked. Creed held his breath, unable to look away.

"Hey, boy!" Jed slurred, swilling another mouthful of liquid. "About time you came looking for me."

Jed's words caught the crowd's attention. An ominous silence followed as every face turned to Creed. Tikka growled, instantly on alert.

"Cat got your tongue, boy? Or are you so high and mighty you won't acknowledge your own father?"

Creed nodded a greeting. He didn't trust himself to speak. He felt as if he were ten years old, anger building in his chest with no place to vent. Jed finished the beer and swaggered toward him. Tikka's hackles rose.

Hoping to gather his composure and not let his temper get the best of him, Creed knelt to smooth the animal's fur. "Easy, Tik. It's all right."

Jed stood a half a foot away, his eyes unfocused. Creed could smell the beer on him, hops and unwashed body intermingling. He was tempted to step back, put space between them, and walk away, but that would only trigger the scene already brewing.

"How are you, Jed?" Creed asked, barely getting the words out. Father was not something he associated with Jed. The man had never acted the part, never been there for him.

"The Mighty Creed!" Jed made an exaggerated bow, the pitch of his voice rising, now that he was assured the crowd's undivided attention. "Gotten too big for his breeches to acknowledge his own father. I live in a boardinghouse while he lords it in a manor." Jed swayed and took another step, closing in. His fetid breath whipped across Creed's face, nauseating him. Tikka tensed, ready to attack. Creed clutched the shepherd's leash, and tried desperately to reign in his own anger.

His is the seed from which I came, Creed reminded himself. *I shouldn't hate him.* But he did. He hated his father for being alive when his mother had been driven to an early death.

"Walking the streets, free as you please. Not a care in the world." Jed continued his tirade, playing to the crowd. "This man," he pointed a finger in Creed's face, "this big shot son of mine's a real ladies' man." He hiccupped loudly. "Every time he puts it to one of them, she up and disappears."

Creed felt the fingers of his free hand curl and uncurl. The veins at the sides of his neck pulsed and the blood pounded at his temples. God help him, he was going to slug his father, flatten him out for all to see. How he wished he could create an illusion and make him disappear. A tug on his elbow swung him around.

Skye Walker linked a hand through the crook of his arm. "There you are," she said. "I've been looking all over for you. You're late."

Her ridiculous dog, outfitted in a smart sweater, white lettering on red, the word "Killer" prominent on his back, snapped at Creed's ankles.

Skye kissed Creed's cheek, then turned to acknowledge his father. "Hi, Mr. Bennett. How's it going? My bet's on you winning the beer contest." She gestured to the booth behind him, where people had ceased drinking and stood frozen, mesmerized by the unfolding scene. Tugging Creed, Tikka, and her terrier along, she approached the person manning the beer booth. Creed remained open-mouthed as Skye withdrew five dollars from her purse.

"Give Mr. Bennett another yard of beer," she said to the vendor. Then to Creed, "We've got to get going, cherie. The dogs are getting antsy and I'm hungry. There's some place we need to be."

Six

"Thanks for coming to my rescue." Creed chuckled, a mirthless sound. "Did you see Jed's face when you intervened? I don't think he knew what hit him." Creed used a poker to turn a log on the fireplace. Sparks shot upward, flames licking at the wood noisily.

"Your father couldn't help himself. It was the alcohol speaking," Skye said, quietly.

"It's always alcohol talking."

Though Creed's voice remained neutral, Skye heard the hurt behind the words—hurt and embarrassment. She'd wandered into the unpleasant scene and felt compelled to get involved. One look at Creed's face and she'd picked up on his mortification. The ugly exchange had reminded her of how humiliated she'd been as an adolescent, taunted about her weight and the zits she simply couldn't get rid of. Jed had behaved abominably to his son. There was no reasoning with an alcoholic.

In silent agreement, Skye and Creed had left the festival. She'd kept her arm linked through his. That small action had felt surprisingly right. In the parking lot, Creed had invited her to lunch, and she'd followed him in her Bronco, never thinking that lunch would be at his house. She'd fully expected they would drop the dogs off at their respective homes and go off to a restaurant. But when she'd followed him up his winding driveway and was waved into his underground garage, she'd been too surprised to protest. She'd been even more surprised when their dogs called a truce. The animals were currently in Creed's kitchen, enjoying a snack under the watchful eye of his housekeeper.

Skye nursed the cup of cappuccino Vilma had brought her. It was amazing that Creed remembered what she'd been drinking at the club. She'd never thought of him as being especially perceptive. Then again, she really didn't know him.

"Want a refresher on your drink?" Creed asked, lowering himself onto the rug to join her. "Lunch should be served soon."

"No, thanks." She stared at the flames, then up at the vaulted wooden ceiling, trying to ignore the tingle that started in her toes and rapidly worked its way upward. "What made you decide to become an illusionist?"

Skye knew he must have been asked that question a million times, but she wanted to hear more than the usual pat answer. She wanted to know why the funniest boy in Mills Creek, and the most handsome, had chosen the life of a magician. It was a difficult career choice at best. Only a handful made it big.

"I've always been good at playing tricks . . . ," Creed said.

"That you were." She of all people should know. She'd been the butt of one of his pranks. He'd made a laughing stock of her.

Creed continued. "Illusions help you escape the realities of life. I was hooked when I saw David Copperfield on T.V. Here was this guy, totally different from everything you expect a magician to be. He was worlds apart from Harry Houdini. He was young, handsome, and had a definite style of his own, rubbing shoulders with the rich and famous, turning the somber business of trickery into something upbeat, fun, and very happening."

"How did you get into the business?"

"I majored in theater at Ithaca, met an illusionist during a work study program . . ."

"You went to Ithaca College? I was at Syracuse. Up until my junior year."

"So close, yet worlds apart," Creed murmured. "How come we were in high school together, but never got to know each other?"

Skye sipped her cappuccino. "Fat, pimply-faced introverts aren't usually very popular. You hung with the in crowd; Mills High's beautiful people. I wasn't in your league."

"Hard to believe. Look at you now." Creed adjusted his position. His shoulder grazed hers. She flushed. The heat of the fireplace was nothing in comparison to the slow burn he'd ignited.

"Where will you have lunch?" Vilma asked, entering with a covered tray.

Tilting his head, Creed deferred the decision to Skye. "We can eat in the dining room or stay here if you'd like."

"Let's stay here."

Vilma cleared a huge Parson's table and set down linen and crockery. She put out trays of cold cuts, assorted cheeses, pickles, condiments, and baked goods.

"I have wine chilling," the housekeeper added.

"None for me. Just water, please."

"I'll have the same," Creed said.

After Vilma departed to do their bidding, Creed pushed himself into a sitting position. He slid on his rump toward the coffee table. Folding long legs, Native American style, he crooked his finger, beckoning her to join him.

Skye came to sit opposite him. He broke a piece of bread and dipped it into the Brie. "Open up," he commanded.

She closed her eyes and did as he asked, allowing him to place the bread between her lips. "Mmmmm. Delicious. Haven't had this since . . ."

"Paris?" For one split second his index finger traced her bottom lip. She shivered. "How well did you know Kristina Brown?" he asked.

Skye's eyes flew open. "What's that have to do with anything?"

Creed ceased his ministrations, and using that same hand, attacked the Brie. "Finding Kristina seems of paramount importance to you. Indicates to me you two were pretty close. You must have stayed in touch long after high school."

She could easily have told him then that Kristina was her cousin. But she sensed he would clam up if he knew she was family. He was already wary of reporters. Even so, she stood a better chance of having him open up if he thought they were school chums.

"We wrote to each other occasionally," Skye said. That wasn't a total lie. They'd written sporadically. "Kris was one of the few people who kept in touch while I was in Paris. Loyal friends normally don't drop off the face of the earth. That's why I want to find her."

Creed chewed on his bread and cheese. "She could be anywhere."

"Not the Kris I know."

"Then you didn't know her well. Turkey or chicken salad?" Creed pointed to the untouched platter. He methodically sliced a roll in half.

"Turkey. And you did?"

For a moment she thought he wasn't going to answer. She'd gone too far. He piled meat on two rolls and added condiments. "Kristina was one of those restless types," he said, "always chasing the next big adventure, constantly on the go. The relationship we shared was special. She was a wild woman with a heart of gold. Made me laugh."

"Kris, wild?" Skye made a wry face. Just how close had the two been?

"Obviously you didn't know the Kristina I knew. That's all I'll say." He handed over her sandwich.

She nibbled on turkey, making a mental note to ask around in case what she'd just heard about Kris was true. She hadn't seen her cousin in six, seven years. Quite possibly, there was a lot she didn't know. Her aunt had invited her over for dinner next week. She would be a good person to question.

Vilma returned with water and set down two bottles. Assured they needed nothing further, she left.

"So tell me," Creed asked, "why the burning desire to go to Paris? What kept you there all these years?"

Skye swallowed a mouthful of turkey. "Sophomore year at college was a difficult time for me. My parents were divorcing. Signing up for an exchange program junior year seemed the thing to do. I'd be abroad, immersing myself in a totally different culture and learning a second language. I narrowed it down to Paris, Italy, or Spain, put the names of the countries in a hat, and pulled one."

He placed a hand on her shoulder, squeezing gently. "Must have been tough having parents split up. I've heard divorce is more devastating to adult children than kids."

"It was difficult," Skye admitted. Even today, she had trouble dealing with the fact that her parents were no longer together. She was an only child and had no one to turn to. She'd dealt with the hurt and feelings of abandonment alone.

Skye wanted to cover his hand with her own, draw warmth and comfort from his touch. She knew she was a glutton for punishment. A young man who could callously lead a teenager on would hardly care about her feelings. Creed wasn't to be trusted.

"You didn't answer the second half of my question," he probed. "Seven years is a long time to be away from home."

"And how long were you gone?"

He polished off the last of his sandwich and pushed his plate away. "I suppose I deserved that. But, seriously, what kept you in Paris all this time?"

"Found a job I loved. Fell in love with the city. Fell in love with a man."

"Lucky fellow."

"Apparently he didn't think so."

"Oh, oh. Broken heart?"

A high pitched yelping, followed by a vicious growl from the vicinity of the kitchen, prevented her from answering. In the midst of the commotion, Skye heard Vilma's shouts.

"Looks like the truce is over. Thanks for lunch . . . and the conversation." She stood, straightened her clothes, and headed to the kitchen to referee.

He followed, footsteps behind. Skye collected Hogan and thanked him again. But even seated in her car, Creed's woodsy scent lingered in her nostrils.

Creed lowered the garage door and retraced his steps, this time making his way to the solarium, by far his favorite room in the house. What a strange day it had been. First, his face off with Jed, then the Walker woman coming to his rescue, and the unexpected camaraderie that had developed between them. Skye was certainly different from any reporter he'd ever met. Of course he'd thought the same about Chantal and look at how she'd betrayed him.

The problem was that he had too much time on his hands or he wouldn't be having these thoughts. Contemplating Skye Walker as a possible—possible what? Romantic prospect?—was a ridiculous idea. If he planned on staying in Mills Creek through the holidays, he needed to keep busy.

An idea niggled the back of his mind. What if he were to contact the Boys and Girls Club and propose conducting some magic clinics geared at teaching young people the basics of his craft? It would be a fun project and a rewarding one. Those kids might never have such an opportunity. He loved children, always had, and if he made a difference in just one child's life, opened up a new world to him or her and provided the guidance he'd never had, he would be fulfilled. The more he thought of it, the more he liked the idea.

He reached for the phone, punching the programmed number. "Come on, Lydia, pick up," he muttered, drumming his fingers against the arms of the over-stuffed wing chair. He would run the idea by his publicist. Lydia was a dear friend, one of the few people he trusted. He also needed to talk to her about where they were in terms of promoting his book, *The Magic in You.*

"Hey, good looking!" she eventually greeted.

"Do you always answer your phone that way?"

Lydia chuckled. "Yup. Thanks to ESP and Caller I.D. I've been meaning to ring you."

Creed listened to her ramble, filling him in on future T.V. and radio interviews, asking if he'd be available for signings at some of the more upscale department stores.

He ran the idea of the magic clinics by her. She loved it. She felt that it would be great P.R. for him. That wasn't the reason he was doing it, though, and he impressed upon her the need for secrecy. He didn't want to use the Boys and Girls Club as an avenue for promoting himself.

"And another thing," Lydia said, when they'd almost completed their business, "there was an article in this morning's paper. Ona DiSantis's body was found in a dumpster in downtown Fort Lauderdale."

"What?" Creed's fingers massaged his aching temples. His cleaning lady had been missing for well over three months. The woman had three young children and no spouse in the picture. "Have they made an arrest?"

"No, and the old story's surfaced again. Your name

was mentioned at least three times in that article. The reporter's got a source in Mills Creek, and says that since you've been home a local girl's disappeared. She even used an excerpt from the Pocono Record to illustrate her point."

Skye Walker! And to think he'd found her fascinating and had even contemplated asking her out.

"Want to hear something sick?" Lydia's voice penetrated the roaring in his ears.

Creed remained silent. She would tell him anyway.

"Ona's body was violated. She was found with a red silk scarf wrapped around her neck and not a stitch on."

"Oh, God! That poor woman . . . her kids," Creed groaned, his head pounding. "These red silk scarves seem to be the murderer's calling card. Could be a serial killer. We need to do something for Ona's children. The least I can do is send a check anonymously. I'm sure the family needs the money."

"I'll talk to Rick about that. Have him handle it. Don't be surprised if the police show up on your doorstep wanting to question you again. I'm calling in favors from the reporters I know. I'm trying to get them to downplay any reference to you. We can only hope."

Creed chatted a few more minutes with Lydia before hanging up. Given the latest murder, it was only a matter of time before the sleepy town of Mills Creek was besieged by journalists.

So much for peace and quiet. So much for coming home.

Seven

Deep in thought, Skye tapped the nib of her pen against the battered wooden desk. Another update had come across the wires. Ona Di Santis's decaying body, wrapped in a garbage bag, a red silk scarf tied around her neck, had been found last week. Now the coroner's office had confirmed she'd been raped and strangled. In their professional opinion, she'd been murdered five weeks ago.

That made two deaths and four women still missing. Creed would have been in Florida around the same time Ona was killed. But it was increasingly more difficult to believe he could be capable of rape and murder.

Skye knew she was jumping the gun, coming to premature conclusions. But her reporter's instincts told her there was a definite link between these murders and Creed Bennett. Each of the women had been involved with him in some capacity. Still, she didn't want to believe he was a violent man. Callous, maybe. But a beast with no regard for human life? That was too hard to swallow. If the animal at large wasn't Creed, then it was someone associated with him. *Or someone who had it in for him,* a tiny voice reasoned.

The phone on Skye's desk rang. Preoccupied with putting the pieces together, she reached for the receiver.

"Skye Walker."

"Ms. Walker, Don Washington." A man's deep voice boomed into her ear. "We went to high school together. My father asked me to call."

Don Washington? Why did that name seem familiar? Skye thought for a moment—ah, yes, Jamie Washington, the missing woman's brother. "Hi, Don, what can I do for you?"

"My parents got mail today. They're pretty shaken up."

With her free hand, Skye fumbled for her notepad. She began to scribble. "Another lead?"

"Don't know if you'd call it that."

"Talk to me," she said, sensing that whatever it was, had shaken the Washingtons to the core. "Tell me what's going on."

"The package held a red silk scarf. No note. Nothing. My mother's hysterical."

Covering the mouthpiece of the phone, Skye whistled softly. Two dead women, a red silk scarf. Sounded like a serial killer at work. The murderer was getting brazen. From everything she'd read about these sickos, they were usually male attention seekers, men who thrived on being in the limelight and craved media notoriety. Creed Bennett. No. She was letting an old hurt cloud her judgment. Creed was already famous.

"Ms. Walker?"

"Skye. Have your parents notified the police?"

"They're talking with Grover Peters as we speak."

"Good."

There was a pause on the other end. Don Washington cleared his throat. "Uh, Ms. . . . Skye. You think we could meet face to face? Our conversation would be strictly off the record. I don't even know if it's relevant, but there are a couple of things about Jamie my parents don't know. I'd rather not discuss them with the police."

After going back and forth, they arranged a time and place. Skye thumbed through her appointment book and made a notation. She hung up, perplexed. The little she remembered of the man, she didn't particularly like. And why would he want to share his sister's secrets with the press?

The clock on the paneled walls indicated the lateness of the hour. Skye grabbed her coat and said a hurried goodbye to the few remaining colleagues, busily working to meet deadlines. She was late for dinner at her aunt's house and still had a half an hour ride ahead of her.

Skye took the familiar winding curves at full speed. Her Aunt Tonia was the only remaining sister living in the old family home. Uncle Tom had died over a decade ago and she'd never remarried. Skye's divorced mom had moved in briefly with Aunt Tonia, then she'd met a visiting contractor, fallen in love, and moved to California with him.

Smoke curled from the chimney of the sprawling redwood home. Skye shifted gears, tapped the accelerator, and steered the Bronco up the steep driveway. No sooner had she parked the vehicle when the front door flew open.

Kris's younger sister, Mariah, screamed a greeting.

"There you are, at last. We're holding dinner for you. I'm starving, girl."

"And hello to you, too." Skye reached into the back seat to remove the bouquet of mums and bottle of wine she'd picked up during her lunch hour when she'd gone home to let Hogan out.

At the door, Skye pecked Mariah on the cheek and sniffed the air. "Something smells wonderful."

"Pot roast," her cousin confirmed. "Ma, Aunt Leona, Skye's here. Looks gorgeous, as usual."

Skye pulled on a lock of Mariah's curly hair. "And you're chopped liver? Just look at you. Most women would kill for that height, figure, and face. Girl, you're definitely supermodel material."

"Think so?" The seventeen-year-old preened, her smile a mile wide. "I've been thinking of getting a portfolio together and going to see Eileen Ford."

"Let me know if I can help. My photographer owes me some favors. We'll set up a photo shoot."

"I love you, Skye." Mariah threw her arms around Skye's neck and whooped loudly.

The teenager's screams brought her mother and aunt from the kitchen. They both hugged Skye.

"Let me look at you," Tonia, Mariah's mother said. "I still can't get over how much alike you and your mother are. Same sultry hazel eyes."

Skye's Aunt Leona pinched her cheek. "Especially now that she's lost all that baby fat."

Skye knew her aunt wasn't being mean. It was simply typical of her to say what was on her mind. Still, Skye's fat phase wasn't a part of her life she wanted to remember. People had been nasty and hurtful then. She would never allow herself to get that heavy again.

"We're so glad you're here. Dinner's already on the table," Aunt Tonia said, leading the way.

"What should I do with these?" Skye held out the wine and flowers.

"Here, I'll take them," Mariah offered, relieving Skye of her gifts.

Skye was seated at the foot of the table opposite Aunt Tonia. Mariah and Aunt Leona sat across from each other.

"Where's Uncle Walter?" Skye asked, noting the extra place setting.

"His knee acted up at the last minute and I suggested he stay home," Leona replied.

After dishes were passed around and a sizable amount of food devoured, dessert was brought out. Skye helped pour coffee.

"Any word on Kris?" she asked carefully.

Aunt Tonia shook her head. "Not a thing. I don't know what to think. And now two women have been murdered." She sighed, struggling to hold back tears.

"You say Kristina left for Fort Lauderdale to visit Creed Bennett?"

"We think so. In the past, she'd visited him."

"Creed says he hasn't seen her in some time.

Aunt Leona spoke up. "That's right, you went to school together. Didn't know you still talked."

They'd never talked. Not until recently. "Upon occasion our paths have crossed," Skye admitted.

Mariah's voice rose. "I know he's good looking but what's he like up close and personal? Think he'd hurt my sister?"

A difficult question. How to answer? She didn't want to believe that Creed was capable of physically hurting a soul. She'd gotten a glimpse of the other side of him—the more sensitive side she'd never guessed existed.

"I don't know why he would," Skye said. "I'm not exactly a fan of Creed Bennett's, but I can't imagine what his motive would be."

"Something terrible had to have happened. Kristina wouldn't abandon her job and give up everything she's worked so hard to attain—her condo, her life—walk away from it all without even dropping a note to me or her sister." Tears rolled down Aunt Tonia's cheeks.

Skye took a deep breath before asking the question foremost on her mind. She squeezed her aunt's shoulder. "How involved were Creed and Kris? There's an awful lot of speculation."

"Kris claims they were good friends," Mariah said. "I think they were more. He bought her expensive clothes, sent her money . . . took her to clubs . . ."

"Mariah! How do you know that?" Aunt Tonia screeched.

"I read her mail," Mariah admitted, "and listened to her phone conversations."

"You didn't."

Skye swirled the liquid in her cup. She'd allowed her coffee to sit and get cold. To diffuse the quarrel brewing, she asked, "Aunt Tonia, have you gotten any strange mail?"

"Like?"

"Maybe a package without a note."

"You're scaring me."

"Nothing to be scared about. Just thought I'd ask." It was time to call it an evening. Skye yawned. "You folks are going to have to forgive me. I have an early day tomorrow and I've got to get home and let Hogan out."

"You'll be here for Thanksgiving dinner?" Aunt Tonia asked, rising and beginning to collect plates.

"Absolutely."

Promising to call, Skye departed with several plates of leftovers.

"The guard at the gate house is on the phone," Vilma whispered, nervously. She stood at the entrance to the solarium, her palm covering the mouthpiece of the cordless phone.

Creed looked up from his position on the floor where he rough-housed with Tikka. "I'm not expecting anyone."

"It's the police. What should I tell them?"

Creed groaned. He sat up, brushing fur and lint from his sweat suit. "Sit, Tikka." The shepherd, looking crestfallen, obeyed. "Good girl. Where's Rick? Have him meet them at the door. I'll be in the den. Bring in coffee."

"Yes, Sir."

If was starting again—cops showing up at his home questioning him. He'd left Fort Lauderdale believing it was all over. His name had been cleared, or so he'd thought.

In the den, Creed seated himself at an antique wooden desk. He stared into the fire Vilma had started earlier that day, the smell of hickory tickling his nostrils. He got no enjoyment from the woodsy odor today, more like a headache. He hated dealing with the police. All that transparent drilling put him on edge.

Rick entered, immaculately dressed, as always, in a grey blazer, cream turtleneck sweater, and black wool pants. "They're he-e-re," he said, wiggling his eyebrows. "Actually, there are two of them. You all right? Want me to stay?"

"I'm fine. Stay if you want, but if you've other things to do, I'll survive."

"I'll stay. Pigs amuse me. Such rigid creatures. Full of their own sense of importance." Rick flopped down on an overstuffed wingback chair. He spread his legs wide and clasped both hands behind his head.

Creed heard a knock on the French doors and darted a glance in that direction. Through highly polished glass panes, he spotted Vilma carrying coffee, accompanied by two plainclothes cops.

"Come in," Rick yelled, rising to straighten the creases in his slacks.

Creed remained seated. All this questioning was becoming tiresome. He now viewed the police as his enemies.

"Officer Grover Peters," the younger of the two undercover cops said, entering, and extending a hand.

Reluctantly, Creed rose to clasp the policeman's hand.

"Stu Malone." A silver-haired older fellow followed suit.

"Make yourself comfortable." Rick waved vaguely to the chairs and ottomans liberally scattered about the room. He resumed his seat, long legs swinging over the arms of his chair. Creed took his original seat.

The policemen produced pens and pads and scribbled furiously.

"I'm a big fan of yours," Grover Peters said, looking up at Creed. "Always have been. My sister went to high school with you. You done Mills Creek proud."

In no mood for small talk, Creed merely nodded.

"This shouldn't take long," Malone said, wetting his index finger, then flipping through the pages of his pad.

"All right, then, cut to the chase and get to the real reason you're here," Creed growled.

Rick flashed him a warning look. Creed reined in his temper. Better to be courteous, answer the questions, and usher them out of his house.

"Did you know Jamie Washington?" Peters asked.

Nibbling on his bottom lip, Creed shook his head.

"Is that a yes or a no?"

"No."

Peters appeared puzzled. "Wasn't she the volunteer you picked out of the audience at the benefit?"

Creed frowned. "I don't recall."

Rick came to the rescue. "Mr. Bennett interacts with numerous people. His stage act requires audience participation. You can't expect him to remember every single soul."

"Maybe this will jog his memory." Peters produced a graduation picture of a pretty dark-skinned woman, smiling from ear to ear. He flicked it in Creed's direction.

Creed glanced at the photo. "I'm sorry. Can't say I remember her."

"But she was on stage with you a full five minutes . . ."

"And during that time, I was working, concentrating on magic, not scoping out volunteers."

"Jamie Washington was seen with you afterward,

at the Halloween party," Grover Peters said, affably, "the one at the town hall."

"She might have been talking to me," Rick interjected. "We're normally besieged with fans after the show. They're curious. They want to know how a particular illusion works, or simply want to get close to Creed."

"I see. What about Don Washington, Jamie's brother?" Malone asked Creed.

"What about him?"

"Says he knows you."

Creed shrugged. "Everyone in this town knows me."

"According to him, you were high school buddies."

"I had a lot of high school friends. Am I being accused of something?"

Malone stroked his chin. "I wouldn't exactly say that. Jamie Washington is missing. We understand you're the last person to have seen her."

"I am?"

"This is a routine follow up, Mr. Bennett," Grover said, seemingly anxious to placate. "Six women you're in some way associated with have mysteriously disappeared. Two have since been found dead."

Creed rose and eyeballed both men. "Gentlemen, this conversation has ended. If you have further questions, I'd like my lawyer present. Rick, please show the officers out."

The men remained unfazed as Creed closed the door softly behind him.

Eight

"So, what you're saying is, you're not sure your sister was abducted?" Skye was seated at Eve's, in a banquette across from Don Washington, nursing a cool cup of coffee. The pungent smell of hamburgers and fried onions hung heavily in the air.

Don, a big, hulking guy in a black leather jacket, nodded. The hoop earring in his right lobe wobbled back and forth with each movement. "That's right. There were things about Jamie my parents didn't know."

"Want to tell me about them?"

As she waited for him to answer, Skye jotted a note to ask if Jamie had disappeared for an extended period before. A waitress swung by with a pot of coffee and refilled her cup. T.T., who'd served her and Creed on her previous visit, was nowhere in sight.

Don chugged his Budweiser. "Mom and Pop haven't a clue that she danced."

"Danced?"

"Yeah. Summers and nights. Said she needed the money."

Skye was slowly getting the picture. "Jamie was an exotic dancer?"

Don nodded, finishing his beer in one easy swallow. "Pays well, and my sister likes nice things. The money my parents give her can't support her lifestyle."

"Don, is there a particular reason you're telling me this?" Skye tapped her pen against the Formica in rapid succession. The longer she sat across from this man, the more she wondered about his agenda.

"I'm concerned, of course. My sister's run off and no one knows where she is. With all the unsavory types at those clubs, well . . ."

Skye sipped her coffee. "What makes you think Jamie ran off?"

"She wasn't doing that well in school. Kept saying she could make a heck of a lot more money if she danced full time. Kristina gave her lots of encouragement."

"Kristina Brown?"

"Yeah, the bank teller—the woman who's missing now. She went to high school with us. Wasn't she a relation of yours?"

Skye didn't acknowledge the question. "Go on."

"Anyway, Kristina's been dancing for years. She and Jamie met at the Psychedelic Pony. My guess is they took off together. They were always yakking about moving down South. The pay's supposedly better, and the cops leave the clubs alone."

Kristina, an exotic dancer? It was the most ridiculous thing she'd ever heard. Skye schooled her expression and focused on taking notes. She'd have to check out this bit of information.

"How come you know all of this?" she asked Don.

Don Washington ran fingers wreathed in gold rings across his shaved head. "I found out by accident, last summer. Me and the guys attended a bachelor party at the Pony and there they were."

Skye drank the last of her coffee and set the cup down. "So, you think Kristina and Jamie are some place down South—Fort Lauderdale, maybe?"

"I wouldn't be surprised."

"Why Fort Lauderdale? Has she gone down there before?"

"Yes, with Kristina."

"Then why not share this information with the police?"

Don gestured to the waitress for another Bud. "My mother couldn't handle the scandal. The way I figure it, with Kris being a relative of yours, you wouldn't want to embarrass your family either. You have a vested interest in finding Kris. Maybe you could call on your contacts, and make some discreet inquiries in, say, the Miami-Fort Lauderdale area. I'd hate to think my sister and your cousin are part of a con."

Skye sensed there was more here than met the eye. Although her brain processed the information, she drew a blank. Tossing a handful of bills on the table, she rose. "Don, you've given me a lot to digest. I'll be in touch."

He winked at her. "I'll be waiting."

Later that evening, Skye massaged the nape of her neck, where tension always seemed to settle. At last, the long, leisurely soak in the tub she'd been looking forward to all day would be hers.

Replaying in her head the conversation she'd just had with her mother, Skye sighed. It made her feel good knowing her mother was happy, but it became increasingly more wearing being asked over and over if there was someone special in her life. She'd become an expert at dodging the question, but somehow the subject kept resurfacing. At the ripe age of fifty, her mother had met the love of her life. Now she'd become obsessed with planning Skye's wedding.

"Never mind there's no man in the picture," Skye muttered, turning on the tap and squirting an overly generous amount of bubble bath under running water. In the last week, the temperature in the Poconos had dropped to the forties—not exactly frigid, but cold enough to bring out the winter coats and an occasional muffler.

As she waited for the tub to fill, Skye stripped off her clothing then lit a vanilla-scented candle. She retraced her steps to the kitchen and poured a glass of red wine. As she headed back to check on the tub, the phone rang.

Skye grabbed the cordless phone on the coffee table.

"Hello."

"Hi, there." A man's rich velvety growl filled her ear.

Skye frowned. The voice dripped warmth. Intimacy. It was certainly no one she knew. She paused, waiting for him to continue.

"Is this a bad time?"

She wanted to say it was, that she was standing in her living room without a stitch on. But at the same time she was trying to place his voice. It didn't sound like Creed. Just thinking about Creed made her treacherous heart do a rapid pit-pat. Keep the man talking. Will her stomach to settle down. "Who is this?"

"How soon we forget."

She'd heard that teasing tone somewhere. Where? For sure, it wasn't Creed. Her disappointment showed in the curtness of her voice. "So, we're reduced to playing guessing games?"

The man chuckled but didn't seem the least nonplussed. "I deserved that. This is Rick Morales."

Creed's right hand. What did he want?

"How are you, Rick?"

"Better than fine."

"Is there something I can do for you?"

"Yes, you can come to Creed's house for Thanksgiving dinner."

She was taken aback by the invitation but made sure to keep her voice neutral. "Thank you, but I have other plans."

"Can't you change them?" Rick wheedled. "Creed's hosting an open house. He sees it as the perfect opportunity to get reacquainted with his high school buddies and the folks he grew up with. Most likely he'll call you himself. He's doing cocktails, a buffet-style dinner, the works."

The adult Creed hadn't struck her as particularly gregarious. An open house didn't seem his thing. There had to be more to it. Curiosity won out.

"I'm having dinner with my aunt. What time is he starting?"

"About six. At the very least, try to make it for dessert. Vilma makes the best pumpkin and pecan pie."

She supposed she could swing it. Aunt Tonia served at about four. Even if she arrived at Creed's around seven, she wouldn't be terribly late. While she didn't necessarily have fond memories of her high school classmates, it would be interesting to see how they'd fared.

"Okay, I'm convinced. I'll arrive late, but I'll be there. Now, what can I bring?"

"Your beautiful self."

She refused to bite. "All right then, I'll look forward to sampling that pie."

"And I'll looking forward to seeing you," Rick said, before hanging up.

Creed scanned the solarium, looking to see if Skye had arrived. Every inch of space was occupied by people—some he'd never seen in his life. He'd had Rick contact Mills Creek's alumni association for the names and addresses of his classmates. Although each invitation to his open house had included one guest, the invitees had taken it upon themselves to bring their entire households and then some.

As his guests swarmed the bar, Creed felt a tension headache building. Why had he allowed Lydia to talk him into throwing this bash? She'd railroaded him into it, that's what she'd done, convincing him he needed as many allies as possible. By opening his home to high school friends, he would send the message that Creed Bennett had nothing to hide. This magnanimous act would endear him to his public and, at the same time, prove he hadn't dropped off the face of the earth. Why had he listened to her?

Creed circled the room, uttering the requisite welcomes. He wandered into the living room, which appeared less crowded, searching for any sign of a tall, honey-skinned beauty with a punk haircut. His eyes wandered to the entrance as another influx of guests arrived. No sign of Skye. The new arrivals melded easily with the crowd. Creed squelched his disappointment. Even though he hadn't gotten around to calling her, he'd hoped she would come.

Actually, he'd looked forward to seeing her, and tonight he had taken extra pains with his appearance. His cream-colored cashmere sweater was brand new; his gray slacks were meticulously pressed. Heck, he'd even gotten a haircut. How, in such a short space of time, had Skye Walker wormed her way into his heart? His head, he reminded himself. His heart was no longer available. It had been broken years ago, shattered beyond repair. Creed glanced at his Baume & Mercier watch. Seven-thirty. Dinner would be served at eight.

"This is some place you've got." A once-voluptuous cheerleader he vaguely remembered linked an arm through his. Creed smelled alcohol on her breath and knew he was in trouble. The blonde pressed still ample, if sagging, breasts against his arm. "Honey, will you show me the rest of the house?"

"Of course." Where was Rick when he needed him? Creed sent a silent S.O.S. across the room. He spotted the back of Rick's taupe suit, but his assistant was having too good a time flirting with a group of women to come to his aid. Looked like he was on his own.

"Pammy Sue Duggan," the brassy blonde reminded him, digging five ruby-red nails into his arm. "Why don't you show me the bedroom?"

Creed suddenly had vivid images of a bubbly girl

with a poodle cut, who'd spent the greater part of
high school on her back, servicing the entire football
team. Not much had changed since then, apparently.

"Maybe your friends would like to join us."
Creed's gesture took in the group of women Pammy
Sue had abandoned. "We can start with this floor,
then work our way up." He flashed her a practiced
smile.

The blonde's limpid blue eyes raked his body. "I'd
hoped this would be a party for two. Just you and
me, like old times."

He must have been desperate back then. Not desperate—horny. A young boy with raging hormones.
Today, barracudas like Pammy Sue made him run in
the opposite direction.

"Now, Pammy Sue, let's not hog Mills Creek's answer to Denzel," a voice behind them said.

Creed smiled, acknowledging the new arrival. Over
the years, the sultry tone hadn't changed. Fiona
Woods had been the brightest girl in his senior class
and the nicest. Beautiful, too. Now she'd grown into
an even more stunning adult. Fiona, a civil rights
attorney, who'd represented some tough cases, lived
in Virginia and was home for the holiday.

Grateful she'd come to his rescue, Creed gave
Fiona his full attention.

"I can't eat another morsel," Skye said, patting her
full stomach, declining the slice of pumpkin pie Aunt
Tonia shoved her way. "I need to leave soon. I promised a friend I'd stop by his place."

The adult family members had relocated to the
den for coffee and dessert. Mariah was down in the

basement with friends. On occasion, peals of laughter and pulsating rap music floated upstairs.

Skye watched Aunt Leona shove pie around her plate. She didn't seem to have much of an appetite. "We haven't a reason to give thanks this holiday," she pronounced solemnly. "Kris hasn't been found."

"Shush." Uncle Walter raised a hand, silencing his wife. "Now look what you've done. You've upset Tonia."

Aunt Tonia wiped the corners of her eyes with a green linen napkin. "I miss Kris so much. If she were here, she'd be . . ."

Uncle Walter put an arm around Tonia's shoulders, bringing her close. "Hush. We've got lots to be thankful for. Good health, a loving family, food on the table. Kristina will turn up eventually."

"How can you be sure?"

"Gut feeling."

Skye wished she felt as confident as he did. Kristina had been gone at least two and a half months, and still no word. Two of the missing women had turned up dead, red silk scarves wrapped around their necks. She remembered Don Washington's comments and decided it was now or never.

"Aunt Tonia," Skye began, gently, "did Kris have any hobbies?"

Tonia cocked her head. "Why, you would probably know that better than me."

"I want to make sure we're exploring all the avenues. That we're talking to the people she knew socially."

Tonia's fingers made circular patterns against her forehead. "She worked out a lot. Went at least three times a week to the gym."

"Didn't she take dance lessons?" Leona interjected. "I thought you told me she went off to Arthur Murray's at night."

"She did. So what?" Aunt Tonia defended.

"Ma, I'm taking a pie and a couple of bottles of soda to the basement," Mariah called, entering the room.

"That's fine, honey."

"Skye, can you help me carry this stuff?" Mariah headed for the kitchen.

"Sure thing." Skye pushed off the couch, smoothing the creases from her burgundy ankle-length skirt, and flicking an imaginary piece of lint off her beige sweater. "After I'm through, I've got to get going. I have a class reunion of sorts to attend."

"Oh?" Aunt Leona raised an eyebrow expectantly. "Who's hosting this shindig?"

"Actually, it's Creed Bennett."

There was a sharp intake of breath on Tonia's part. "I didn't know you were that friendly. Is there any way to discreetly ask him about Kris? I know he's no longer a suspect, but he and Kris were close, and I'm sure he knows more about her disappearance than he's letting on."

"Skye," Mariah called from the kitchen, "I really need your help."

Excusing herself, Skye answered the call.

"Okay, tall stuff," she said, when they were alone in the kitchen. "Shoot."

Mariah sniffed, pretending to be offended. "Am I really that transparent?"

"In the same league as Saran Wrap. What's on your mind?"

"I couldn't help overhearing the conversation."

"And?"

Mariah stage whispered, "And that story Kris told Mom about going off to Arthur Murray's dance studio is a crock. She needed an excuse to get out at night."

Skye folded her arms and leaned against the refrigerator. "Talk to me, girl. Why would she do that?"

Mariah balanced a pecan and apple pie in each hand. "Kris is an exotic dancer."

"How do you know that?" Skye eyeballed her cousin until Mariah squirmed uncomfortably.

"I listened in on her phone calls."

"Shame on you."

"A girl's got to do what a girl's got to do. I needed money too, and she was making tons of it."

Skye was slowly getting the picture. "Don't tell me you blackmailed Kris?"

"I wouldn't call it that. She could well afford fifty here and there. Mom would have been hurt if she knew she was entertaining men at sleazy night clubs."

"That's a pretty rotten thing to do to your sister," Skye said, shaking her head.

Mariah appeared indignant. "Why—because I charged for my silence?"

"Yes. Plus you invaded her privacy. By chance, were any of these calls from the club?"

"Yup. Usually it was this guy called Jason. He owned the Pony. He was always calling with some type of schedule change. Kris would then call Creed Bennett and cry on his shoulder. She confided in him. He knew about her problems with the men at the club."

Before Skye could ask another question, Uncle

Walter appeared in the doorway. "Came to check on you girls. Thought maybe you got lost."

Skye smiled sweetly and relieved Mariah of one pie. "We were just on our way out, weren't we?"

Mariah's angelic smile was meant to disarm. "We most certainly were. Now, Uncle Walter, if you'd hold this pecan pie, I'll get the soda out."

Forty minutes later, Skye turned over the keys of the Bronco to a hired valet. Using the long walk to Creed's front door to check her appearance, she snapped open her compact and made sure her nose wasn't shiny. Reassured there were no remnants of spinach imbedded between her teeth, she belted her long black leather coat and secured the mohair scarf around her neck.

A car door slammed nearby. A deep male voice called, "Wait up. We're both late; might as well do this together."

Skye turned to see Don Washington covering the short distance between them. "Hi, Don," she said, inwardly grimacing. He was the last person she wanted to be alone with. Even so, she allowed him to take her arm and guide her around several nasty patches of ice.

"Happy Thanksgiving. I was hoping you'd show up. We need to talk."

His too-bright eyes and the faint odor of alcohol on his breath told their own story. Only a few feet to the front door, thank God.

"Happy Thanksgiving to you too," Skye said, picking up the pace.

"What's the hurry?" Don flashed a mega-watt smile.

He's obviously used to having his way with women. "It's freezing out here."

Steps from the entrance, Creed's housekeeper opened the door, ushering them in. She took their coats. Don showed no sign of leaving Skye's side as they picked their way through what seemed like all of Mills Creek.

"Let's get a drink." He kept a firm grip on Skye's elbow, steering her in the direction of a rolling bar.

"Good idea. I can use one." Skye scanned the room, looking for a familiar face, preferably male, who was willing to strike up a conversation. Maybe she could lose Don Washington in the process.

Her gaze locked with a pair of eyes so dark in intensity, she felt the room close in. Creed made no effort to hide his interest. Waves of desire radiated across the room right at her. Like a magnet, she felt pulled to him, drawn by some invisible force, an inexplicable deep-seated attraction that must remain just that—an attraction. She couldn't afford to have her professional judgment clouded.

"Skye." Don Washington tugged on her arm. "Come on. There's a bottle of champagne over here with our names written on it."

Nine

"Who's the guy with Skye?" Creed asked, commandeering Rick's arm, and tugging him away from the bevy of women surrounding him. Creed had abandoned Pammy Sue Duggan and her friends after a quick walk-through of the house.

Rick stroked his beard and looked in the direction of Skye and her escort. "Darned if I know."

A man with a linebacker body had a proprietorial grip on Skye's arm. The two didn't seem to fit. Still, something about the man seemed familiar. Creed was too far away to see his face.

"Can you discreetly find out?"

Rick shot Skye's companion a dismissive glance. "Hardly competition for me. Why would you care?"

"I don't," Creed lied. "I just want to make sure I'm not slighting someone I grew up with. I prefer to greet old friends by name."

"Right." Rick seemed skeptical, but set off in the direction of Skye and her date. He was back within minutes.

"He's Don Washington. The name was on the alumni list. Ring a bell with you?"

"Yes. Don and I were in school together. He's the

missing coed's brother. I don't recall him being that
buff—looks like he's been pumping iron."

"Given the circumstances, I'm surprised he
showed up."

Creed shrugged. "Perhaps he has his reasons."

A heavy hand slapped Creed's back. "Hey, brother,
always knew you'd live large."

Creed turned and enveloped Kareem Davis in a
bear hug. "Kareem, glad you could make it, man."

"Never got to say thanks for lending me your car
on Halloween. I would never have made it to the
hospital so quickly if you hadn't. Ma's still sick, so I
extended my leave. That's why I've been out of cir-
culation."

"How's she feeling?"

"Well enough to have dinner at my sister's. How
come we never get together in Florida?"

Kareem was a sportscaster, residing in Naples.

"You know what they say. The closer you live, the
harder to stay in touch."

"Any of these honies available?" Kareem eyed the
women grouped throughout the room.

"Ask and you shall find out."

"I know one that's definitely single," Rick interjected.

Remembering his manners, Creed introduced
Kareem to Rick.

After shaking hands, Kareem said, "Point her out
to me."

"Check out the fox in the burgundy skirt. The one
with the gorgeous hazel eyes."

Kareem's gaze followed Rick's. "Tenderloin."

"Porterhouse. Don't even think of it, buddy, she's

taken. Gotta get over there before Washington moves in." Rick took off.

A transfixed expression on his face, Kareem stared at Skye, practically drooling. Creed resisted the urge to tell him Skye was his. He longed to go chasing after his assistant and lay claim to his turf. All in good time. As her host, Skye could hardly ignore him.

"Is she new in town?" Kareem asked.

Creed pursed his lips, debating whether to fill him in. Kareem's interest was obvious. "Remember Luke?"

"Skywalker? No-oo-oo. The chubby girl with the braces? The one I played the joke on, making her believe you were her date for the prom?"

Creed nodded. "It was a rotten thing to do. She's changed quite a bit, and you two do have something in common—you're both in the media business."

Kareem's colorful expletive was cut off by the arrival of a waiter bearing champagne. Helping himself to a glass, he moved away, throwing over his shoulder, "In that case, I'm going to offer the lady a long overdue apology."

Determined to shake Don once and for all, Skye raised her wineglass in a mock toast. "I'm making the rounds, see you later."

"I'll come with you."

Skye bit back a groan. Don was worse than chewing gum stuck to the sole of a shoe. She couldn't seem to get rid of him.

"Hey, Skye, how's it going?"

A woman in a black velvet dress and thick glasses

blocked her progress. Skye remembered the red-head from her biology class. She'd been pleasant but dense.

"Hi, Vivian, what are you doing these days?"

"I'm a nurse. I got married last year to an intern at the hospital." She pointed vaguely in the direction of the crowd. "Louis is some place over there with his buddies."

"That's wonderful; congratulations. You must know Don?" Skye prodded her self-proclaimed escort forward. "While you two catch up, there's someone I need to say hello to." She bounded off.

Skye circled the now uncomfortably warm room, conscious that Creed was somewhere amongst the milling groups of people. She stopped to admire the lit fireplace. Someone had done a truly wonderful job of turning the solarium into an autumn garden. Golden chrysanthemums overflowed huge terra-cotta pots, replacing many of the plants previously crowding the solarium. Sheaves of corn and colorful leaves rimmed the ceilings, and two pilgrims guarded the exit leading to the dining room. A delicious smell of baked goods tempted the palate. Skye sipped her wine and stared at the golden-blue flames.

"Skye Walker?"

Turning, she recognized one of Creed's high school buddies, a large handsome man with a dimpled smile; one of his inner circle. He came to stand beside her and extended a hand.

"Hi," Skye said, taking his outstretched hand. "I'm sorry, I don't remember your name."

"Kareem Davis. We went to school together." Engulfing her palm in his, he flashed another flirtatious smile. "Creed tells me we have something in common."

"What might that be?"

"Careers in the media."

"Ah," Skye sipped her wine. Confidence oozed from every pore. It was safe to say the man was a player. "What exactly is it you do?"

Kareem continued to clutch her hand like a lifeline. "I'm a sportscaster. And you?"

"A reporter, formerly with Le Monde. I'm with the Record now."

"Kindred spirits, destined to meet again." Kareem's eyes sparkled. "Can we talk?"

"Sure." The man had something on his mind. And it was definitely not business. Skye allowed him to guide her through masses of people and into the living room where several couples chatted. They stood in front of huge window walls, looking out onto the mountains.

"I owe you a big apology," Kareem began.

Skye frowned. "For?"

"A prank that I played a long time ago. It's bothered me for quite some time."

Perplexed, Skye remained silent.

"Look, I was the person who called you pretending to be Creed. I invited you to the junior prom. Back then, I had a pretty sick sense of humor. It probably wasn't much fun being stood up."

"No, it wasn't." Skye swallowed the lump at the back of her throat. She wouldn't admit just how much his cruel trick had hurt her. To think her resentment had been directed at the wrong man! All these years she'd cultivated an unhealthy hatred for Creed Bennett.

"Why did you do it?" Skye asked, careful to keep the emotion out of her voice.

Kareem Davis shrugged. "Guys can be insensitive clods at that age. I was too busy trying to be popular. I hope you'll accept my apology and at least allow me to buy you a drink later."

"Sorry, Skye will have to take a raincheck. We have plans."

Creed had approached so quietly that neither of them had heard him.

"W-w-we do?" Skye stuttered.

"Yes, darling, we do. We're Billy Lee's guests at Top Of The World. He's doing the midnight show."

Darling—where had that come from?

Kareem hid his disappointment. "Now there's another classmate that's done well. Who would have thought skinny Billy would become a successful jazz musician?"

"If you care to brave the dozens of women mobbing 'skinny Billy,' you might share your thoughts with him. He arrived five minutes ago."

"I think I'll do just that. Later." Kareem took off.

Skye turned to face Creed. "Did I look like I needed rescuing?"

"Ummm hmmm."

She inhaled his woodsy fragrance. He smelled like the outdoors. When he touched her arm, the tips of her toes tingled and her mouth went dry.

"I'm glad you came," Creed said in a voice several octaves lower than she remembered. "Rick told me you had another engagement."

"I'm glad I came too." Skye smiled at him, her first genuine smile, one that was actually warm and welcoming. She might have been wrong about him.

He wasn't the callous, self-centered person she'd initially thought. But could she trust him?

Creed glanced at his Baume & Mercier. "Dinner's
buffet style. Food's being served in the dining room
and solarium as we speak. Hungry?"

"Stuffed, and I've gotta watch my calories." She
patted her hips.

"Hardly." Creed's blue-black gaze roamed over
her. The heat in her face settled in places that
throbbed. "Then let's skip dinner. I've supervised
the preparations and sampled everything all day."

"What do you have in mind?" Skye asked, inten-
tionally flirting.

"You and me spending time together. The Top Of
The World is a pretty noisy place to get to know each
other."

No way could she pass up an opportunity to be
alone with Creed. Somehow she would subtly bring
the conversation around to Kris and see what she
learned. "So, your invitation to hear Billy Lee play
is genuine?" she asked.

"Surprised I'm asking you out?" Creed's index finger playfully touched the tip of her nose.

"Taken aback." He was more relaxed than she'd
ever seen him, and he was flirting outrageously. Skye
knew playing with Creed was like stepping on quick-
sand; she could easily get sucked in.

"I'll grab a plate of hors d'oeuvres and a bottle of
whatever you're drinking and we'll hide in my suite."
He smoothed an escaping tendril off her forehead.

Skye pretended to think about his proposition.
"That may not be such a good idea."

Creed wiggled his eyebrows. "Half an hour. What
can happen . . . unless you want it to?"

"Plenty. The door remains open."

"Scouts honor."

Skye laughed out loud. "Creed, I don't ever recall you being a scout."

With exaggerated movements, he snapped his fingers. A red handkerchief floated in the air. Creed deftly caught the material and folded it around his neck. "Always wanted to be. That, and a knight in shining armor." He took her hand, edging her toward the exit.

A red handkerchief. A scarf. Her imagination ricocheted out of control. "I'm not one of your damsels in distress," she managed to get out.

Upstairs in his sitting room, while Skye reclined on an emerald-green divan gazing at the fire, Creed popped the champagne cork. He poured them both a glass. Through that process, Skye's eyes remained closed. He'd never seen her so relaxed.

"Have you made plans for the holidays?" Creed asked.

Skye's hazel eyes flickered open, quietly appraising him. "I'd considered going out west and visiting my mother, but the more I think about battling airlines and airports, I'm tempted to stay put. I haven't seen a white Christmas in awhile and I'd like to ski and tube."

"Maybe we can do both together?"

"Possibly."

Creed could tell by her slightly raised eyebrows he'd surprised her. He'd surprised himself too.

She seemed dubious. "You'll be here that long?"

"At least through the first of the year."

Skye sat up, swinging long legs off the divan. She reached for the glass of champagne he'd placed on the coffee table. The split in her skirt parted, giving Creed an unfettered view of silk-clad thighs. He felt a tug in his groin and forced himself to think of the lover who'd betrayed him—Chantal, the woman he'd planned on spending the rest of his life with, who'd sold him down the river for a story. He'd never forget the hurt, the feeling of betrayal. The mockery she'd made of his heart. He was attracted to Skye, yes, but no way would he trust a reporter again.

"Did you know Kristina Brown was an exotic dancer?"

Creed was taken aback by the abrupt switch in conversation but was determined not to show it. He sipped his wine and gazed at the woman across from him.

"You did. Didn't you?" Skye persisted.

"What makes you say that?"

"You were friends. I found out she danced at the Psychedelic Pony nights and weekends. Did she dance at clubs in Fort Lauderdale, too?"

Creed shrugged. "Look, I was never Kristina's keeper. What she did on her own time was strictly her business. It wasn't for me to make judgments."

"So you did know." Skye rose and began pacing the circumference of the sitting room. Eventually she squatted in front of the fire. Creed left the comfort of his chair and crouched beside her. The flickering flames of the fireplace danced across her head and features, illuminating her lovely hazel eyes and turning her hair an appealing shade of auburn. Was she even the tiniest bit interested in him or was she just using him?

"I don't want to talk about Kristina Brown," Creed said, tilting Skye's chin up toward him.

"But I do," Skye persisted.

"You've got an obsession with the woman."

To silence her, Creed brushed his lips against hers. She tasted like champagne, slightly tart but heady. He increased the pressure until her lips parted.

"Oh my," Skye sighed.

She wasn't protesting. She seemed to enjoy his kiss. His tongue swept the insides of her mouth rhythmically. Gently, he lowered them to the floor, deepening the kiss in the process. Skye wound her arms around his neck, pulling him closer. Her heart beat a rapid pitter-pat, and her sharp intake of breath smelled of champagne. When her nipples stiffened against his chest, he reached down to cup one full breast. She purred like an overfed kitten, and instinctively he knew she was his for the taking.

Good judgment flew out the window. Skye was no longer a reporter. She was a woman—and a sexy one, at that. They were both consenting adults caught up in the moment. Who was to stop them from taking the next step, then deciding whether to continue from there? She would be a willing and involved partner, he sensed, as he nudged her sweater upward.

Footsteps sounded behind them, then a rapid retreat.

"Uh, excuse me, I didn't know you would be . . . uh . . . occupied."

Rick's voice. Rick.

"What is it?" Creed scrambled upright, his voice husky.

Skye rolled over and made a valiant attempt to straighten her clothing. After a second or two, she bounded to her feet and pretended to be mesmerized by the fire.

"Your father's downstairs," Rick said, quietly. "Vilma's been able to keep him in the kitchen so your guests aren't disturbed. I don't know how long she can hold him there."

Creed felt a familiar anger surface. Trust Jed to show up uninvited, bent on ruining his party.

"How did he get in?" Creed managed.

"He convinced the guards at the gatehouse you'd invited him. As you have so often said, this is a small town and everyone knows who he is."

"Did you ask him why he's here?"

"I did. He claims he wants to thank you for the food you sent to his boardinghouse."

"A likely story."

"This is none of my business," Skye interjected, touching Creed's arm, "but why risk a scene? Go down, wish him a happy Thanksgiving, and send him home in a cab."

"Will you come with me?"

"If you'd like."

Though Rick's face remained expressionless, his eyes were cold, hard pebbles. Without another word, he left them.

Ten

An unsmiling Creed faced his father. "Why did you come?"

His tone was uncompromising, challenging, spawned by years of hard feelings and ancient hurts. Skye hung back as the two men stared each other down. Finally, Jed looked away. They would have to work it out, she decided. This wasn't her fight. She'd only agreed to accompany Creed because he'd asked, and because she sensed he needed support. But she wouldn't take sides.

Jed took an unsteady step forward. Skye smelled alcohol and almost gagged. If someone lit a match close by, he might very well ignite.

"What—I'm not welcome in your home?" Jed slurred.

"I never said that." Creed struggled to hide the revulsion on his face.

It must be difficult seeing your father in this condition, Skye decided. Jed had made a concerted effort to tidy up. He wore trousers from an ancient suit, a starched shirt with a slightly frayed collar, and a pair of suspenders that held the pants on his gaunt frame. His worn overcoat hung over a kitchen chair.

"Then why wasn't I allowed inside? I'm not good enough?" He puffed out his chest.

"Look, you're drunk."

"Says who?"

"Says me."

Both men's index fingers stabbed the air. They were like two kids in a schoolyard, vying for power. Before the exchange grew more heated, Skye stepped in. "Maybe Jed would like something to eat."

Creed thought about it and relaxed. "Da—are you hungry?"

It was the closest she'd heard Creed come to addressing his father as dad. The old man's face softened. With an imperceptible nod of his head he indicated his willingness to eat. He jerked a thumb at Skye. "She your woman?"

Creed smiled a devilish smile and turned to her. "Are you?"

The conversation had spiraled out of control. This wasn't about her or about "them." A heated kiss and some intimate groping did not a relationship make.

"Sit down, Jed, and I'll fix you a plate," Skye said, narrowing her eyes at Creed.

"Think I will. A beer would go down nice, too."

"Sorry. Can't help you there." She sent a silent S.O.S. Creed's way.

He opened the refrigerator, removed a can, and set it in front of his father, who'd plopped into a chair. As Skye heaped food onto a plate, she watched the men. It was the first time she noted any similarity. Jed's eyes were bloodshot, but they were the same midnight blue as Creed's. They shared the same caramel-colored skin. She placed the plate in the microwave.

With a piffing sound, Jed popped the tab. The noise punctuated an awkward silence. Jed took a long swallow and put the can down. "Good stuff. Expensive. You in trouble with the law, son?"

Creed frowned. "What gives you that impression?"

"The newspapers. Talk around town."

"Shouldn't believe everything you hear."

Jed tossed back his beer and belched loudly. "I don't. Might be able to help though. I get around."

Skye's reporter's instincts kicked in. "How so, Jed? What have you heard?"

"There've been a couple of undercover cops at the Pony asking questions. I don't go there much, you understand, only now and then. My friends fill me in."

"And?"

"The police have been nosing around, asking about Creed. Whether he's ever shown up at the club and stuff like that."

Skye made a mental note of all she'd heard. Kristina and Jamie, dancers? Creed's patronage at adult clubs? What did it all mean?

"There's also talk that the Brown girl's been seen in Fort Lauderdale at one of the clubs."

"Wishful thinking," Creed muttered.

Skye's attention snapped back to him. He'd said the words with such certainty. Like a man who knew more.

"Blood's got to look out for blood," Jed said. "This information must be worth something to you."

Creed dug deep in his pocket and threw a fistful of bills on the table. A disgusted look on his face, he snapped, "Finish your meal and I'll have my man drive you home."

Without another glance at his father, he grabbed Skye's hand and pulled her from the room.

"And now I give you Mills Creek's Billy Lee," the owner of the Top Of The World boomed.

An enthusiastic burst of applause followed, then high-pitched whistles and stamping feet. A spotlight shone center stage as the musician bounded on. The chanting began: "Bill-y, Bill-y, Bill-y."

A full house, Skye registered. Every table and chair was occupied. Standing room only. She and Creed had been lucky to have a table up front, prearranged by Billy, most likely.

Skye shouted over the noise. "You and Billy stayed in touch?"

"Through our agents mostly. Early in our careers, we shared the occasional gig."

The subject of their discussion brought the shiny saxophone to his lips and blew a few tentative notes. The room quieted. Billy's tune began softly, slowly, building in intensity. Skye was mesmerized by his agile fingers, his mouth, the expression on his face, as he became lost in his music—totally absorbed. The notes trembled, then with crystal clarity, reached out and wrapped themselves around her soul. She relaxed, the tension slowly eroding, letting his music work its magic. Her eyes shifted momentarily to the people around her. They, too, seemed mesmerized as Billy made musical love to his saxophone and audience.

Skye finally dared look at Creed. He, too, had

fallen under Billy's spell. He'd let his mask down and his expression reflected raw emotion. She'd never seen him so vulnerable. There was a tender side to Creed Bennett, she realized.

At the tables close by, a few couples held hands, while some of the more brazen kissed. Others simply looked dreamy-eyed, bowled over by the beauty of the music and unsure what hit them. It dawned on Skye that she was on a date with Creed Bennett. The Mighty Creed. The man most women would give their eyeteeth to go out with. She shot Creed a not-so-subtle look. He winked at her.

Billy's tempo picked up. He blew short, sweet notes now, touching her emotions with his music, his fingers. He smiled and waved to them. Creed flipped a thumb up, acknowledging the musician's greeting, letting him know he was more than satisfied. Billy's eyelids lowered, his head tilted back. His fingers stroked the saxophone, sensuality oozing with each movement.

"Let's get out of here," Creed whispered.

Skye immediately snapped back to the present. She was safe in this crowded room. Alone, well . . . who knew? "We're Billy's guests; wouldn't that be rude?" she whispered back.

"Half of the people here are Billy's guests. That's the crux of the problem, or he could be bigger. He does this all for love."

"And you don't?"

He threw her a simply dazzling smile. "Love and money. I learned early on, success isn't always about talent. It's hard work, good P.R., and keeping an eye on your business." He retrieved their coats, then took her hand.

With some trepidation, Skye followed him from the club. She saw Don Washington standing at the bar, but avoided eye contact.

Once in Creed's car, Skye faked a yawn. "It's late; aren't you tired?" she asked.

"No. Are you?"

"A little."

Creed started the automobile. "My small talk needs improvement, obviously." He squeezed her shoulder and flashed that killer smile again. "Just a while ago you were wide-eyed and captivated by Billy's music. You appeared to have fallen under his spell."

"Right!" Skye slapped his thigh. When her hand made contact with hard sinew and muscle, she immediately regretted it. What would it be like to . . . No, better not think of it.

Creed steered the car in the direction of his home. He tapped a finger against the clock on the dashboard. "It's not quite midnight. Didn't you say you had the day off tomorrow?"

"I didn't. Reporters never have time off."

"Or are off," Creed said, softly.

She decided to ignore the jab. "All right. All right. Technically, I have tomorrow off."

"Good. I don't have an appointment until midafternoon. Perhaps we can enjoy a nice leisurely nightcap and talk."

Creed brought the Jag to a brief stop in front of the guard gate and waited to be let in. He followed the meandering driveway, coming to a stop in his underground garage. Skye felt the slightest trepidation as the garage door lowered behind her. Creed would have to be stupid to lure her here under false

pretenses. Several people had seen them leaving the
restaurant together. Even so, she needed to take control of the situation, and soon, before he got the
wrong idea. One quick drink, then she'd thank him
for a lovely evening, get into her Bronco, and drive
away.

They sat next to each other in the solarium, a fire
in the fireplace, shadows flickering across the walls.
Creed poured them two Sambucus and Skye took
small sips of the licorice liqueur.

"Do you think Kristina Brown is dead?" she began,
savoring the warmth the drink produced.

Creed shrugged. "I'd rather not talk about
Kristina. Let's talk about you and me."

"What's there to talk about?"

Creed pierced her with those brooding dark eyes
of his. "Let's not play games. Before Rick interrupted, we were going at it pretty hot and heavy."

"And you brought me back here to continue
where we left off?"

He rose and went to stand by the fireplace. "Not
necessarily. Although I wouldn't be opposed, if that's
what you want."

Talk about laying your cards on the table! Skye got up,
moving closer to him. "You know, there was a time
in my life when I hated you." She trailed her fingers
against the mantle.

The back of Creed's hand brushed her cheek.
"What made you change your mind?"

She hesitated, sensing they were at a pivotal point
in their tentative friendship. "Kareem admitted he
was the one who'd called to ask me to the prom. All
these years I thought it was you."

"It was a cruel trick to play. You must have been

terribly hurt." He linked his hands around her neck and drew her closer. His body heat sent off dangerous signals, and the woodsy scent of pine filled her nostrils, causing her senses to whirl.

"I was devastated," Skye admitted. "What little self-esteem I had went down the toilet."

"Oh, honey, I'm sorry."

Honey! His lips brushed hers. She put caution aside, ignoring the voice in the back of her mind warning her to proceed carefully. This man could be dangerous, and not just to her physical well-being. He had the power to flip her heart inside out, and wreak havoc with her emotions.

"I want to make love to you, Skye," Creed said, boldly.

His voice penetrated the warm cocoon she'd been wrapped in. So it had come down to this. This whole night—this incredible evening—was all about having sex.

It had been a while since she'd been with a man. When her romance with Jacques ended, she'd dated an Algerian photographer, but had been reluctant to take their relationship to the next step. Yet, here she was actually considering Creed's rather ungarnished proposition.

"Skye, look at me. I won't do anything you don't want me to."

She snapped out of her reverie, focusing on him. His incredible eyes swept her face, raw passion reflecting in their depths. He would be an artful lover, she sensed. God, was she tempted. He just might help her believe that the overweight girl with the pimply face no longer existed—the one none of the boys wanted.

"All right."

He seemed stunned that she'd so readily agreed and, after a beat or two, said, "Come with me." He held out his hand.

Skye entwined her fingers in his. Together they headed for the staircase.

Upstairs in his bedroom suite, they faced each other. A Luther Vandross song played softly in the background and two scented candles burned on the mantle of the unlit fireplace. The rest of the house was blanketed in darkness. It was deadly quiet—eerily so. Rick and Vilma were most likely asleep.

Creed's fingers played with the buttons of her shirt. He undid the top one, then paused to caress the hollow at her neck. A flash of liquid heat coursed through her. With certainty, she knew she wanted this man and would give anything to feel his hands on her body. Why did it have to be him?

Creed's eyes remained hooded as he slowly undid one button, then another. It was sheer madness on her part to think she could readily turn off her emotions and hop into bed with him. There would be consequences. Feelings.

"Skye," Creed whispered, his fingers circling her flesh, plucking at the Victoria's Secret bra she'd changed into at the last minute.

"Yes?"

"Did anyone ever tell you you're beautiful?"

Lots of men had, but she'd never believed them. Skye wasn't sure she believed him now, much as she wanted to.

He worked the shirt off, and his lips soon replaced his roaming fingers, teasing her nipples. His tongue left wet trails in its wake before diving downward to find her cleavage. She arched into him, inhaling his scent, enjoying the heat sizzling between them. Luther hit a high note and held it, just as Creed's hands cupped her buttocks, bringing her even closer. She felt a pulsating hardness against her flesh.

Refusing to let her brain take over, Skye reached for his belt buckle. His sharp intake of breath surprised her when she loosened the notch and proceeded to unzipper him. He wore black briefs.

As he stepped out of his pants, Skye unsnapped her bra.

"God, baby," he panted loudly, soft palms circling her globes.

This time when he kissed her, both feet left the floor. She molded herself against him.

"I'm taking you to bed."

A pounding at the door slowly penetrated.

"Open up, Creed. It's important."

Rick's voice, an urgent demand, couldn't have come at a worse time.

There was a muttered expletive on Creed's part, a frustrated sigh on hers.

Removing his hands from her quivering body, Creed stepped into his pants and headed for the door.

Eleven

"What do you want?" Creed said, cracking the door several inches and peering through the opening.

"Sorry. Did I wake you?"

Rick's tone dripped sarcasm, and he didn't sound sorry at all. Creed wondered what the attitude was about. Ah-ha! He'd wanted Skye from the moment he'd laid eyes on her. And now, the entire town of Mills Creek, having seen them together, had fabricated their own story.

"It's late to come knocking." Creed held an arm out, pointing to the illuminated face of his watch. He smothered a loud yawn, hoping Rick would get the message. "It's after one. Has something happened?"

"Plenty. If you'd allow me to come in, I'll tell you."

"Can't we discuss it tomorrow?"

His assistant shook his head. "Look, Lydia's phoned several times. She said it was extremely important you get back to her tonight."

"Sounds like trouble."

"Just call her, okay? And don't forget, you have an appointment at two this afternoon. I got the executive director of the Boys and Girls Club to fit you into his calendar. See you at breakfast."

Rick retreated and Creed shut the door firmly behind him. When he turned back to Skye, he saw she'd used those few minutes to dress and now faced him. "I'd better get going," she said, picking up her purse.

"I'm sorry that happened. Bad timing on Rick's part."

Skye flashed a wan smile and Creed wondered if she might be grateful for the reprieve. Rick's untimely arrival might have actually been a blessing in disguise. It allowed them a cooling off period. Bedding Skye Walker would not be without its consequences, that was for sure. He knew that. She knew that.

"I'll walk you to your car," he said, taking her hand. "Let me get our coats."

"Thanks."

Without saying another word, they crept downstairs and out of the house.

Preoccupied with the pending phone call to Lydia, Creed placed a perfunctory kiss on her lips and waited while she started the car. "I'll call you," he shouted, just as she rolled up the window and put the automobile in gear.

Retracing his steps, he made a quick stop in the kitchen, where he poured himself a glass of water. But even downing the contents didn't take the edge off his thirst.

"I'm glad you called," Lydia said, in a tight little voice.

"What's so urgent?" Creed flopped onto the couch, cradling the receiver against his ear.

"I've got bad news. The cops just found Tammy's decomposed body."

She sobbed non-stop for a couple of seconds while he remained silent, digesting the news. Tamara Linley had been his administrative assistant; a pretty girl with a head full of problems. Tammy was a single parent working diligently on her masters. Creed, on more than one occasion, had tried to help her out, throwing extra money her way, offering her overtime when he didn't really need it.

"Where was she found?"

"On Hollywood Beach. A surfer discovered what was left of her body on the sand. She had a red scarf wrapped around her neck."

"The family must be devastated."

Lydia sniffled. "Her ex-husband is a mess. I saw him on Live At Seven. He swears he'll get the person who killed Tammy."

"I didn't think he cared one way or the other."

"Oh, Creed, that's cold. They may not have been together, but a bond still existed. They shared two beautiful children, a boy and a girl. It's an awful ending. She was so young and had her whole life ahead of her. Naturally, the media's hyped up and speculating like crazy. Now all the old stories are surfacing again, and reporters are swarming all over your Fort Lauderdale property. It's just a matter of time before they head North."

Creed's free hand massaged his aching temple. Was there no end to this nightmare? "Take care of the funeral arrangements, Lydia. Make sure the family doesn't have to lay out a penny," he ordered.

"I anticipated you'd say that; that's why I brought Rick into the loop. He'll take care of it."

"You're a good and loyal friend," Creed said.

When he hung up, he headed for the bar and poured himself a double Scotch, downing the drink in one swift motion.

"What are you doing here, gal?" Pete Martini stubbed out the cigarette he defiantly smoked, ignoring the huge "No Smoking" sign above his head. The Record was a smoke-free environment, but you couldn't prove that by Pete. "Thought you were taking the morning off," he added, looking at Skye with red-rimmed eyes.

"I lied. What's going on?" She yawned and fanned the air around her. "Pugh! That thing stinks."

"What stinks?" Pete pocketed the butt of his cigarette and gave her an innocent look.

"That smelly thing you're hiding." She slung her Coach briefcase onto a desk already overflowing with papers and booted up her computer. Yawning again, she asked, "Did you make coffee?"

"Yup." With a slight raise of an eyebrow, Pete tossed aside the paperwork he'd been scribbling on. "Anything you want to tell me?"

"Nothing I know of." She tossed a quizzical glance his way. It wasn't like Pete to fish.

"Like what's going on with you and your magician friend?"

"You just crossed the line." Skye pretended to glare at him and he chuckled.

"Get me a coffee too, will ya?"

Ignoring his smirk, she crawled past him, muttering. She made her way down an unending row of empty cubicles. Everyone must be off the day after Thanksgiving. She returned from the staff lounge with two steaming mugs and set Pete's down. She'd kept it jet black like he liked it. Gulping her own coffee, she flopped into her chair and typed in her password.

Pete came to stand beside her. She could smell the remnants of last night's partying on him.

"Had I known you'd have front-row seats at Billy Lee's shindig," he said, snidely, "I'd have had you review him."

Turning toward him, Skye narrowed her eyes. "And just how did that piece of information come your way?"

Pete slurped his coffee, making gurgling noises. "If you'd been less preoccupied with Creed Bennett, you would have noticed me sitting in the back with one of the local bimbos."

Skye made a tsking sound. "What a way to refer to your date."

"Just calling it like it was. Body that would stop traffic but no brain. Bored me to death." Pete's eyes searched her monitor, scanning her e-mail. "Didn't you once tell me you despised Bennett?"

"I don't recall saying that." Using her mouse, she arbitrarily clicked on a message.

"You sure did, and a whole lot more." A stubby index finger stabbed the screen. "Who's that from?"

Skye glanced where he was pointing. "Altarboy? That's a new one." She read the subject out loud. "Creed Bennett's women disappear. Could you be next?"

Pete's fingers pressed into her shoulder. She could

tell he was concerned. "Someone's trying to warn you, gal." The grip on her shoulders eased, turning into a pat instead. "Creed Bennett's no killer. Someone's out to frame him. I can smell it."

How could he be so sure of Creed's innocence when she wasn't? Who was this Altarboy who'd taken it upon himself to warn her? What if the person was right and she was next?

Later that day, Creed was shown into the shabby office of Miguel Santiago, executive director of the Boys and Girls Club, by an awed receptionist.

"Cr-cr-eed Bennett! Is it really you?" the brunette stuttered. "I can hardly believe it." A dimpled hand clutched her ample bosom.

Santiago, a stocky Latino of indeterminate age, rose from behind a battered desk. "Mr. Bennett, thank you for coming. My entire staff is thrilled at the idea of working with you. Seldom does someone of your stature seek to give back to the community." He pumped Creed's hand energetically.

"I consider it a pleasure, Mr. Santiago." When he was able to, Creed retrieved his hand, inwardly grimacing at the discomfort the director's firm handshake left behind.

"The name's Miguel. Have a seat."

"Call me Creed." He sank into a vinyl armchair that showed evidence of losing its stuffing. "Miguel," he said, to the overly enthusiastic director, "I've wanted to work with young people most of my adult life. I just haven't had the time until now."

"Coffee?" Miguel's receptionist interrupted, re-

turning with a pot. She filled her boss's cup and undulated in Creed's direction.

"No, thanks. Water if you have it." As the tittering
receptionist left to do his bidding, Creed turned up
his smile a megawatt.

Miguel eyed Creed over the brim of his cup. "What
did you have in mind?"

"Putting together a series of magic clinics. The
kids will be out of school in a few weeks and this
would give them something to do. My stage assistant,
Felicity, and I will gladly teach the basics of the
craft."

"Love it," Miguel Santiago said, jumping to his
feet and rubbing his palms together. "Maybe at the
conclusion, we can have a holiday show and charge
admission. We're a not-for-profit organization but
can sure use the funding."

"Done deal. When would you like me to start?"

Miguel's index finger worked the lines on his forehead. "I just thought of something. What if the parents are hesitant to . . ."

". . . to have me work with their kids?" Creed
shrugged, then splayed his hands wide. "Look, I can
only tell you that despite all the media hype, I haven't been arrested. Hopefully, the adults of this
town are intelligent enough to draw their own conclusions."

"Let's hope so. Dina," Miguel bellowed, "bring me
in the December schedule."

After the receptionist returned bearing both water
and calendar, Miguel Santiago turned his full attention back to Creed. "Let's pick some dates that will
work for you."

"Sounds like a plan," Creed said, releasing the breath he didn't know he was holding.

"This is getting stranger and stranger," Skye muttered, tossing copies of the Sun Sentinel's articles on the floor. A colleague at the Florida newspaper had scanned more recent articles and forwarded them to her via e-mail. While scrutinizing the pieces, Skye had learned that in addition to being Creed's administrative assistant, Tamara Linley had been an exotic dancer.

First Kristina, then Jamie Washington, now Tamara. Nibbling on her bottom lip, she tucked away this new piece of information to mull over later. So far the evidence didn't look good for Creed. A few weeks ago she would willingly have believed anything about Creed Bennett. Now, she didn't know. She reached down to scratch behind Hogan's ear. The dog licked her face then nuzzled his nose deeper beneath the comforter they lay wrapped in.

It didn't all compute. Creed Bennett had the world by the bazookas. He'd achieved more than most mortals ever would: fame, fortune, international acclaim. Plus he was handsome. What could possibly be his motive for killing these women? He'd have to be nuts. Then again, logic often didn't come into play with an emotionally unstable person.

Hogan shifted and made a whimpering sound. Skye smoothed the animal's silky fur, making soothing noises. She really should get up and throw another log on the fire, instead of lying here, staring at the dying embers. So much for coming home early to sort out her crazy mixed-up feelings; if anything, she was more confused.

Just thinking about Creed Bennett made her body ache for his touch. The adult Creed was different from the spirited teenager she remembered. He was much more complicated, and definitely more intriguing. Even the information strewn across her floor had not caused her to think differently of him. She wanted to know this man. Too bad Rick Morales had chosen that moment to knock on the door.

Hogan's insistent growling penetrated her inertia. The little dog's ears stood straight up, and his sharp claws dug into the tender spots of her chest. Some uninvited person was at her home calling her name.

"Skye."

Creed's voice. Skye flung the old comforter aside as Hogan raced ahead of her. Willing her queasy stomach to settle, she placed one foot in front of the other. So much for working this thing through; the object of her thoughts had arrived on her front steps.

A series of rat-a-tat-tats shook her door. Skye tugged at the sweatsuit she'd slipped into, adjusted the top over her hips, and slid the ragtag sleeves up her arms.

"Open up," Creed called. "Your car's out front. I know you're home."

"Hang on a minute. I'm coming."

Hastily, she ran her fingers through her hair, nudging the spiky haircut into some semblance of order. What if he was here to pick up where they'd left off earlier? She threw the door open as Hogan bayed and began circling Creed's ankles.

"Sit," Skye admonished. The dog sat. Skye raised her eyes and met Creed's stare head on. For a long moment, neither said a word. Eventually, she tore her gaze away.

"May I come in?" Creed asked, rubbing his palms together and blowing on them.

Skye stood aside to let him by. His arrival brought with it the blustery evening air and the faint smell of pine. Magically, Hogan's whining ceased, but the suspicious terrier's stare followed Creed every step of the way.

"I had an appointment nearby," he said, by way of explanation. "I figured it was as good a time as any to come by and apologize." He removed his mohair coat and flung it over the arm of the sofa. Crossing over to the fireplace, he bent to retrieve a log and tossed it on. Red and yellow sparks, like the ones behind her eyes, shot up the chimney.

"Apologize for what?" She asked, not wanting to make things easy for him. It didn't take a genius to know that he was here to tell her that last evening had been a huge mistake. The Mighty Creed had gotten in way over his head and now wanted out.

"For the rather abrupt ending to our evening, of course."

She knew her mouth hung open and heat flooded her face. Pushing aside memories of how he'd made her body come alive, she kept her voice even. "Sometimes things happen for a reason."

"Do they, now?" He was so close, she could feel his warm breath searing her face. When he tilted her chin up, she shuttered her eyes.

"Yes."

The pad of his thumb skimmed her jaw, making her insides wobble. "Stop fighting your attraction to me. You and I have been on fire for each other from the moment we became reacquainted." He dipped his head, and she shifted so that his lips made contact with her neck instead. She wasn't ready to let him play with her emotions.

"You mentioned you had an appointment close by," she said, breathlessly.

"Yes." The tip of his tongue skimmed her lower lip. "I'm working on a project with the Boys and Girls Club."

"Sounds intriguing." His tongue plunged into her open mouth and common sense took wings.

When she came up for breath, she picked up Hogan and held him like a barrier between them. She said the first thing that came to mind. "You drove way out of your way. The club's got to be a good fifteen miles from here."

Creed's devilish smile tugged at her heart. "I'm busted. Truth is, I needed an excuse to see you."

Her head and heart weren't ready to handle this. "You must be thirsty. I'll get us something to drink." She practically raced from the room.

When she returned, Creed's head was buried in the papers she'd discarded. She set down the tray of drinks and took a moment to observe him. He wore a black pullover sweater and gray corduroy pants. His ears still bore the effects of the frigid November temperatures that had settled on Mills Creek. Tinges of pink showed under the caramel of his skin, and, although he reclined on her sofa, long legs splayed out in front of him, she could tell what he was reading did not make him happy.

"I see you found the articles," she said, matter-of-factly.

He tossed the papers shut and stood up. "Are you checking up on me, Skye?"

"What?"

He picked up his coat. "Those articles are from The Sun Sentinel. Hardly a local paper."

"I'm a reporter."

"How could I have forgotten?" His icy smile told her that whatever opinion he'd had of her had plummeted. "Your kind would do anything for a story, even sleep with a man you consider a murderer."

"Please let me explain."

"No explanation necessary. Save those wide-eyed innocent looks for someone easily conned. I'm out of here."

The door practically slammed in her face as he let himself out.

Twelve

Hands gripping the steering wheel, Creed catapulted the Jag up and down the treacherous mountain roads. An ancient Pointer Sisters tune blasted from the stereo. He vented his anger by pressing the accelerator to the floor. *How could she do this to him?* The expensive automobile shot forward as he hurled through the dusk with no particular destination in mind, his sole goal to put as much distance between himself and Skye as possible. Just as he'd begun to trust her, she'd failed him.

Focused on keeping the car on the road, his knuckles practically popped from their sockets. Maneuvering a sharp curve, he gripped the steering wheel even tighter. Skye was what he'd thought of all day. Even during his meeting with Santiago, visions of her haunting face and enticing body had taunted him. He'd left the meeting wanting to see her so badly, it had become a physical ache. And though he'd been unsure of his welcome, some invisible force had prompted him to show up at her door.

"Dammit!" Creed yelled, pounding on the steering wheel as the shrill scream of a siren penetrated.

He hit the brake just as the cop car came into sight, revolving amber lights illuminated.

He eased the automobile onto the side of the road, and the police car came to a rolling stop behind him. Reaching for his wallet, he removed both license and registration. A circular beam illuminated the interior of the Jag and a dark silhouette loomed before him. He hit the automated button, rolling down the window.

"Yes, Officer?"

The policeman approached the driver's side. "License and registration, please." He shone the flashlight directly in Creed's eyes.

Creed held both out to the man. The light flickered across his face briefly. "Creed Bennett! Who would think we'd meet over a traffic violation? Any idea how fast you were going?"

"Not a clue," Creed said warily, resigned to getting a ticket.

The cop leaned into the open window, elbows resting on the ledge. "Buddy, you were doing close to eighty in a thirty-mile zone."

"I must have been preoccupied."

"Pretty lame excuse. In our high school days, you could come up with a much better tale." The cop lowered his flashlight but made no move to take his license and registration. "You don't remember me, do you?"

"Should I?" The voice was vaguely familiar, but in the rapidly darkening evening, the policeman's face was a blur. "Freddy. Freddy Newton." The name finally popped into his head. "That's me, bud."

"The Incredible Hulk. How are you, man?"

"Holding my own. I hated to miss your party, but

couldn't get the time off. Heard there was a nice turn out."

"Almost all of the old gang showed."

They chatted for a few minutes then made plans to get together.

"Speed limit's thirty," Freddy reminded, before zooming off.

Creed waited until the police car had disappeared before putting the Jag into gear. Thank God they'd been friends in high school. Any other cop would have given him a ticket. His thoughts turned back to Skye. He'd acted irrationally. What if she'd had a perfectly logical explanation for requesting those articles? He was tempted to return to her place and get it all sorted out. No. He'd go home. Tomorrow was another day; he'd deal with it then.

As he approached the narrow path leading to the guard house, he noticed several cars parked off to the side. Instinct told him something wasn't right. He made a sharp U and turned on his cell phone. The phone rang almost immediately.

"Where are you? I've been trying to reach you," Rick Morales said.

"About a half a mile away. My phone was off."

"Don't use the main entrance. Take the back way. The guard says he's being harassed by reporters. He's had to call backup security."

"Oh, boy."

"Go to dinner, just don't come home. I'll call you when it's safe."

After the conversation ended, Creed found himself steering the car in the direction of Skye's house.

* * *

Skye bit into a juicy chicken breast, savoring every morsel. She was eating non-stop, a sure sign she was upset. She chased the chicken with a mouthful of sweet tea, heaped her fork full of potato salad, and closed her eyes. No one made potato salad like Food For The Soul. No one.

The tiny restaurant had been around forever. It was nothing more than a hole in the wall but had survived the chic gourmet invasion. Supposedly it had been the meeting place of the few African Americans in Mills Creek who'd found Black Power. Today, it was managed by an interracial couple, who, judging from their vintage clothes, were throwbacks from the seventies.

The place had a definite sixties feel and reminded Skye of an East Village eatery. Black lights gave off a surreal glow while at the same time shielding the patrons from prying eyes. The scent of Patchouli lay heavily in the air, and Stokely Carmichael posters were mounted in prominent places.

Skye shoveled food into her face while staring at the rainbow colors of the lava lamp. She'd made a real mess of things with Creed. He had every right to feel deceived, and calling her a con artist had been justified. But how could she explain to him that reporters had an insatiable curiosity? How could she turn her back on a story of this magnitude? Her entire professional career, no one had ever taken her seriously. She'd been assigned fluff. Accepting the job at the Pocono Record had been a step in the right direction. She'd finally had the opportunity to do some real reporting.

"How's your meal?"

Skye registered the voice of one of the owners—a

shapely woman with a large salt-and-pepper Afro. Her husband, a bottle-blonde with a waist-length ponytail hovered at her heels.

"Every bit as good as I remembered."

"That's what we like to hear. You're not a tourist, then?"

"Hardly. I've been gone from Mills Creek a while. Now I'm back."

"Well, don't be a stranger," the husband interjected. "And to ensure you're not, dessert's on us." With a nod and a smile they walked away, leaving Skye to attack her chicken.

She had just sunk her teeth into a particularly tender piece of breast when there was a commotion at the entrance. Squinting in that direction, the low lighting prevented her from getting a clear view of the new arrival. From the sounds of whispered conversation, this person must be important. Skye focused on her potato salad and bit into her collard greens. If she didn't stop eating soon, she would never stop.

The blonde owner, his wife bringing up the rear, led a man by her table. Skye clutched a chicken wing as if she would never let go and ventured a look up. The patron's black sweater was familiar; so were his grey corduroy pants. Creed. What was he doing here? With any luck he would not notice her.

"I'll send that dessert over in a minute," the male owner said, stopping abruptly in front of Skye.

"Thank you." She mouthed the words, hunkering down in her seat, hoping they would move on. Quickly.

"Skye, fancy seeing you here."

Dammit! Creed had spotted her after all.

"You two know each other?" the solicitous owner deigned to say. "We can arrange for you to sit together. It'll take my waiter a second or so to set up."

She didn't have time to protest or even offer a lame excuse. She just nodded and smiled wanly.

"I'd like that very much," Creed said, his long fingers curling around the back of the empty chair, and pulling it out. "May I?"

"Of course." What else could she say? He'd backed her into a difficult spot.

"I'll send your waiter over, Mr. Bennett," the owner said, leaving them alone.

When the owner was out of earshot, Skye ungraciously snapped, "What are you doing here? Are you following me?" Suddenly sated, she pushed her plate away. She couldn't imagine why he'd chosen to sit with her.

"I'm sorry I walked out on you," Creed offered, settling into his chair. "I thought we were friends. Finding those articles rattled me badly."

"We are friends," she reluctantly admitted.

"Apology accepted, then?" He snapped his fingers and a white flag appeared. He waved it at her. "Truce?"

"I suppose." She grinned at him. Despite not wanting to be a pushover, she gave in to his humor. Magically, his presence had made everything right with her world. She didn't want to feel this way. Not if she was going to do some objective reporting.

Reaching across the table, Creed covered her hand with his free one. "I drove all the way back to your house. When you weren't there, I came here on a whim."

"You must have needed comfort food," she said, jokingly.

"That, and a place to hide. I've got reporters swarming all over my property."

"Oh, Creed." She squeezed his hand, hoping that small action would let him know that she was there for him.

Why did she have such confusing reactions to the man? Why didn't she listen to the alarm bells going off in her head? Why was she turning to mush? She could easily have told him she was done eating. Seeing them together two nights in a row would only set tongues wagging. Still, maybe, just maybe, she'd get a chance to explain that she'd simply been curious about the murders. And, in the course of conversation, she'd find out whether he knew if this latest victim—his ex-administrative assistant, had been a stripper.

Their waiter, a high school student from the looks of him, appeared at Creed's elbow. Cutlery and crystal clinked as he set down a knife, fork, spoon, and pre-folded napkin in a glass. Seeming overly awed, he gushed, "Mr. Bennett, you're my idol. I want to be just like you."

"Why is that?" Creed's wide smile softened the directness of the question.

"You didn't have a rich daddy or nothing, yet you made it out of Mills Creek. Now you're famous." He removed the napkin from the glass and poured water.

For one fleeting moment, Skye thought she saw a look of abject sadness cross Creed's face. It wasn't there when she looked back. "Is that your primary goal, to make it out of Mills Creek?" he said to the young man.

"Yup. Nothing's happening here. I want to be an actor." The boy stuck his chest out, proudly. "I can't accomplish that unless I go to New York."

"What's your name, son?"

"Malcolm."

"Any chance you might have a piece of paper, Malcolm?"

Reaching into the pocket of his apron, the youth retrieved a notepad and handed it to Creed. He scribbled for a moment and gave the pad back. "That's my personal assistant's number. Call him. I'm doing a project with the Boys and Girls Club. I may need your help."

"For real, Mr. Bennett?" Malcolm's brown eyes widened.

"For real. Call me Creed."

Unable to contain himself, he let out a loud whoop and hurriedly took Creed's order. "I'll bring your dessert back when you're ready," he said to Skye.

"You made one young man very happy," Skye commented, after the boy danced off.

Creed's eyes met hers briefly. He answered reflectively. "I was once that young man, full of aspirations and unfulfilled dreams."

"But you made it." All her concentration now focused on the man across from her. She'd lost interest in the remnants of chicken, salad, and greens on her plate.

"Thank God," he said, so softly she almost missed the comment.

Skye sipped her water and decided to let it go.

Creed had his own issues to deal with—one of them being his father.

"I wasn't checking up on you," she said, switching the subject. "A colleague at the Sun Sentinel knew that a Mills Creek girl was missing. She knew I'd be interested in the story. She e-mailed me those articles."

Creed appeared to listen intently. He nodded but didn't say a word.

"Did you know Tamara Linley was an exotic dancer?" Skye asked, hoping to nudge him out of the strained silence that had descended.

"No. I didn't."

"Dancing seems to be the one thing the victims have in common."

"Maybe the guy has a whore-madonna complex," Creed contributed.

"I wonder if Marla St. James or Ona Di Santis, the housekeeper, stripped?" Skye said, thinking out loud.

"That wouldn't surprise me."

"Do I detect some animosity?" She immediately went into reporter mode, noting the way he now sat ramrod-straight.

Creed shrugged. "Hardly. My former makeup artist was more a figure to be pitied."

"Why is that?"

"She had her problems."

"Is that why you fired her?" Skye had read that somewhere.

Creed removed a biscuit from the basket and crumbled it in half. "This is beginning to sound more and more like an interview. Is it?

"Sorry." She picked up the abandoned flag and

waved it at him. Old habits didn't die easily. She was inquisitive by nature and sensed a good story. Why let someone scoop her?

"How long has Rick Morales worked for you?" Skye asked.

"A little over a year. Why?"

"He acts as if he's known you a lifetime and seems to look out for your interests."

Creed devoured the remaining half of his biscuit. "He's loyal. He also has a thing for you."

She tilted her head in acknowledgment, but didn't say a word. She was thinking about how it felt to have his full lips on hers, and the reaction his touch elicited.

Creed continued. "Rick watches my back. At the same time, that breezy style of his puts people at ease. He's the antithesis of Tammy."

"What was she like?"

"You're at it again," Creed said, giving her an amused look. "Probing, prying. You can't help yourself."

Malcolm's return saved her another apology. "Chow's on," he announced, setting down a gravy-laden plate in front of Creed. "Ready for that dessert?" he said to Skye.

"Not yet. I'll wait until he's done."

Creed winked. "Must mean my company's palatable. Mal, my boy, anyone ever tell you women were temperamental?"

Skye whacked him with the handle of the flag.

Their waiter maintained a surprisingly straight face, but had the good sense not to respond.

Thirteen

"Let's start off with the pea shell game," Creed said to the handful of children attending his workshop. "It's easy once I show you the secret."

A chubby pre-teen boy, with his cap on backward, waved frantically.

"What is it, son?"

"My name's Marc. We aren't interested in some dumb trick involving shelling peas." He turned to his audience of two girls and five boys. "We came to learn the good stuff. Not woman's work, didn't we guys?"

The children hooted, shouting their agreement.

"All right, listen up," Creed said, dryly. "We're in agreement this isn't a cooking class. But if you stay with me you might learn a thing or two. Like how to pay attention."

The children snickered as the boy grew red in the face. Creed was disappointed by the meager attendance, but never let on. Had he not been viewed as suspect, there would be three times the number of kids here.

"I'll wait until you settle down," he said, crossing his arms and eyeballing the inattentive children. If he didn't show them who was in charge, he'd lose control forever, and there would be no respect.

Removing three identical bottle caps from a paper bag, his stage assistant, Felicity, handed them to him. Creed set them on a table covered by a black cloth. "Perhaps we can begin now. Why don't you come on up front, Marc." He beckoned to the insolent boy.

"Moi?" The pre-teen made an elaborate bow and mouthed something to his peers. Another outburst of laughter ricocheted across the room. Creed realized the child was an attention seeker. He kept a straight face and waited for the room to quiet. The boy's behavior mirrored his at that age, except he'd never had a smart mouth. His mother simply wouldn't allow it.

"Yes, you," he finally said. "Hold on to this nickel." He flipped a coin in Marc's direction.

"Chump change," Marc said, palming it. "Up it ten bucks and we're talking."

That smart retort set the group off again. Creed waited for the hooting and hollering to die down.

"Okay, Marc, lay that nickel down under one of those caps."

With an exaggerated swagger, the boy complied, placing the coin under the cap farthest right.

"Now mix up the caps," Creed ordered.

Marc took his time maneuvering the bottle tops back and forth.

"Felicity," Creed said, "which cap has the nickel under it?"

His assistant's jaunty ponytail bobbed back and forth as she selected the middle one.

"Is she right?" Creed asked his audience.

"Ooh! Ooh! Ooh!" A dark-skinned girl, whose hair appeared neglected, bounced up and down. She was so excited.

"Latisha, what do you think?"

The child raced forward and lifted the cap on the left. Her face dropped when there was no sign of money.

"Dam . . ."

"What was that?"

"Doggone it," she quickly corrected.

Felicity removed the center cap and showed the children the nickel.

"How did you do that?" the girl asked. "I had my eyes peeled and I knew that money was under there."

Creed patiently explained that a tiny black hair had been glued to the coin. It was long enough to protrude from underneath, but the dark tablecloth made it invisible to the eye.

"Awesome. I'm goin' to try that soon as I go to school."

Creed ruffled the child's nappy head. "You do that and you'll be one popular young lady."

"Think so?" The girl's eager smile revealed two missing front teeth.

"I know so."

"Shall we try the broomstick suspension trick?" Felicity asked, leading Latisha back to her seat.

Creed nodded. "Yes. Can we have another volunteer?"

Skye entered the room as a gangly boy climbed onto a stool. She remained at the back, watching Creed patiently give instructions. He was good with these difficult kids, she decided. Two broomsticks lay on the floor, and the boy was instructed to stand, arms outstretched over the bristles.

Oh a whim, she'd decided to drop by. During dinner, Creed had matter-of-factly mentioned he would be at the Boys and Girls Club two nights a week, just until school ended. This way, kids would have ample time to polish their skills in preparation for a Christmas performance. He'd suggested she stop by, so she'd called the club to see what nights he'd be there.

As she watched Creed explain how the illusion was achieved, an idea began to percolate. What if she were to write an upbeat piece about Creed's involvement with the community? It could countermand the damage caused by the Tamara Linley story and help get attendance up. She jotted notes and made a mental note to discuss it with Pete.

The woman working alongside Creed spotted Skye. She whispered something to him. He looked up briefly and raised an index finger. Skye made herself as comfortable as she could on a folding metallic chair. She pulled off her beret, loosened her coat, and stuffed the gloves she was holding into her pockets.

"Switch places with Felicity," Creed said, helping the child down. He placed his hands around his assistant's waist, and hoisted her onto the now vacant stool.

Considering the coldness of the night, the woman wore an awfully skimpy outfit. She was model-thin and thigh-clinging leggings accentuated mile-long gams. She wore a man's cotton shirt over the tights. Was the oversized shirt Creed's?

What if it was? She had no claim to him. They were

simply two people caught up in an inexplicable physical attraction—lusting after each other. Yet, watching Creed touch another woman had set several emotions loose—feelings she didn't even want to examine: envy; insecurity—neither pretty traits. Skye squelched her ugly thoughts and continued to scribble.

"This is a surprise," Creed said, coming to stand beside her.

"You said I should stop by, so here I am." She snapped the book shut and smiled brightly at him. "I thought Malcolm had agreed to help you." She scanned the room looking for signs of the waiter they'd met at Food For The Soul.

"Thursday nights aren't good for him. He'll join me when school gets out. May I buy you a drink when we get done?"

Creed's navy gaze swept over her, leaving a tingling feeling in its wake. He made her feel discombobulated. She said the first thing that came to mind. "Uh . . . don't you have to take *her* home?"

Creed glanced in the direction of his assistant, wrinkling his nose. "Who? Felicity? She has her own car."

The cellular phone clipped to his belt rang. Turning away, he barked a greeting.

Skye heard him say, "Chill, will you? It's a prank call. Let the machine pick up." He snapped the flip phone shut.

"Problem?"

"Nah. Some idiot keeps phoning every fifteen minutes but doesn't say a word, and just keeps hanging up on Rick. What about that drink?"

"Sorry. I have to be someplace. Maybe another time?"

"As you wish."

She refused to acknowledge the disappointment flickering across his face. While his invitation was tempting, she already knew how the evening would end. He'd try to convince her to come home with him, and she'd be forced to say no, just like the other night after dinner. She couldn't allow lust to get in the way of a good story. She needed to remember that.

An idea niggled at her. What if she were to go the Psychedelic Pony and check out her hunch? Russ would gladly accompany her. The photographer seldom asked questions.

Skye circled the parking lot, surprised to see the number of Mercedes, Jaguars, and Lexuses present. She hadn't known what to expect, but, judging by the types of vehicles, the clientele was far more upscale than she'd anticipated. She'd had visions of pickup trucks, Harleys, and souped-up cars with chrome wheels, not Mitsubishis, sports utilities, and pricy vehicles.

"There's a spot two rows down." Russ pointed out the space. Skye stepped on the accelerator, cutting off a red corvette.

"I thought we didn't want to draw attention to ourselves," Russ said dryly, as he watched her bulldoze her way into place. He'd laughed when she'd asked him to escort her but hadn't asked questions.

"You're right. We don't."

After getting out of the car, Skye took a moment

to survey the plain brick building housing the Psychedelic Pony. She hadn't expected it to be factory-like in its ugliness, nor clear across town. It had been difficult to access from most of the major highways.

A braying sound came from the roof. Skye focused her attention in that direction. Above her, a garishly lit wooden pony, with a blousy mannequin astride, rocked back and forth. The blonde's postage-stamp halter barely covered two sizeable assets. A mechanized contraption caused the pony to buck and bray. For one New York minute, the halter and skirt shifted, giving the viewer a glimpse of outrageous scarlet nipples and a thong-clad behind.

"The Pony's not known for its subtlety," Russ said, closing the car door and coming to stand beside her. "It's hardly a gentlemen's club. I'm sticking close by." His hand cupped her elbow.

Skye took a deep breath. "Have you been here before?"

"I plead the fifth." Russ's grip on her arm tightened as he hustled her along. "Might as well look like a couple. If not, someone's going to think I'm your pimp."

Skye giggled. The thought had never occurred to her that red-haired Russ, accompanying her into a strip joint, might seem suspect. "Do couples come here on dates?" she asked.

"Some do. Depends on what they're into."

Skye decided it was best not to ask what that might be. She already had the feeling she was in for an education.

They entered through huge double doors and faced a massive bouncer. His grim expression and tattoo-wreathed biceps reminded her of a wrestler.

He gave them a speculative once over before exchanging glances with the slender, effeminate man at his side. After what seemed a lengthy time, he waved them in.

Dense clouds of smoke billowed across the room, hanging like heavy drapes over the heads of patrons. Skye covered her nose to block out the metallic smell of tobacco filling her nose and throat. She squinted into the thick cloud, unable to see anything other than the two ramps projecting out into the room. They beckoned customers like welcoming tentacles. On each raised platform, costumed women in various stages of undress jiggled their wares. Russ's grip on her arm tightened. He steered her around small groupings of tables.

"Overwhelmed?"

"I can handle it."

Sure she could, she reminded herself, sidestepping a cluster of bandanna-clad Hell's Angels playing pool. She pretended not to see when one of them winked at her. Instead, she concentrated on placing one foot ahead of the other while loud raucous music played, mostly top forty hits. Russ, hurrying her along, didn't notice when she'd stumbled. A Big Daddy-type came to her aid.

"Easy, honey," he said, his paws on her hips.

Grateful for Russ's presence, she thanked him.

"There's a table coming vacant over there," Russ hissed. "We'll need to be quick."

Skye's attention returned to the action on stage. A Raggedy Ann look-alike had just lifted her pinafore, revealing garters and not a lot more.

"Okay. Let's go for it." Russ tightened his grip on her arm and sprinted them across the room.

Entranced by the action on the runways, Skye let him pull her along. She slid into the chair he held out, in time to see a woman dressed in a studded dog collar being led on stage. Her handler's knee high boots and bright red bustier drew every eye. Bringing her charge with her, she pirouetted. Back to the audience, she bent over and planted spiked heels apart. The leashed woman was ordered to sit and the audience was given an unfettered view of the handler's naked buttocks. By the rustle and sighs in the audience, Skye gathered this was a popular act.

"I'll be right with you," a waitress called, racing by, nose ring bobbing.

Good, she could definitely use a drink.

"Is this what you expected?" Russ asked.

She hadn't known what to expect. Her only experience with a strip joint was what she'd seen on TV.

The bar off to the side was populated with gawkers. An eclectic group downed drinks while keeping an interested eye on the runway. Some were obviously blue collar, but others could be anything. Something drew her attention to a man hemmed in by two big-haired women. He bore a striking resemblance to Rick Morales. Would Rick hang out in a joint like this?

A voice came from behind her. "Fancy finding you here."

Swivelling, she saw Don Washington, his hand on the vacant chair. "Mind if I sit down?"

"Uh . . . Skye." Russ looked to her uncertainly.

"Is this something that can wait, Don?" Skye asked.

He slugged his beer and shrugged. "I wanted to say hello and fill you in on the latest."

"Stop by my office tomorrow. We'll talk."

"Okay." Don cast a hostile look in Russ's direction. "If you're on a date, I wouldn't take up your time." Without a backward glance, he slinked away.

"What'll it be?" their waitress asked, returning, her pen and pad poised to take their order. "Your drinks are taken care of," she said to Skye.

"But how? Why?"

"Gent at the bar said it would be his pleasure."

"What gentleman?"

The woman shrugged. "Fancy type. Manicured nails. You pay me, I don't ask questions."

Skye's gaze shifted to the bar again. The man she'd thought was Rick had disappeared. The two big-haired women were making time with his replacement.

Skye placed her order, then looked to Russ. He ordered a beer.

"Any idea how I can get a job here?" she asked the waitress, before she turned away.

"Ya gotta talk to Micky. Depends on what kind of job ya looking for."

"Like hers." Skye pointed to the stage. "I have a friend who dances. Claims she makes a mint."

Russ raised an eyebrow but remained silent.

"Anyone I know?" The waitress's nose ring wobbled with curiosity.

"Kristina . . ."

"Brown? Jason's girlfriend?"

Skye struggled to keep her face expressionless. "Yes. She and I are tight."

"She and Jason left to chase the sun. Last I heard, they were in Fort Lauderdale. If you happen to speak to them, tell them things are different now that Jason's not around. The mice will play when the owner's away."

"Jason owns the Pony?"

"I thought you knew him. I gotta go." She shoved off, then turned back. "Why don't ya talk to Micky? If you tell him you're a friend of Jason and Kristina's, he's bound to hire you."

"I'll do that."

Fourteen

"Rumor has it someone resembling Skye Walker's been hanging around the Pony," Pete said, clutching a smoldering cigarette.

Skye read her e-mails while fanning the noxious air. In a small town like Mills Creek, word tended to get out quickly. She discarded unwanted messages and placed others in folders.

"You hear any more from that Altarboy?" Pete asked, standing over her shoulder to peruse the monitor.

"Who?"

"The prankster. The guy who sent you that strange e-mail"

"Oh, him. Not since the last one." Skye had dismissed the whole episode as some joker's feeble effort to scare her off a good story. She wouldn't put anything past the competition.

Bitterly cold December had settled in, colder than any Skye could remember. Earlier that week, an unexpected snowfall had paralyzed the town, and now the roads were icy, making driving dangerous. That might be the reason Don Washington had not shown up as promised.

"So, what you doing for Christmas?" Pete asked.

Skye continued scrolling through her messages. "It's two and a half weeks away. I haven't given it much thought."

"No dinner with relatives? No plans with lover boy?"

Lover boy meant Creed, whom she hadn't seen or heard from since that night at the Boys and Girls Club. Not hearing from him had mattered more than she thought it would.

"I may have dinner at my aunt's," she said, carefully.

"Well, I'm taking off. Gotta do my Christmas shopping."

That got her attention. "Shopping? You?"

"My ex and kids claim sending them money's okay, but gifts add a more personal touch." Pete's stubby fingers clutched her shoulders, squeezing. "Come with me. I can use feminine advice."

She and Pete Christmas shopping together? A hilarious thought. Still, it would get her out of the office, and she did have her own gifts to buy.

"All right. Where are we heading?"

"Downtown. The area that's gentrified."

Skye shut down the computer and scooped up her mail. Shoving the lot into her pocketbook, she followed Pete from the room.

"All this shopping's getting to me," Pete huffed, not even an hour later. "I need a beer."

"One more stop," Skye pleaded. "I want to go into Victoria's Secret then we're off to the Tap House."

"Okay. If we have to, we have to." Even though he grumbled, his eyes lit up.

Twenty minutes later, they were waiting in line to

pay when Pete muttered, "Don't look now, but Creed and his man just came in."

How could she not look? Creed Bennett's presence in the lingerie store had created a minor stir. Skye overheard snippets of female conversation.

"I don't care what they say. The man's fine."

"Oh, yeah, honey, he's da bomb."

"Wouldn't exactly toss him out of my bed, if you know what I mean."

Both men were already busily scouring the racks, fingering teddies and assorted silk robes. Skye felt minor irritation build. She wondered who they were shopping for. Pete's voice in her ear only added to her agitation. "I'll hold your spot. Why don't you go say hello?"

"No."

He shrugged. "Suit yourself, but I'm going over. Here." He thrust at her the satin robe and elegant lounging pajamas she'd convinced him to buy his ex-wife. "Pay for them if I'm not back, and I'll reimburse you."

"Don't you dare . . ."

Too late. He was already off. Skye stared straight ahead, praying the line would move quickly. With any luck, she could make her purchases and be out of there before Pete invited the men to join them for drinks.

She was next in line, tapping her foot impatiently, when she sensed Creed's presence.

"I take it you weren't planning to say hello?"

"Well . . . uh . . . I didn't want to lose my place in line."

"Right."

"Next," the cashier bellowed.

Arms filled with stuff, Skye hustled to the register. Creed followed. When she was through paying, he said, "Pete mentioned you guys were off to the Tap House. He asked us to come."

"That's great." What else could she say?

Creed's hand cupped her upper arm. "Look, I've still got some shopping to do, so I'm going to pass. Could we have a late dinner, alone?"

Skye thought quickly. In a couple of hours she had an interview at the Pony. She'd called up the manager, Micky, pretending to look for a job. He'd agreed to see her at eight.

"I'm sorry, I have an appointment afterward," Skye said.

His grip on her arm tightened. "You seem to have a lot of those lately. How about tomorrow night?"

"Tomorrow, uuuh . . ." She needed to think quickly and come up with a good excuse.

"What about going with me to the mayor's holiday dinner-dance? It's formal. The proceeds go to the local orphanage. I purchased a table so I'd better show up. I need a date."

"We have a reporter assigned to the event," Pete said, returning, a pair of thong panties hanging off his pinky.

"We do?" Skye's eyebrows rose. It was the first she had heard of it. "What are you doing with that?"

"An extra gift. Just in case . . ."

She could tell by the way Creed's lips twitched, he was amused.

"In case what?" she asked Pete.

"I get lucky. As I was saying, we have a reporter covering the dance and I'll be there."

"You will?" Pete stuffed into a tuxedo was something she'd never imagined.

"Well, what do you say?" Creed waited for an answer while Rick hovered in the background, listening to every word.

"Come on. Break out one of those fancy Parisian gowns in your closet," Pete urged. "Prepare to party."

"What time is this thing?"

"Seven."

"Fine. You'll pick me up when?" Skye asked Creed.

"Quarter of seven."

"And she'll be dressed to the nines," Pete interjected. "Won't you, Skye?"

She shot the editor a look that said, "Enough already." What she really wanted to do was strangle him.

Micky Caldwell took a long drag of a cigarette then flicked his ash into the nearby Philodendron. "You strip before?"

Skye blew the bangs of the ash blond wig out of her eyes. "Yup." Tamping down on her discomfort, she snapped her gum.

"Where?"

Micky's feet were propped up on the cheap Formica desk cluttered with cheesecake magazines. He was the same effeminate man she'd seen with the bouncer.

"Paris and Fort Lauderdale. I also dance in New York."

"You danced in Paris, France?"

An important message from the ARABESQUE Editor

Dear Arabesque Reader,

Because you've chosen to read one of our Arabesque romance novels, we'd like to say "thank you"! And, as a special way to thank you, we've selected four more of the books you love so well to send you for only $1.99.

Please enjoy them with our compliments, and thank you for continuing to enjoy Arabesque...the soul of romance.

Karen Thomas
Senior Editor,
Arabesque Romance Novels

SPECIAL OFFER!
4 BOOKS FOR ONLY $1.99

ARABESQUE

A PRODUCT OF

BET BOOKS

Check out our website at www.arabesquebooks.com

3 QUICK STEPS
TO RECEIVE YOUR "THANK YOU" GIFT
FROM THE EDITOR

Send back this card and you'll receive 4 Arabesque novels!
These books have a combined cover price of $20.00 or more,
but they are yours to keep for a mere $1.99.

There's no catch. You're under no obligation to buy anything.
We charge only $1.99 for the books (plus $1.50 for shipping
and handling, a total of $3.49). And you don't have to make
any minimum number of purchases—not even one!

We hope that after receiving your books you'll want to
remain an Arabesque subscriber. But the choice is yours to
continue or cancel, anytime at all! So why not take us up on
our invitation to receive 4 Arabesque Romance Novels, with
no risk of any kind. You'll be glad you did!

Call us
TOLL-FREE
at 1-888-345-BOOK

THE EDITOR'S "THANK YOU" GIFT INCLUDES:

- 4 books delivered for only $1.99 (plus $1.50 for shipping and handling)
- A FREE newsletter, *Arabesque Romance News*, filled with author interviews, book previews, special offers, and more!
- No risks or obligations. You're free to cancel whenever you wish... with no questions asked.

BOOK CERTIFICATE

Yes! Please send me 4 Arabesque books for $1.99 (+ $1.50 for shipping & handling, a total of $3.49). I understand I am under no obligation to purchase any books, as explained on the back of this card.

Name _____

Address _____ Apt. _____

City _____ State _____ Zip _____

Telephone ( ) _____

Signature _____

Offer limited to one per household and not valid to current subscribers. All orders subject to approval. Terms, offer, & price subject to change.

AN050A

Thank you!

Accepting the four introductory books for $1.99 (+ $1.50 for shipping & handling, total of $3.49) places you under no obligation to buy anything. You may keep the books and return the shipping statement marked "cancel". If you do not cancel, about a month later we will send 4 additional Arabesque novels, and bill you a preferred subscriber's price of just $4.00 per title (plus a small shipping and handling fee). That's $16.00 for all 4 books for a savings of 33% off the cover price You may cancel at any time, but if you choose to continue, every month we'll send you 4 more books, which you may either purchase at the preferred discount price. . . or return to us and cancel your subscription.

THE ARABESQUE ROMANCE CLUB: HERE'S HOW IT WORKS

ARABESQUE ROMANCE BOOK CLUB
P.O. Box 5214
Clifton NJ 07015-5214

PLACE
STAMP
HERE

He leered at her. "They get pretty down and dirty there, I hear."

Skye giggled. "I'll never tell."

"So, show me your stuff," he said, shoving back from his seat and clearing a path on the overcrowded desk. "Get up there."

"I didn't bring my music," she said, thinking quickly.

"Who needs music?"

Skye stood, tugging on the micro-mini skirt worn with thigh-high boots. She blew a bubble at him. "I do. To set the mood. You gonna hire me or what?"

Micky took a long toke on what remained of his cigarette. Skye's too-short skirt and snug-fitting sweater didn't seem to make an impression. Despite the girlie magazines strewn about, she didn't think he liked women.

"Depends. Where do you know Jason and Kristina from?" he asked.

"I danced with Kristina at Pure Platinum in Fort Lauderdale," Skye said, boldly.

"They're good buds of mine. At least they used to be. I haven't heard from them in awhile, though Jason hits the ATM regularly. That's how I know he's still down there. If he recommends you, that's good enough for me. You still goin' to need to audition." Micky stubbed his cigarette out in an overflowing ash tray. He turned his attention back to Skye. "When can you do that?"

"Before Christmas."

"When before Christmas?"

"Look. I gotta give the New York job notice. Can't just walk out on them."

He cocked his head, eyeing her warily. "My girls

ain't that loyal. Be here on the 15th for rehearsal. Five o'clock sharp. Bring your music and whatever you're wearing. If you don't cut it, sayonara. Understand?"

"Understand," Skye said, gathering the red vinyl clutch purse that matched her boots. "Thanks, Mick, I wouldn't let you down." She tossed her ash blond hair, then, wiggling her hips provocatively, left the room.

Creed sat on the couch waiting for Skye. She'd been dressed in a bath robe when she'd hurriedly ushered him in. Hogan played sentinel at his ankles, emitting low growls if he flexed so much as an ankle. The little beast hadn't tried to nip him, though. He should be thankful for small mercies.

"Make yourself comfortable," Skye said, waving him onto the sofa. "I shouldn't be long . . ." Yet fifteen minutes had elapsed with no sign of her.

On the far side of the room, Creed spotted a stereo. A pile of what looked like today's mail was heaped next to it. He ignored Hogan's warning growl and rose from the couch. The dog remained at his heels as he tinkered with the radio's dials, searching for a jazz station. The sleeve of his tuxedo jacket brushed the envelopes, sending the stack toppling. Under the watchful eye of Hogan, Creed bent to retrieve the mess.

He was busy scooping up Christmas cards and bills, and stacking them into piles, when a postcard with an enormous red heart got his attention. It was the type of card a lover might send. Did Skye have a lover?

After he'd placed the mail back on the table, he held onto the postcard. A quick peek only revealed a hastily scribbled, "I've been thinking about you." He scanned the bottom for a signature. *Altarboy?* Could that possibly be someone's real name? It had to be a joke. No self-respecting male would carry around that handle. Still, he didn't like the thought of Skye having an admirer. Not one bit.

"Is there something I can help you with?" she asked, surprising him.

Embarrassed to be caught snooping, Creed turned to face her. "I was just . . ." The words stuck in his throat. "God, you look lovely."

"Thank you."

She wore a strapless form-fitting golden gown that made her amber skin glow. A gossamer scarf cascaded down her back. Her punky haircut had been jelled into a neat cap, and a jeweled butterfly peeked from behind one ear. The wings of the insect fluttered. Her only other adornments were the diamond studs in her lobes. Creed drew in a breath, inhaling an expensive perfume he couldn't quite place. Eau de Skye. Heavenly.

"Can I have that?" she asked, referring to the card he still held.

"Sorry."

He handed it to her, watched her glance at it briefly, frown, and toss it aside. "Ready?"

"If you are." He helped her into her coat then shrugged into his. Offering her an arm, he headed for the door.

The phone rang.

"I don't feel like getting it," she muttered.

"Then don't. Let the machine pick up."

A forlorn Hogan followed them. They closed the door as a foreign male voice said, "Skye, are you there?"

"Everybody, I want you to meet Skye Walker," Creed said, pulling out her chair and waiting for her to sit.

Skye acknowledged the occupants of the table with a nod and a smile. Every chair held someone she knew or recognized. Rick Morales was accompanied by a woman the newsroom guys would have called a Hootchie Mama—a title probably well deserved, given that her breasts poured over the top of a tight lycra number. Rick had an arm draped around the back of the woman's seat. He smiled vaguely in Skye's direction but seemed engrossed in his date.

A mocha-colored man, who Creed introduced as Miguel Santiago, executive director of the Boys and Girls Club, sat next to his wife, a dumpling of a woman. She beamed at Skye and commented, "Dynamite dress." The remaining two seats were occupied by Kareem Davis, still on leave. His date, Pia, an elaborately coiffured woman, ran one of the town's hot new boutiques.

Distracted, Skye looked around town hall's cavernous interior. Enormous Styrofoam snowflakes hung from the ceilings, and garlands of greenery and glittering pine cones rimmed the room. A tremendous Christmas tree, limbs bowed by elaborate fans and netted bows, held intricately wrapped gifts. This was supposed to be a festive occasion, she reminded herself. She'd been looking forward to the evening, up until Creed had handed over that card with its cryptic message. On her way out the door, the answering machine had clicked on, and a voice from her past had almost caused her to lose it. What could Jacques possibly want? It had been years since she'd heard from him.

A waitress cleared her throat nearby. "Drinks?"

"Skye?" Creed's fingers brushed her forearm, getting her attention.

The spot tingled. "Chardonnay, please."

"I'll have the same," he added.

After drinks were served and dinner orders taken, Skye sensed Kareem's interest. She looked over, caught his wink, and smiled back. Creed must have noticed the exchange. She saw him waggle a not-so-discreet finger at Kareem. Womanizer or not, Kareem was at least personable. It had taken some courage to confess to an insensitive prank.

In the background, an eight-piece orchestra played a medley of carols, and on the dance floor, a handful of mature couples swayed to "White Christmas." Skye glanced around the room, registering that things had indeed changed during her seven-year absence. Judging by the forty or so African Americans in attendance, more upwardly mobile blacks had moved to the Poconos; they represented twenty percent of the patrons. Considering the hefty ticket price of one hundred and fifty dollars per head, their presence said a lot.

Entrees, consisting of prime rib and lobster tails, were served and rapidly consumed. Rich chocolate and berry desserts were laid out and scooped up. The volume around her had risen noticeably, signifying that many were well on their way to inebriation. Spotting Pete, Skye waved, but a buxom brunette had his attention and he did not acknowledge her presence.

To take the edge off, she downed her third glass of wine and was now feeling exceedingly mellow. She looked up and saw a tuxedoed Don Washington beaming down at her, his shaved dome glistening under the twinkling lights. How on earth had Don wangled an invitation? His parents were business owners, she remembered; most likely they'd paid for the table.

"Dance?" he said, extending a surprisingly well-tended hand.

With seven pairs of eyes looking at them, how could she say no? It would not only embarrass him, but would be exceedingly rude on her part. "Certainly." Dancing with Don was the last thing she wanted, though.

Under the watchful eye of Creed, Don escorted her to the dance floor. Tonight, his gold hoop earring had been replaced by a twinkling diamond stud. They free-formed to a pulsating tempo, but soon the music changed and Don drew her close.

"Weren't you supposed to stop by my office?" Skye shouted, over the old Temptations song.

"Yeah. But I got busy and the roads were bad."

"What did you want to talk to me about?"

"A buddy just came from down South. He thinks he saw Kristina and Jamie at some club." Don jutted his jaw in the direction of Skye's table. "You move in some pretty interesting circles. You and Bennett are tight, and Tiffany's a friend."

"Tiffany?"

"The woman with Bennett's sidekick. She does a pretty interesting routine at the Pony."

"I had no idea . . ."

The music changed to something slow and sultry—Al Jarreau at his best. Don's arms tightened around her. As she debated discreetly extricating herself from his grip, she heard Creed say, "My turn."

Skye was never so glad to see anyone. She smiled brightly at him, stepped into his arms, and fitted her head against his shoulder. Matching each other's movements, they waltzed across the floor, dancing as if they'd done it dozens of times before.

Skye closed her eyes and inhaled the clean, fresh scent of him. Pine. The smell conjured up memories of joyous occasions and goodwill to all men. There was no denying the attraction between them and the pull he had on her.

"I'd like to leave," Creed whispered after they'd danced through several numbers. "Come home with me. Rick won't be back, and Vilma's visiting a friend."

Now or never. Should she take the chance?

"Alright."

His hand caressed the small of her back, fingers drumming against her flesh. "You have no idea how long I've been waiting to hear that."

"And just how long is that?" Skye teased, the wine and man dulling her inhibitions.

"Forever and a day," Creed sang, twining his fingers around hers, and hustling her off the floor.

Fifteen

"You must be freezing," Creed said, wrapping his arms around Skye and holding her close. It was a bitter cold night and the valets were hustling to turn over cars to a few shivering people.

Across the street, the retail stores were battened down tight. The few remaining people on Main Street patronized the liquor store and the town's only pizza parlor. Creed noticed a group of men clutching brown paper bags in front of Garrison's Liquors. He swore Jed was amongst them and prayed he wouldn't see him.

"Isn't that your father?" Skye confirmed, pointing to a man huddled in a shabby overcoat, swigging from a paper sack.

Creed shrugged. Even when his father didn't know it, he managed to embarrass him. "Looks like him," he said, evenly.

"It is," Skye insisted. "Go on, Creed. Go say hello. I'll get the valet."

"Some other time." He nuzzled the side of her neck, hoping she would change the topic. Her honey and almond shampoo titillated his senses, triggering his imagination. He wouldn't let Jed ruin tonight.

Skye narrowed her eyes, but remained silent. What she must think of him. How could he explain that Jed wasn't the father he wanted, and never had been. But even thinking those thoughts made him feel guilty. He made a mental note to find out Jed's address at the boardinghouse. Although he'd vowed not to be an enabler, it was the holiday season. He'd have Rick pay the rent and send an anonymous care package. From the looks of things, his father could use a good coat.

"Mr. Bennett?"

The valet waved his keys at him. As he held the passenger door open, waiting for Skye to get in, Creed gave the man an overly generous tip. Delighted, the man loped off, turning to wave and smile in acknowledgment.

"You made one person happy," Skye said, scooting into the car's already warm interior.

"Hopefully he isn't the only one I make happy." Creed grinned before pushing the button for the seat warmers.

"Promises. Promises."

A sole light came from an upstairs room as they started up his driveway. He parked in the underground garage and helped Skye out of the car. Keeping his hand on the small of her back, he guided her upstairs.

Tikka bounded out to greet them. Creed petted the shepherd. "I've got Chardonnay chilled," he said, leading her to the kitchen, his dog at their heels.

"Great. I'll have some."

"That'll make your fourth."

"Who's counting?"

"Not I." Creed traced her full lips with his index finger. Keeping her prisoner with his arms, he backed her up against the refrigerator. Slowly, he bent over and claimed her lips. Their kiss went on forever.

Skye's hazel eyes remained wide as he deepened the kiss, sliding his tongue between the opening she allowed. In and out and in again. He felt his excitement rise and pressed his groin against hers, flattening her against the cool refrigerated surface.

"What about my wine?" Skye managed, during one of those rare moments when he allowed her up for air.

"Who needs wine when we have this?" Bending over, he resumed where he'd left off.

"Cool it, cherie," she said, backing him off with a hand. "Time to deliver."

"Darling, I have every intention of doing just that." He let his tongue play across her lips, deliberately teasing her.

"So you say," Skye said, melting. She trailed copper-colored nails across his crisp white shirt.

Creed grabbed the Chardonnay and took her hand. "Better go upstairs while we can." Tikka bounded ahead of them, looking back as if to say, "What's taken you two this long?"

Upstairs, Skye lounged on the emerald divan while Creed worked on getting a fire started. He'd shed his tuxedo jacket and rolled up his sleeves. Smooth, dark hairs covered his forearms. Straightening, he rubbed his palms together and stood back to admire his handiwork. Gold and red flames shot up the chimney.

He crouched down again, retrieved the silver

mules she'd discarded, and placed them next to the
door. Skye crossed her arms, protectively, shielding
her chest. He regarded her through lowered lids.

"If you're not warm enough, I'll get you a blan-
ket," Creed said.

"I'm plenty warm. Here, sit." She patted the space
beside her.

He tugged off his bow tie, dropped the tiny scrap
of silk on an accent table, and popped in a CD. Sitting beside her, he eased his feet out of shoes that
looked suspiciously like Gucci. "Long day?" He
wrapped an arm around her.

"Brutally long."

"More wine?"

"Not for me."

"Did you have a good time tonight?"

"The best."

It had come down to this. The two of them making
mundane conversation—a prelude to sex.

Creed's fingers drew circular patterns on her bare
shoulders. He bent his head and kissed her clavicle,
his tongue leaving a moist trail in its wake. The raw
sensuality of Marvin Gaye's "Sexual Healing," filled
the room. It had been a while since she'd had that
kind of healing,

"Come," he said, pulling her up. His warm breath
caressed her cheeks and his chest rose and fell er-
ratically. When he reached for her zipper, she tensed
up. There would be no turning back now. No time
for regrets.

"You don't have to do this," Creed said, picking
up on her unease. He paused, zipper in hand.
"Skye?"

She squeezed her eyes closed. "It's okay. I want to."

The rest of the zipper slid down easily. Creed helped her out of the strapless dress. Folding it carefully, he placed it over the back of the divan. He cupped a hand over her bare buttocks, where the thong underwear left her exposed. "We'd be more comfortable in the bedroom," he said, squeezing gently.

She didn't feel the least bit uncomfortable following his lead. She sat on the bed and watched him hurriedly undress. In a matter of seconds, he'd shed his shirt and slacks, then whipped off his socks. When only his black briefs remained, he knelt on the floor in front of her, his warm palms on her thighs. A gold chain nestled in his chest hairs. A ring, looking far too small to be his, hung from it.

"Why has it taken us this long to get it together?" he asked.

No answer was required. Tonight she wasn't a reporter, or he a possible murder suspect. She was a woman who wanted to trust again.

Creed unsnapped her bra and tossed the scrap of silk over her shoulder. He buried his face in the hollow of her chest, his fingers drawing tiny circles around her breasts. "I've wanted to make love to you ever since I saw you again."

"You had a funny way of showing it."

He groaned. "Here we go again, needing to get the last word in." His fingers returned to her breasts. He captured a nipple in his mouth and tugged gently. Skye rubbed the back of his neck and arched into him, letting him have his fill, allowing him to lave one bud then the other. Tiny sighs escaped her.

When Creed's hands moved lower, plucking at the thong underwear that was hardly a barrier, she opened her legs wide. His willing fingers slipped beneath the elastic, exploring and probing her secret places.

"I need to get you to bed," he grunted, his strong fingers cupping her bottom, the tips driving her wild. She laid back on the bed and pulled him down on top of her. Every thick inch of him ground into her. It would take remarkable restraint to slow down. Creed Bennett was a sensitive, considerate lover, she decided. The best she'd had by far.

Sure she'd been made love to, but not like this. She'd known men before, but none like him. It dawned on her that what she'd feared the most had happened. She'd fallen in love with him.

No time to think. No time to ponder this certainty. Skye's hands reached under his briefs, cupping his buttocks. She rubbed against him, nipping the sides of his neck, pressing her full breasts against the rough hairs of his chest, enjoying the friction that movement created. It was as if the closer she got to him, the closer she could get inside his head. It made no sense. But this thing she was feeling made no sense either.

Gasping like a man thirsting for water, Creed rolled off her. He slid off his underwear and, with an equally rapid motion, tugged down her panties. Using his knee, he parted her thighs. The palm of one hand cupped her throbbing core, testing for dampness. The other slipped a condom on. She'd been ready for him the moment he walked through her front door.

"Creed," she cried, when his tongue probed her center.

"What, honey? What?" He surfaced and looked at her with what she thought might be adoration.

"I can't wait anymore."

Then he was inside her, filling her up, sliding in and out, and in again. Building friction, hurling her over the top, taking her on a wild galaxy ride where only the two of them existed. She held on tightly, an eager participant, slowing down when he slowed down, speeding up when he did. She was right with him when he toppled over the edge.

As the reality they'd made for themselves faded, she imagined she heard him say, "Skye Walker, I love you."

But that was impossible.

Skye took time dressing. She'd already discarded several outfits, considering them too severe. She needed something warm but sexy. A unitard might do. She tugged on the one-piece outfit and slipped a bulky sweater over her head. Smart black ankle boots, with three-inch heels, followed. She tossed the ash blond wig into her tote, and tucked an old Supremes tape beside it. She had an audition at the Pony. A date with Creed followed that.

Skye drove through the pitch black evening. Earlier, a heavy sky had alluded to the possibility of snow. She pulled into the almost empty parking lot with twenty minutes to spare. It was too early for the horse and rider to be lit up, and thankfully the annoying braying sound had been turned off. Wig firmly in place, she stepped out of the car.

When Skye entered the club, an eclectic group of women, in various stages of undress, were warming up. Several had their own boom boxes propped against the wall. There was no sign of Micky. She spotted Rick's date, Tiffany, amongst the group, and prayed the woman wouldn't recognize her. Even though she'd layered the make up on, she whipped out her sunglasses. During the drive she'd gotten the brilliant idea to use glasses in the act.

"Hi there." A woman with wild red hair made space for her against the wall. Limbering up, she had one leg curled behind her. "You trying out?"

Skye nodded.

"Your first time?"

"No. I've danced before."

"Where?" her chatty new friend asked.

Skye gave her the same story she'd given Micky.

"Wow! Paris, France. You must be good."

Skye flicked a lock of ash-blonde hair back and smiled at her. "How about you? How long have you danced?"

"Going on five years now," the woman said, brightly. "Money's good. I'm Veronique and you're . . ."

"Sable," Skye said, thinking quickly. "Kristina Brown and I go way back. We danced at another club. She said she was pretty happy here."

"That's cause she had it made. Jason looked out for her. Kristina's not with us anymore," Veronique said. "But I suppose you know that."

Skye removed her sunglasses and made her eyes wide. "No kidding. Where did she go?" She shed her sweater and tightened a belt around her waist.

Veronique shrugged. "Fort Lauderdale. She and Jason were doing the nasty. They headed down

South. Before she went missing, she was dancing at some club down there—Club Nirvana, I think."

"Missing? Did you say missing?"

"Yeah, up and disappeared into a big black hole. She and Jason. The police are looking for her."

"You think something bad happened?"

"Sounds like it. The cops used to come around questioning the girls. Then when Jamie Washington went missing too, they swarmed down like locusts. You got a nice figure. Big boobs." Veronique gave Skye the thumbs-up sign. "Micky's gonna want to see them. How you planning on getting outta that thing?"

Skye hadn't planned on getting out of anything. But she'd gleaned vital information during their small talk. Nirvana was a club in South Florida. It was a lead worth exploring.

"You think I have too much clothing on?" She said to Veronique, eyeing the woman's mini skirt. "I'll run home and change, then. If I don't make it back in time, can I call you? You'll let me know when Micky's auditioning next? I'm a really good dancer."

Veronique bent over, retrieving something from her bag. Her snug lycra top unsnapped, and when she straightened, her considerable assets hung low. She handed Skye her card. "Call me anytime. A pal of Kristina's is a pal of mine. This is a cut-throat business. You'll need friends to survive."

The man on stage clapped and shouted, "Let's get this show on the road." Micky vaulted onto the stage, joining him.

Skye used that small distraction to make a discreet escape.

* * *

"Mommy, Mommy, how much longer till they light the tree?"

Creed watched the young mother lift the child into her arms. She pointed to the giant clock dominating the town square. "Be patient, Tommy. When the long hand's on twelve and the short hand's on seven, the Christmas tree will light up like a giant sparkler."

That conversation reminded him of the ones he'd had with his mother when she'd taken him and his brother, Tyler, into town. Seeing the tree lit had been their favorite event. Those were happy days then. It was all he and Tyler talked about for months. Now there was no Mom and no Tyler. His brother had died of AIDS almost five years ago, only months before their mother's own passing. It was ironic that Jed was still alive.

Ten minutes to seven. Skye was running late. He'd had plans for them to grab a quick bite at Eve's. Creed blew on his gloved hands, but even that didn't help. He turned up his coat collar and stuffed frozen fingers into the pockets of his cashmere coat. The smell of roasted chestnuts brought on another wave of nostalgia. A street vendor, blue from the cold, sold little paper packets to those waving dollar bills at him. His mother used to buy him and Tyler chestnuts.

Where was Skye? She'd promised to meet him here. Things were progressing nicely between them, and he'd decided not to pressure her. He'd sensed that if he boxed her in, she would bolt. It had been a whole week since they had slept together. An entire week to get used to the fact that he'd fallen for a reporter with a wry sense of humor and tremendous street smarts. A woman who cut to the chase and wasn't afraid to stand up for herself. A woman more beautiful than he'd ever imagined.

"Sorry I'm late," Skye said, linking an arm through his, and offering her lips to be kissed. "I had an appointment clear on the other side of town and then I got stuck in traffic."

She appeared flushed and tasted slightly of mint. "You work much too hard," he said.

Skye was huddled into a bright red coat. She had a black hat pulled down over her ears and wore cherry red mittens. "Oh, look, Creed," she said, tugging on his arm. "Look. They're lighting the tree."

The mayor, a portly sort, addressed the crowd. In the background, carolers sang a somber rendition of "Silent Night." Ten days until Christmas.

Creed wrapped his arms around Skye and brought her close. The big spruce tree came ablaze, white lights twinkling off massive branches. Children cheered. Adults clapped. The voices of carolers soared, beginning a soulful rendition of "White Christmas."

When the cheering and applause finally stopped, Creed asked, "Did you eat?"

"I haven't had a chance."

"We'll take care of that right away. Eve's is close by."

They wove their way through an enthralled crowd and crossed the street. The diner was jampacked and the outer vestibule held hungry patrons vying for seats.

"Average wait time's twenty minutes," the woman at the register said, when they entered, "and we're all out of meat loaf."

Creed thought quickly. The occasion presented

the perfect opportunity to have Skye to himself. "Come home with me? I'll have Vilma whip you up something."

"How about you come home with me, and we'll send out for pizza?"

"Sounds like a plan." It had worked out even better than he'd hoped. He wouldn't have to deal with a curious housekeeper, or, for that matter, his overly nosey assistant. "Where did you park?"

Skye motioned to the municipal parking lot.

"Good. I'll follow you."

It took longer than expected to get to Skye's home. Stores had extended their hours and all of Mills Creek was out Christmas shopping.

The moment Skye opened her front door, Hogan bolted. The little dog headed for the woods and relief.

"Looks like he had to go badly," Creed commented.

"Poor dog's been locked up most of the day."

Skye flipped on the lights, set her tote down, then hung their coats. She ignored the blinking red light on the answering machine and picked up the phone. She placed their pizza order.

"Aren't you going to check your messages?" Creed said, pointedly.

"Not tonight. I don't feel like allowing reality in."

"I'm flattered. You've put me ahead of work."

She remained silent.

"I've been meaning to speak to you about something," Creed said, stretching out on the couch and motioning for her to join him.

A bulky sweater hung almost to Skye's knees. She lit a candle, then perched on the arm of the sofa, not quite next to him, his proximity no doubt making her uncomfortable. Their attraction had burgeoned way out of control. Even the slightest brush of flesh had the potential to lead to other things.

"Have you made plans for Christmas?" Creed asked.

Skye shrugged. "I'd thought about going skiing, then maybe having dinner at my aunt's. But nothing's written in stone."

"How about we go into the city?"

"City, as in Manhattan? I'd like that."

"Yes. We'd take a suite at the Waldorf or Ritz. If we left on Christmas Eve, we could go in and maybe have a late dinner. Then we'd sleep in the next morning—maybe have breakfast in bed." His fingers kneaded her thigh. "We could see what the rest of the day brings. Maybe take in a show. What do you say?"

"I say it sounds tempting. One problem. I promised Pete I would work on Christmas Eve."

"Not a problem. Manhattan's a little over an hour's drive. If we leave late evening we could still have dinner. And we'll miss the holiday traffic."

The sound of scratching at the front door got their attention.

"Hogan," Skye said, jumping up.

Creed grabbed her wrist. "I'll get him."

Skye shot him a wry smile. "Okay by me. You two need to work out your issues."

Trailing something red in his mouth, the Jack Russell raced in. He sent the bag on the floor toppling. A blond wig and dark glasses fell to the floor. Creed barely had time to register their significance.

His attention returned to the dog, who deposited his gift at Skye's feet.

"What do we have here?" he said, bending to retrieve the item as the animal growled a warning.

Skye was even quicker. She snatched up the soiled material and stuffed the wig and sunglasses back in her bag. "A red silk scarf," she said, waving the filmy material at him. "The same kind of scarf the dead women were found with. Am I being overly paranoid?"

Creed simply stared at her.

Sixteen

"Don't be silly." Creed rose to pry the cloth from her clenched fingers. "It's just an old rag."

"I don't think so." Skye relinquished the fabric and plunked down on the sofa. Her front teeth worried her bottom lip. Picking up on her distress, Hogan circled her ankles. The little dog cocked its head, whining piteously. Creed tossed the cloth on the coffee table and eased himself down beside her.

"There's something else bothering you," he said, astutely. "You're overly jumpy and stressed."

She debated whether to tell him that her life had suddenly become very confused. Kris's disappearance had definitely been a stresser, plus she was dealing with these new feelings for him. Jacques' sudden reappearance in her life had added to the turmoil. Her ex had taken to phoning, trying to convince her to come back to Paris. On top of that, she'd come so close to stripping earlier. Only quick thinking had gotten her out of that audition.

Attempting to gauge his reaction, Skye began. "Some guy called Altarboy sent me a cryptic e-mail." She was sure Creed's eye ticked. But when she looked at him again, there was nothing but concern on his face.

"Was he the same guy who sent you the Christmas card?"

"Yes."

"Then why haven't you notified the police?"

She shrugged. "What am I going to tell them? That I got an e-mail from a man with the screen name, Altarboy. He wrote 'Creed Bennett's women disappear. Could you be next?' That's hardly a threat."

"It's an attempt to intimidate. That same fellow also sent you a card with a big red heart on it, and a rather suggestive message." He cracked his knuckles and muttered, "If I get my hands on him . . ."

"You'd what?" Skye seized his chin in one hand and turned his face in her direction. You're jealous. You *are* jealous."

"I'm worried," Creed insisted. "Look, Skye, you and I have been under a lot of pressure. We need to get away—go some place where we're not under scrutiny. Where we can relax and get to know each other."

"I thought we'd agreed to spend Christmas together."

"That's one day, maybe two. Not exactly time to unwind. When we return, the whole hectic cycle begins again. Can't you take a few days off after Christmas? We'll go to New York and fly to Fort Lauderdale from there. By then the media should have backed off. You and I will do nothing more stressful than lie in the sun and get to know each other."

She'd been presented with an invitation too good to turn down—an excuse to go to Fort Lauderdale.

It was a way to follow up on the leads she'd been given and an opportunity to find Kris.

"Oh, Creed, what a delightful invitation." She nibbled her lower lip. "Now I just have to convince Pete to give me the time off."

"Just think," Creed said, the tip of his tongue tickling her inner ear. "Seventy degree temperatures, fun, sea, and sun."

"I'm visualizing it," Skye said, snuggling against him.

He worked a hand under her sweater and ran his palm across her stomach. The first tingle began working its way down. It settled in her core. "It would be nice not to be under a microscope. I can show you the sights. And you wouldn't need this in Fort Lauderdale." He tugged at her sweater. "Take it off."

Skye felt her mood lighten. Even Hogan sensed it. The little dog seemed less irritable. He lay quietly, eyes closed. Springing out of her chair, she held her arms up. "Help me with it."

Creed willingly complied. Soon she stood before him clad in a formfitting body suit. His eyes practically bulged. She twirled, giving him a full view of her well toned body while Hogan raised a wary ear.

"Dance class?" Creed asked, dubiously.

"Something like that."

When she stopped spinning, he reached for her, pulled her close, and pressed her up against his length. "How about dancing for me?"

"There's no music."

"We'll make our own. You'll be my private dancer." He kissed the sides of her neck and her shoulders.

"Mmmmm. Don't stop."

Creed's palms cupped her buttocks, bringing her even closer, forcing her to feel what she was doing to him. Skye swayed against him, falling easily in step. He waltzed her about, humming the Tina Turner song, "Private Dancer," in her ear.

Before she knew it, he had waltzed her into the bedroom—a place that he'd never been before. Skye thought briefly of the unmade bed, the clothing she'd draped over the back of a chair that needed hanging, the old photos she'd scrutinized then left scattered across her dresser.

The backs of her legs were pressed up against the bed. Creed kissed her eyelids, cheeks, and jaw. His hands roamed her entire body, caressing, soothing, exploring. She couldn't think anymore. She just wanted to feel. She would keep her eyes closed and give in to these exciting sensations. Let him take her away.

"This thing you're wearing is a pain. Help me get rid of it," Creed said, in a husky voice.

Skye slid the shoulders of the unitard down. She wasn't wearing a bra. As she rolled the material down her stomach, Creed fastened his mouth on her breast, teasing the nipple. He stroked the other with his free hand. Everything pulsed. Hurrying, she struggled out of the bodysuit, almost tripping in her effort to be free.

Creed ground his groin into her. He was still fully clothed, but not for long, if she could help it. She tugged at his belt and fumbled for the zipper on his mocha colored slacks. He groaned. The pants slid to his ankles and he kicked them free. Stepping back from her, he tugged the cranberry crew-neck sweater over his head, taking with it the gold chain he wore around his neck. Every sense heightened, Skye heard their rapid breathing and smelled the cinnamon of the candle. She felt the feathery touch of Creed's fingertips trailing up and down her arm. She couldn't wait to have him inside her.

Picking up on her thoughts, Creed whispered, "I can't wait to love you."

"Then love me," she boldly invited. She'd agreed to spend the holidays with this man. At some point she had to trust him.

He stepped out of his black briefs and tugged at the elastic on her panties. "Are you planning on getting out of these, or do you need help?"

She threw him what she thought was a wicked look. "No, I need help."

No need to repeat herself. He was on top of her, hands sliding into her panties, cupping her mound, fingers probing her hidden recesses. He peeled away the skimpy red underwear and, in unspoken agreement, they climbed into bed.

Skye sat on top of Creed, savoring the feeling of being held in his arms, of having him inside of her. His slow yet calculating strokes were designed to drive her wild. Their kisses had been nonstop, continuous, matching the maddeningly slow pace he made love. She wanted him to pick up the pace, to drive her to the type of climax she'd envisioned but never experienced. She took charge of the situation, clamping her legs around him and gyrating her hips. The speed of exit and entry picked up. His hands tightened around her breasts, plucking, teasing, loving. At last they matched each other move for move.

The first ripple of pleasure washed over Skye. "Creed, come with me . . . pleeease," she cried.

"I'm coming with you, honey. I'm with you all . . . the way."

In a powerful whirl of emotions they hurled over the top.

"Your magician did a good job with those kids," Pete said, stabbing a finger at the article Skye had written. "It was a terrific show. Still has Mills Creek talking." He rattled the pages of the newspaper and beamed at her. "Good copy, gal. Why don't you cut out early?"

"Soon as my ride comes, I will." Skye straightened up her desk and hefted the suitcase, stuffed with mostly summer clothes, at her feet. "Let's get one thing clear. Creed is not . . . *my* magician. We happen to be friends. And yes, I agree with you, he did wonders with those kids. It was a nice performance."

"Yeah. Yeah. He's not *your* magician and I'm Pope John Paul. Who did you say was picking you up?"

"I didn't."

Quinn, occupying the cubicle next to Skye, piped up, "Can I cut out, too? It's Christmas Eve and I still haven't done my shopping."

"Sounds like you got a problem." Pete clamped a hand on the reporter's shoulder while dragging on the eternal cigarette. "Your wife needs to buy you one of those time management courses as a gift."

Quinn groaned. "Don't tell her that. Hey, I almost forgot," he said, thrusting an elaborately wrapped package Skye's way. "This came for you. It was delivered to the front desk. I picked it up on my way back from lunch."

Thanking him, Skye accepted the package. She

wandered into the staff lounge and made a quick call to Creed. He told her he would be delighted to come and fetch her early. She decided to wait in the lobby.

"Merry Christmas," she called to the few remaining reporters, glued to their computers. "You be a good boy." She kissed Pete's cheek and waggled a finger at him. "Try to stay out of trouble. Now, don't forget, if anyone needs a free meal Aunt Tonia's hosting an open house."

"Bye, gal. You have a nice holiday with your young man. If Tonia needs help with Hogan, call me," Pete replied.

"Thanks for the offer. I may take you up on it another time. Hogan adores Aunt Tonia. He's horribly spoiled by her." Was Pete just guessing or did he know she was spending time with Creed?

"Bye, Skye. Hope Santa's good to you," the remaining crew sang.

A giant Christmas tree dominated the lobby. A haphazard arrangement of decorations had been tossed on by the fourth graders who made it their annual project. Skye smiled at the sullen guard seated behind the circular desk. Reluctantly, the guard's face creased into an answering grin. "Merry Christmas, Ms. Walker."

"Have a nice holiday, Ken."

"Looks like someone's been good to you."

Skye nodded, shifting the gift Quinn handed her into a more comfortable position. There wasn't a tag, at least none that she could see. She didn't have time to open it now. Maybe later at the hotel.

Out front, a Ford Explorer pulled up. Her heart

raced as Creed poked his head out of the open window. The man behind the wheel would be hers, for at least the next six days.

Hers? Hardly. He hadn't committed.

"Gotta go. There's my ride," she said, wheeling her suitcase out to the curb, and carrying the cumbersome package under her arm.

Creed greeted her with a brief peck on the lips—a friendly one. "Figured it would be easier to rent a car. That way we could just drop it off at the airport."

She hid her disappointment that the kiss hadn't been longer, and hugged him loosely. He relieved her of the suitcase and kissed her again, this time with purpose. It was a kiss filled with promise, all his pent-up desire barely held in check. Holding the passenger door open, he waited for her to be seated. Soon the entire building would know she and a packed suitcase had left with Creed.

The hour-and-twenty-minute ride into Manhattan actually took three hours. They'd left earlier than planned, and, as expected, the toll plazas were filled with impatient motorists. Broken-down cars made travel even more hazardous, and a heavy sky held the promise of rain. To pass the time, they swapped memories of Christmases past. Skye told Creed about her Parisian Christmases, of eating roasted pheasant instead of turkey, of strolling down the Champs Elysee sipping cafe au lait and listening to strangers exchange Joyeaux Noel—Merry Christmas—greetings.

Creed told her of bundling up in bed with his late brother and pretending to be asleep when their mother crept in with armloads of presents. Of taking that initial peek, then rewrapping the presents to make them appear untouched. She wanted to ask him how his brother had died but sensed to do so would ruin their time together.

While Creed was lost in his memories, Skye stared at his hands. He maneuvered the vehicle effortlessly through the tunnel, long slender fingers holding the wheel. She remained mesmerized by the fine dark hairs at his wrists, his skillful steering. His touch evoked a sensuality she hadn't known she possessed. She bit the skin of her inner jaw, hoping the pain would center her. Heaven help her, she had fallen for the man. And there wasn't a thing she could do to change those feelings.

They arrived in midtown, the poignant smell of Creed's woodsy cologne heavy in her nostrils. He placed a possessive hand on her thigh as she tried her best to focus on the scenery flying by the window. Most stores had already closed down for the night. A few late shoppers waited at bus stops, arms filled with bundles. The occasional couple strolled the streets, stopping to smooch before ducking into restaurants. On the sidewalks, urban con artists made a last ditch effort to hawk cheap trinkets. Wound up gorillas, in full Christmas gear, danced at their feet.

"We got Tommy, Karan, Dooney. Cheap, cheap, cheap," one of them yodeled.

Skye was tired, but alert. Falling asleep wasn't part of the plan—not with Creed's palm burning a hole through her black wool slacks, and her entire body throbbing for his touch. She wanted to savor everything the city offered, eat every last morsel of the delicious dinner he had promised and make love to him like he'd never been made love to before. She'd learned a thing or two in Paris—from Jacques, whom she wished would stop calling. When would he get it through his head she was no longer interested?

The Waldorf loomed above them and Creed pulled into the Kinney Garage servicing the hotel. When he popped the rear door and turned the key over to a fawning valet, a cluster of bellmen snapped to attention.

"Mr. Bennett, I'm a big fan," the attendant said, snapping his fingers to get one of the men moving. "I think you're even better than Copperfield."

"Thank you," Creed said, flashing a smile that lit up his navy-black eyes and made her heart race.

"Welcome to the Waldorf, Sir, we've been expecting you." A uniformed bellhop cast a quizzical glance about them. "You are . . . alone?" He stowed their suitcases and Skye's gift on his trolley.

"Not exactly." Creed angled his chin to indicate Skye.

The bellman blushed. "What I meant was, I thought there would be more people. An entourage. Maybe even bodyguards."

"Not this time." Creed placed an arm around Skye's shoulder before claiming her mouth. Averting his eyes, the man scurried away. He waited at the elevator and, when they got on, inserted a key for the 30th floor. Bypassing the lobby, they headed straight for their tower suite.

"Tired?" Creed asked, when they were alone at last.

"Exhausted."

"Too worn out for dinner and midnight mass at St. Patrick's Cathedral?"

Skye smothered a yawn. "Both sound heavenly. Maybe I'll get a second wind."

She watched him play with the stereo until he found a jazz station. Placing an arm around her waist, he nibbled on her lobe. "I'd say a short nap's in order, then perhaps room service. Afterward, we can think about church."

"Sounds like a plan."

He led her to a cream-colored bedchamber. Warm burgundy drapes and complementing wingback chairs gave it an old English feeling. Creed shed his clothes, first slipping his formfitting turtleneck over his head, then stepping out of his dark gabardine slacks. He stood before her naked, and beautiful. The gold chain and its ring for a pendant were noticeably absent.

Playing the role of the aggressor, she wrapped her arms around his waist and rubbed against him, slipping her tongue into his mouth. His hardness, pressed against her belly, told its own story. For now that was enough. No point in forcing the relationship to the next step—not until she found Kris. After that, she might want more.

Skye's sixth sense had never failed her. The man she'd come to know wouldn't hurt a fly, much less another human being. Getting to know Creed was like reading a fascinating book that had grown increasingly harder to put down. She was a reporter caught between a rock and a hard place. Emotions weren't supposed to color her objectivity.

"That was a spectacular mass the Cardinal gave. I'm glad we went," Creed said, drawing Skye onto his lap and using that opportunity to kiss her soundly. "Merry Christmas, love."

"Merry Christmas."

Love? She wrapped her arms around his neck. He captured her tongue and drew it into his mouth, nipping gently. She tasted of almonds and honey, just like the cookie he'd bought her on the way home.

"What a nice way to bring in the day," she said, when she could finally speak.

"It was."

She seemed totally relaxed, more at ease than he'd ever seen her. It had been a good decision to get her away from the Poconos and bring her here. "I'll pour the champagne while you open your presents."

Her hazel eyes widened. He could almost hear the wheels in that overactive brain of hers turning. "Presents, I didn't expect . . ."

"Shush." His kiss silenced her. "Didn't your mother ever tell you to accept gifts gracefully?"

He'd been so thrilled at the prospect of having her to himself, that the moment she'd said yes, he'd rushed out and done some heavy duty shopping. Choosing the right gifts had been an agonizing process. But they'd had to be right. Perfect. Everything with meaning. Nothing frivolous. Except one. Maybe two. Skye wasn't the frivolous sort.

Not that he wouldn't have bought her the sun, moon, and stars if that's what she wanted. Instead, he opted for chic but practical: a Coach portfolio to match her briefcase and stow the sheaf of notes she so often carried; a Mont Blanc pen in deep burgundy; a butter soft leather coat lined in ermine that would look absolutely delicious on her; and a hot red mohair sweater to bring out the cinnamon of her skin. Then there was the impractical gift from Victoria's Secret.

After that, he'd gone just a little bit crazy, and wrapped up the gift he'd been saving for someone special—his mother's ring. He'd hold onto that for last. He was already taking a huge risk by presenting her with so many high-priced items. But Skye Walker was the type of woman you wanted to spoil and, as infatuated as he was, common sense no longer came into play.

"What do you suppose Jed's doing for the holiday?" Skye asked, sipping on the bubbly he'd poured.

The question took him by surprise, and he tried to keep his voice emotionless. "Probably doing what he always does. Drinking. It keeps his beasts at bay. I'm certain he's passed out by now."

"You're awfully hard on him."

"Am I?"

"Yes. Regardless of what's happened between the two of you, he's still your father, Creed."

He debated telling her that Jed had ceased being that a long time ago—the moment he'd become old enough to reason. The father he once adored was a weak man, dependent on his wife to smooth the way, and vodka to get him through.

Be that as it may, he'd dispatched Rick to take care of Jed's rent and provide him with enough groceries to feed a small army. The Bon Ton, the best store in town, had been ordered to wrap up a warm coat and a half-dozen sweaters. Despite his better judgment, an unsigned Christmas card with five crisp one-hundred-dollar bills had been couriered to Jed. He'd bet his life on it, by now his father was in drunks' heaven.

Creed preferred not to think about Jed.

"Aren't you going to open that gift?" he urged,

pointing to the elaborately wrapped package resting on one of the conservative wingback chairs. Skye had been lugging the thing around like it was the crown jewels.

"Why so interested? Did you send it?" She raised a curious eyebrow at him.

"Not me. I'm just dying to see if the competition's creative." He kissed her soundly, immersing himself in the smell and feel of her. "We need more champagne," he said, moving away so he wouldn't ravish her.

The Perrier Jouet awaited, draped in white linen, the bottle propped at an odd angle in the wine bucket. Creed replenished their drinks, casting a glance at the oversized basket of fruit wrapped in cellophane. The concierge had sent it to them with a note wishing them the nicest of Christmases.

Skye fought not to ruin the paper, inserting a well-manicured finger under the bow and tugging on it. She finally pried the ribbon loose and gingerly attempted to peel back the wrapping.

"Oh, just rip it," Creed said, anxious to see the contents.

The sound of paper shredding didn't quite drown out the sultry Winton Marsalis tune. Outside, the rain beat down. Creed crossed the room, throwing the drapes wide open. He resisted the urge to press his nose against the window pane and regress to childhood behavior. Back then the pitter-patter of rain had washed out the loud arguments. Almost.

His room had been the safe place he used to escape to. The simple magic tricks, self taught, lulled him into believing he was in control. Powerful. He'd come to love this world of make believe. People didn't get hurt there. At least they hadn't, up until recently.

"Creed?"

Reality intruded with the sound of his name. Skye held out a slightly smaller box wrapped in the same paper as the other had been.

"Some wise guy's idea of a joke," he said, biting back the jealously he'd tried so hard to control.

"I don't know," she said, hesitantly, her fingers working rapidly. Her second attempt yielded more wrapping. Another box. "Damn," she muttered, adrenaline fueling her as she tore the paper apart and pried the lid off a rectangular white box with Lord and Taylor written across the cover.

"Oh no," she said. Creed moved in closer, watching her shred tissue and remove red silk. She held it out.

"No mistaking what this is," she said, waving the scarf like a matador would to a bull.

He saw red. "It's time to get the police involved." He bent to retrieve the note that floated to the floor. She didn't seem to notice.

"And tell them what?"

"Tell them . . . tell them . . . some unknown person is sending you a warning."

"Are they?"

"Sure looks like it," he said, quickly crumpling the note and stuffing it into his pocket.

Seventeen

Skye hung up the phone. No point in leaving a message. She'd called, hoping her old friend, Freddy Newton, would be home. Instead, she'd gotten his answering machine. He would tell her if she had cause to worry. Outcasts tended to stick together, and it was logical that the Incredible Hulk and Luke Skywalker had found each other. He was the only cop she trusted to tell about Altarboy. Freddy wasn't into the egotistical cop thing. She'd relied on his level-headedness to get through school.

Skye had been overwhelmed when she and Creed had pulled up in front of the huge white house, with its wrap-around decks, which he called home. She'd stared awestruck at his mansion with its unfettered view of the intra-coastal. No zero-lot lines here. Just water, as far as the eye could see. Water and other expensive homes.

After they'd gotten settled, Creed had taken her by the hand and given her the ten cent tour of the place. He was immensely proud of his home and seemed anxious to have her like it. As he'd whisked her around, he'd appeared nervous and bashful, as if his excesses embarrassed him. She'd decided the suave performer of international acclaim was really a vulnerable man who wanted to be liked, though not necessarily for what he owned. She'd found that side of him touching.

Skye returned to the patio, where Creed lounged in the mid-morning sun, a pair of Tommy dark glasses perched on the end of his nose and a New York Times bestseller clutched in one hand. It was the day after Christmas.

They'd left the Waldorf earlier then planned, taking the first flight into Fort Lauderdale. The red silk scarf had dampened Skye's enthusiasm about opening her other presents. Even now, Creed's wrapped gifts remained on the dining room table. He'd said tonight would be their Christmas. Meanwhile, he was perfectly content to sit on the patio soaking up the morning sun.

The household help had been given the holidays off. When hunger struck, Skye was dispatched to a nearby restaurant for takeout. Creed didn't want anyone to know he was home, so having anything delivered was out of the question. It had turned into a peculiar Christmas—certainly different from others she'd experienced.

The thought that his was a lonely life saddened her. Despite his wealth, she would never change places with him. Living isolated from others just wasn't her cup of tea. Although worshiped by many, Creed trusted so few. Kareem Davis was the only friend she'd ever heard him speak of. Rick, close as they seemed, was still an employee.

She was grateful for her mundane existence, for a mother who loved her, and relatives who cared. What was the point of having a huge mausoleum of a house if you were alone and lonely?

"I've been thinking of taking the boat out," Creed said, snapping her back to the present. He lowered his designer glasses and smiled at her.

"Sounds like fun."

Pulling up his legs, he made room for her, waiting until she settled into the inverted V of his thighs. He wrapped his arms around her and pulled her down on top of him, stroking the sides of her breasts and whispering suggestively in her ear.

"No way, you sex-crazed fiend." She slapped his wandering hand.

"I didn't hear you complain earlier."

Skye snorted. She loved making love with him. She loved the way he made her feel. But everything in its own time. She had other thoughts on her mind, like how to find Club Nirvana and get the information she needed.

Inside, the phone rang. It had been ringing non-stop since they arrived.

"Aren't you going to answer it?" Skye asked, for what seemed the hundredth time.

"No. No one knows that I'm here, except Rick. The answering machine's been turned off. If it's urgent, he'll call on the cellular. How about that boat ride?"

"Sounds divine."

Later, after returning from their trip up the Intracoastal, Creed left to take a shower. Skye searched for the Yellow Pages and eventually found the phone book stashed in a kitchen cupboard. The red silk scarf had left her feeling uneasy. Queasy. The rag Hogan had brought her could be anything. But there was no mistaking what this was. Someone had purposely selected a scarf and sent it to her anonymously. She couldn't imagine anyone being that unconscionable.

Skye leafed through the C's until she found Club Nirvana, the strip joint that Veronique, the dancer at the Pony, said Kris used to work at. She didn't know how she was going to manage it, but she planned on going there. She had some specific questions that needed answering. Maybe she could go after Creed went to bed.

"Skye," Creed called. "Where are you?"

"Getting a drink of water." She bent the page of the book and quickly snapped it shut. She'd copy the address later.

"Open that one first," Creed said, handing over an elaborately wrapped box with a big silver bow. He watched Skye struggle with the paper and turned his attention to his own gift, a small square box, wrapped in red gilt.

Dinner had been a barbecue out on the patio. He'd found enough in the refrigerator to make a surf and turf dinner. Skye had rustled up a salad. It tasted like nothing he'd ever tasted before. He hadn't known she could cook.

"Oh, Creed, you shouldn't have," Skye said, her hazel eyes misting over. She hugged the portfolio to her. "I love Coach. How did you know?"

He shrugged. "You're just a Coach kind of girl. Besides, the briefcase was a sure give away." He removed a pair of butter-soft leather gloves that must have cost her a fortune. "These are wonderful. Perfect. I needed a pair." They kissed.

The phone rang, as it seemed to do at fifteen minute intervals.

"Aaaagh."

He was determined that nothing would ruin the mood they'd created. Not the press. Not Rick. Not anything.

"I suppose you're not going to pick up." Skye moved out of his arms.

"Nope. Why let the outside world in?"

When the phone stopped ringing, they returned to their gift giving. He was surprised that she'd thought to buy him anything, but was delighted she had. It had taken a lot of thought and time to find the hand-carved antique box with the secret compartments, another of her gifts. The present would be put to good use. His cherished collection of antique playing cards needed a home.

He was still undecided about what to do about the ring. While it wasn't quite an engagement ring, he knew it would scare her off. Still, he needed a way to communicate how he felt about her—that she wasn't just a passing thrill. Skye Walker was a woman he planned on holding onto, if she would have him. She was a woman he was slowly beginning to trust.

She seemed pleased with the Mont Blanc pen and red sweater and went gaga over the coat. She tried it on, strutting the length of the room like a runway model, making exaggerated poses. Creed held up a pink, white, and gold box, which he hadn't bothered to wrap. "Wait until you see this," he called.

"Victoria's Secret? You must be a regular there."

She raised a quizzical eyebrow at him. He knew

what she was thinking—that he had a string of women that he needed to appease. Was she wrong, though. He'd gone into the lingerie store at Lydia's urging. His publicist had suggested buying lounging pajamas for Felicity and the other female members of his entourage. Then Skye had walked in. On impulse, he'd decided to fulfill his fantasies and buy her a gift. Intimate and impractical as it was, he knew she would look gorgeous in it.

Skye took the package he held out. She reached in and removed a champagne-colored garter belt, matching camisole, and minuscule thong bikini, edged in lace. She held them up to her. "What if they don't fit?"

"They'll fit. I asked the saleswoman for help."

"And she just happened to know my size?" She gazed at him, a half-smile curving her lips.

"I pointed you out."

"You didn't. With Rick hanging around?"

"He was busy selecting his own gifts. I don't think he put two and two together."

The cellular phone he'd left on top of the outdoor bar rang. He didn't feel like getting it. Skye was closer. "Grab that," he ordered.

"What if it's Rick?"

"What if it is? It's no secret we're seeing each other."

She returned, holding the phone to her ear, looks of abject surprise, concern, fear, and bewilderment flashing across her face simultaneously. Something horrible had happened. He could tell by the way she clutched the receiver tightly. Gone was the relaxed young woman he'd held in his arms and made passionate love to a few hours ago. She was back in full reporter mode.

"Hold on, Jed," he heard her say. "You'd better talk to Creed." She held the receiver out to him.

He accepted it reluctantly. What did the old man want? Surely he hadn't called to thank him for the gifts. Jed had never been big on thanks. How would the old geezer have gotten the number of his cell phone anyway? Not from Rick. Rick was smart enough to know he wouldn't want his father to have it. With a few drinks in him, Jed would give that number to anyone.

As he prepared to greet his father, Skye picked up the remote and aimed it at the T.V.

"What is it, Jed?" Creed grunted.

"No Happy Holidays? Nothing?" The old man sounded lucid—clear as the day, and more coherent than he'd been in ages. Was this a new Jed? Creed looked up to see Skye pretending to surf the channels.

"How did you get my number?" he asked carefully.

Jed chuckled. "I have my ways. Nothing's sacred in Mills Creek, remember?"

Creed didn't like playing games. "Is something wrong?"

"You haven't heard?"

"What?"

"There's an almighty ruckus going on up here. The Washington girl's body was found in the woods last night. Red scarf tied around her neck. A hunter stumbled across her remains. The reporters have taken over this town. They're asking all kinds of questions about you."

"Have you contacted Rick?" Creed asked, wondering why his assistant hadn't called him.

"Couldn't find him. I stopped by your house as soon as the news broke. It was battened down tight. The guard at the gate told me he's having the devil of a time keeping reporters out. The T.V. anchor says they expect to make an arrest shortly."

"The T.V. anchor? You mean this mess is on T.V.?"

"It's all over the news. One of the hunter's found a man's jacket nearby, covered in blood. He turned it in to the cops. The owner is probably the killer."

Rick had chosen a bad time to go missing. Creed pinched the bridge of his nose with his thumb and index finger. He could imagine the tumult Mills Creek was thrown into. Gruesome murders didn't happen in the tiny borough. They happened in places like New York, Philly, New Jersey—not in a small Pocono town where most people didn't even lock their homes.

Skye was riveted to the T.V., the garter belt dangling from her fingers and the matching panties and camisole slung over one shoulder. He watched her expression as a picture of Jamie Washington, the way she must have looked at graduation, flashed across the screen. A beautiful girl—wide eyed, intelligent, innocent.

Another picture of the coed replaced the sophomoric one. The real Jamie Washington, perhaps, braids swinging freely to a frenzied beat and teeny bikini bottom covering the essentials. A black rectangular line covered her naked breasts when she straddled a pole. Muted applause could be heard in the background.

The brief flick had obviously been videotaped by a patron and sold to the highest bidder.

"Creed, son? Are you still there?"

"Yes, I'm here."

"No matter what they say, I know you didn't do it."

He hadn't even considered that his name and reputation might be at risk again. He hadn't made the association that Jed had called to alert him that he was in trouble. He chanced a look at Skye. How was she taking it? She appeared to be listening to the newscaster—intently.

"I have to go, da . . . thanks for calling."

"You need some place to hide, boy, you come to me."

"Hide?" Why would he do that? He was innocent, and there was no way that he would allow anyone to pin this heinous crime on him. No one.

"The cops are out for blood," Jed said, before hanging up.

Creed stood for a long time holding the phone in his hand.

"Are you all right?" Skye asked. Using the remote, she cut the newscaster off mid-sentence. She came to his side, arms open wide. "Whatever the outcome, we're in this together. I believe you, Creed. I believe in your innocence."

All the months of tension finally got to him as he was enveloped in her arms. He was a little boy needing comforting. He listened to her soothing voice and clung to her, swaying back and forth. He'd just discovered another side of Skye Walker: nurturer, soother of an anguished soul.

The only person he'd been able to let go with totally had been his mother. Skye was rapidly replacing her as confidante and friend. But what he felt for Skye wasn't the love of a son for his mother. It was much more. He'd come to need Skye as much as he needed the air that he breathed or the adulation of an audience. She validated his existence. She made him feel alive and whole again.

The tears he hadn't allowed himself to shed when his mother died fell. He hoped she didn't notice. He suddenly had the absurd need to make love to Skye, to be in tune with her mentally and physically. He wasn't entirely convinced she felt the same emotional need. Considering that, it would be ridiculous to tell her his true feelings until this nightmare of a situation was over, and the emotional baggage stashed. For now, just having her here was enough.

"Creed, I think we should think about getting back to Mills Creek," Skye said, holding his chin between her palms and forcing him to look at her.

He blinked and pulled away, refusing to acknowledge the confusion and hurt reflected in her eyes. "I'd think that would be the last place you'd want to be."

"My job's there. The police are going to want to ask you questions. Better to be available than not available. Call your attorney. Have her meet you at the airport."

So it all came down to this. Her job. A potential story.

Nothing good ever lasted. Nothing ever had.

Eighteen

Club Nirvana was a cavernous place with Eastern decor and big screen T.V.s. Oversized lithographs from the Kama Sutra, sporting positions that Skye thought weren't humanly possible, hung on the walls. Her arrival at almost closing time hadn't raised an eyebrow. A few diehard drinkers were grouped around the bar, the remainder worshiped at a gyrating stripper's feet. Skye took a seat next to a construction type and ordered a wine spritzer.

She'd waited for Creed to fall asleep then pocketed the keys to his Jeep. Not that she'd known where she was going. But with the aid of a map and a quick stop at a gas station, she'd managed to find her way.

They were leaving for Mills Creek tomorrow and a black mood had settled around them. Creed had changed their plane reservations, then brusquely told her of the arrangements. After that phone call from Jed, their make-believe world had come toppling down.

Skye nursed her spritzer and tried not to become maudlin. Creed's mood change frightened her.

"Hey, sweetness, you looking for company?" A cowboy type, dressed in faded Wranglers, pointy boots, and a conch shell belt, hoisted himself onto the vacant stool next to her. He'd either just come off the ranch or could be heading there.

"Not particularly."

"Ah, don't be like that." He leaned in close enough for her to smell the beer on his breath. "So, what are you doing here, alone?"

"Did I say I was alone?" Skye sipped her spritzer.

"You work here then?" Roy Rogers fished.

Dodging the question, Skye smiled at him. "Why? You a regular?" She needed any information he might have.

"Ummm hmmm. But I never seen you before. I would have remembered."

"I took a little vacation. Used to dance when Kristina Brown was here . . ."

"You did? That Kristina was a fine piece of a . . . I mean, a good-looking girl. Every man's fantasy. Knew how to move her assets and use that whip. How come I never seen you?"

"I stripped part time. Probably danced nights when you weren't in."

"That would be Wednesdays and Fridays—when the old lady refused to cut me loose."

Bingo. She'd found someone who remembered Kristina.

"Then you must have known Jason?" Skye asked, crossing a leg and straightening the tight mini-skirt she wore.

Cowboy licked his lips. His eyes never left her thighs. "Big guy. Sat in the back. If anyone got fresh with his woman, he moved in."

Skye took another gulp of spritzer. She watched a handful of people shuffle to the door. "Yep. That's him. I came here trying to hook up with them but no one seems to know where they went."

"Hey, Nathan," Roy Rogers called to a huge black man built like a wrestler. "Remember the stripper, Kristina? The one whose boyfriend was always hanging out here. This here's her friend. Know where she went?"

"Last I heard it, was up North. Money was better and her man had a business to run."

Skye turned to Roy Rogers. "Why involve him?"

Her new acquaintance squinted his eyes suspiciously. "Nate's been here since the place opened. Knows everything and everyone. Come to think of it, how come he don't know you?"

"I cut my hair," Skye said, quickly. "Colored it, too. I got a new career—modeling."

"Is that a fact." Roy placed a suggestive hand on her thigh and squeezed hard. "You're a hot babe. Let's you and me go someplace where the booze is free and we can get comfortable."

"I don't think so," Skye said, sliding off her stool. "My boyfriend's not going to like that. He's outside. His nickname's Looney Tunes. Believe me, you don't want to mess with him."

In search of a more comfortable position on the king-sized bed, Creed flung his arms wide. He reached for Skye but grasped only a plump pillow. Realization dawned, there was only emptiness next to him.

"Skye, where are you?" he called, sitting up and rubbing his eyes.

After waiting an appropriate time, and no answer,

he flung the covers back. He fumbled for the switch on the lamp. Light flooded the room. Perhaps Skye was downstairs watching T.V.

The media room was blanketed in darkness when he entered. A silent television commanded no audience. And a thorough search of the house left him more perplexed. Skye couldn't have disappeared into thin air, could she? She wouldn't have left without telling him, would she?

Purposeful steps took him back into the kitchen. One of the cupboard doors was slightly ajar. Normally he wouldn't have given it another thought, but a bulky phone book prevented the door from latching. Someone had perused the directory then shoved it back haphazardly. Curiosity, more than anything else, made him open the book. A bent page got his attention. Club Nirvana and a number of others had been circled in red. Could Skye have gone off in search of night life? How insensitive of him not to realize she was bored.

Club Nirvana—wasn't that the place Kristina had danced? A second glance at the directory confirmed his worst fears. They were stripper joints. Many of them known for cosmetically enhanced dancers and back room sex. Creed's whistle was long and low. Why would Skye be interested in exotic clubs? Why would places like that draw her?

He remembered the wig and dark glasses that had fallen out of her bag. She'd needed the disguise for a reason. Kristina Brown had apparently become an obsession.

Upon reflection, he realized Skye had jumped at the offer of accompanying him to Fort Lauderdale. What if spending time with him had not been utmost in her mind? Rick had mentioned seeing her at the Pony one night. He hadn't believed him. Women like Skye Walker didn't hang out at exotic clubs. Unless . . . unless . . . they were on a story.

Suppose she were using him? Suppose she had accompanied him to Florida with a specific agenda in mind? He retraced his steps, threw on his clothes, and searched for the keys to his Jeep. They were gone. Luckily, he had another vehicle.

Only one way to get his questions answered: Go to Club Nirvana and confront her.

What a waste of time this had been. She'd left Nirvana no wiser than when she'd arrived. Now she had the oddest feeling she was being followed. It had all begun with a slammed car door in the parking lot, then footsteps trailing her, and the eerie sense of someone in hot pursuit. A surreptitious glance in the car's rearview mirror revealed nothing out of the ordinary, just a slow stream of traffic inching its way out of the lot. Still, she couldn't shake that jittery feeling.

Skye put the car in reverse then remembered to turn on the interior light. She perused the map, noting that I95 was only a short distance away. If she headed north, she'd be home in less than twenty minutes and Creed wouldn't be any wiser.

Her attempts to find the highway took her down poorly lit streets, past rundown warehouses, and ramshackle tenements. Cheap Christmas decorations dangled off bent lampposts and hung from battered wooden doors. It saddened her to think of those less fortunate than she having to celebrate in these surroundings. Not that her holiday had been a picnic so far. But at least she was spending time in a beautiful home with a man she had come to care for.

A Saab maintained a discreet distance behind her, turning when she turned, slowing down when she did. Crime in the Miami-Fort Lauderdale area was something she'd only read about. She hoped the stories were exaggerated and put the weird feeling down to nerves.

The Saab maintained a respectable distance but followed her up the ramp. It merged with her onto I95 then zoomed into traffic. She stepped on the accelerator, zipped into the middle lane, and wove her way in between cars. Assured she'd left the vehicle behind, she crossed over to the left lane, put her foot to the pedal, and sped off. She knew she was taking a chance, driving like a demon in an unfamiliar state, but she couldn't shake the uneasy feeling that she was being pursued, and the person behind the wheel meant her harm.

After a while, she began to relax. She whooshed air out of her lungs and turned on the radio. Music might be a welcome distraction. But something made her glance at the mirror again. The Saab was back, inches behind her, headlights on bright. Skye's stomach flip-flopped. She felt nauseous. What good samaritan would come to her rescue if she were forced off the road? Who would be willing to put his or her life at risk at this late hour?

Jumping lanes, Skye successfully ended up in the far right. In the process, she cut off a truck driver. Brakes squealed. Horns honked. She could only imagine the ugly expletives being yelled at her. Still, she was better off in front of the truck than behind it. At least if the Saab tried to nudge her off the road, the trucker, given his height advantage, would see and possibly come to her aid.

Signs for Sterling then Griffin Road whizzed by. Another ten minutes and she would be home. The truck driver picked up his pace. He was on her tail now, dangerously close to her bumper. Better him than the Saab; at least she knew why he was angry. The foreign car moved alongside, keeping up with her. The driver had the audacity to honk.

"Oh, God!"

At any moment she could be killed. She was boxed in by both vehicles with no way out. Adrenaline kicked in. She pressed down on the gas. The Jeep shot forward. So did the Saab. The speedometer indicated she had hit the eighty mile mark. She was flying down a pitted highway, two vehicles in hot pursuit.

The high-pitched sound of sirens pierced the night. Flashing lights headed her way. Skye eased her foot off the accelerator waiting for the cop car to catch up. She'd never thought of a ticket as a Godsend. The vehicles behind and alongside her slowed to the speed limit. She whooshed the aching breath out of her lungs as the truck was pulled over. The Saab got lost somewhere in the process.

Who would ever have thought the police would be a welcome sight?

He'd just pulled into the parking lot of Club Nirvana when he spotted her. "Skye," he called. She ignored him or simply hadn't heard.

"Skye," he shouted again, garnering the attention of several tipsy patrons.

"If she don't want you, buddy, plenty more will," a man shouted, gesturing to inside the club.

Skye's pace quickened. He hopped out of the car and slammed the door of the Saab. It was humid outside, and the smell of exhaust fumes clung heavily to his clothes. He sprinted, trying to catch up with her. It was crucial they talk. By the time they were in conversational distance, she'd already jumped into the Jeep, windows wound tightly shut, headlights on. He didn't want to alarm her. He'd catch her at home.

He loped back to his car, put it in gear, and followed her from the parking lot. Lucky for him, she drove slowly, since she was unfamiliar with the neighborhood. A plus this time around. He followed her onto I95 where she immediately picked up speed. He tried to let her know that he was there and would lead her home if necessary. Pressing down on the accelerator, he covered the distance between them. She bolted like a frightened deer, cutting off an angry truck driver.

The driver's colorful oath floated through his open window. "Damn woman driver!"

The heavy vehicle bore down on her. No one would get away with talking to his woman like that. He would let her know he was there and would protect her if he had to. He forced the Saab alongside her, honking his horn. His presence made her panic. She pushed the Jeep forward. The truck driver kept at her, practically kissing her bumper. He barely kept up with them.

He heard the whoo-whoo of sirens and saw the

flashing lights behind them. Slowing down, he prepared himself for the ticket that was bound to follow.
But the police seemed bent on getting the truck.
The cop car practically hooked itself onto the
trucker's bumper, forcing him off the road.

"Pull over," an amplified voice ordered.

He hadn't realized he was holding his breath, or
that the taste of rust in his mouth meant he'd bitten
his tongue. The close call served a purpose, though.
From then on he kept to the speed limit, maintaining a discreet distance, following Skye home.

"Merciful God, he's still behind me," Skye said,
pulling into Creed's winding driveway, edged by
flower beds. Visions of a too-short life flashed before
her eyes. In each vignette, she wore a red scarf tightly
wound around her neck.

The lights of the trailing vehicle cast eerie shadows
against the trees and cascading foliage, making the
most mundane greenery look like boogie men. Why
hadn't the person backed off?

Too late, Skye thought of the cell phone she'd left
on Creed's dresser, of the staff released for the holidays. He'd told her he sometimes kept bodyguards
on hand to ensure his personal safety, that security
often patrolled his vast grounds. She could only pray
that a few of these people were still around.

She continued up the driveway. The Saab followed.
What were the odds that Creed would be waiting out
front? Never mind that she'd have to come up with
an excuse for her nocturnal excursion—anything
was better than ending up another Florida statistic.

Motion sensors went on as she threw the car into

park. The grounds flooded with light. In that brief second, the estate turned into a veritable wonderland, all emerald foliage and twinkling lights. The driver of the Saab didn't seem the least bit fazed. He parked his car inches from her bumper. She sat immobile, afraid to get out. Finally she sprang into action, hitting the horn. The rude noise succeeded in startling her.

The Saab's door slammed. The driver crunched his way toward her. She pressed harder on the horn. He knocked on her window. She felt the bile build in her stomach, rise up, and invade her chest. She heard the loud rat-a-tat of a hand hammering on the glass. At last, she ventured a look up.

"Creed! Why were you following me?" The tears she'd held back finally fell. After a moment, she leapt from the Jeep. She pounded on his chest. "What the hell are you doing in that Saab, trying to scare me?"

His arms encircled her, trapping her, as a gentle hand wiped the tears from her face. In spite of her anger, she melted.

"Hush, baby. Hush. I didn't set out to frighten you." He pulled her close and tucked her head against his chest. "I woke up. You were gone. I found the phone book. I got the car out of the garage and came looking for you."

She lifted trembling hands to her aching temples. "That's how you knew where I was?"

"Yes." He led her to the front door, opened it, and shooed her in. "It's time we talk," he said, when she was seated on one of the sunshine-yellow chairs in his den. "Start from the beginning. Tell me why Kristina Brown is so important to you."

Could she tell him the truth? Honesty was essential

to a relationship, if that's what they had. She'd lied by omission—by necessity, actually. If she told him Kris was her cousin, would he forgive her or trust her again? The cellular phone clipped to the waistband of his slacks rang.

"Hold it for a moment. Let me pick up." Creed tugged the phone free. He held the receiver to his ear. "Hello."

One look at his face told her something even more horrible had happened.

Nineteen

"If you knew this was coming down, why the hell didn't you call me?" Creed yelled.

He listened to his assistant ramble on, offering every excuse in the book.

"I tried the Waldorf but you'd checked out."

"You know I always carry my cell phone."

"Yes. But it wasn't on. Believe me, I've tried reaching you repeatedly. Since you have Skye Walker with you, I assumed you didn't want to be disturbed."

Creed took deep breaths and counted to ten. Nothing was sacred in Mills Creek. Nothing. "Jed said he stopped by the house. No one was at home."

"Yes. I took Tikka with me. We spent the holidays with Tiffany. You remember her? She was the woman I brought to the dance."

"You're back now, I assume."

"Yes. Lydia's left a slew of messages. You need to turn your T.V. on. Your jacket was found at the murder site."

Creed massaged his aching head. "My jacket! You dropped off the face of the earth the moment I disappeared. That was pretty irresponsible of you. I pay you to keep me informed." Rick was supposed to be his eyes and ears. He counted on him to watch his back. He would have expected him to call the moment the news about Jamie Washington broke—even if it meant putting his personal life on hold.

"Come on, Creed, give a guy a break," Rick wheedled. "You told me to get lost—take time off and enjoy my holiday. How was I to know all hell would break loose in my absence?"

"Where did you go to, Timbuktu? There isn't a place in the world that doesn't have televisions. If, as you say, the media's sunk their teeth into this, how come you didn't know earlier?"

How come he *didn't know? Lucky for him, Jed had called. He'd immersed himself in Skye and gotten carried away by their loving.*

"I assure you it won't happen again," Rick responded, chastened.

"You bet it won't. Get Doreen Salazar on the phone. Have her meet me at the airport. I'll be in tomorrow." He gave the details of his flight.

Creed knew Skye was hanging on to every word. He'd purposely not mentioned Doreen was his attorney, and he hoped his body language didn't communicate how upset he was. Rick's bombshell had just rocked his world. The logical next step would be for the cops to question him. Maybe they would even apprehend him. His entire world was turning upside down.

Who could hate him so much they'd want him out of the way? He didn't have any enemies he knew of. Yet four women had been gruesomely murdered. The finger in each and every case had pointed to him. Most of these women had lived a double life, making good money as exotic dancers. While he'd never been the judgmental type, and personally felt it was a woman's right to do with her body what she saw fit, the killer plainly felt otherwise.

Skye tugged on the tail of his T-shirt. "Is there anything you want to tell me? Can I get you water? An aspirin, perhaps?"

"I'm okay," he said, gruffly. "Stop fussing." He moved away.

His distress must show on his face. His only concern now was to get her as far from him as possible. She didn't need to be dragged into this mess or associated with a nasty scandal. He didn't want her there if he was arrested.

"No. You're not okay." She followed and tried linking her arm through his. "Talk to me. What's going on?"

He tugged away. "What's it with you women?" he growled. "Sleep with you a couple of times and you want to get inside a man's head."

Skye's face registered her mortification. She stepped back and flashed him a look of bewilderment and hurt.

"What's with you?" she shot back. "Intimacy scares you so much, you're afraid if anyone gets too close they won't like the real you?" She hugged herself, looking as if she ached. Tears welled in her eyes.

He hated to hurt her. But at least he'd succeeded in making her mad. She was angry enough to leave for Mills Creek without him, hopefully. She didn't need to have her name linked with his. The publicity would only kill her career. And she didn't need her picture plastered across newspapers.

"Our little fling is over. It wouldn't have worked

anyway. You might as well pack your things and catch the first flight tomorrow."

"You bastard," she said, turning to face him.

Creed refused to acknowledge her hurt expression or the fact that his brutality had caused the unshed tears in her eyes. It had killed him to be that cruel. And it took every ounce of willpower not to gather her in his arms and kiss that stricken look off her face—to tell her that she was the only thing in the whole wide world that mattered to him. She and Tikka.

"I'll make sure your reservations are changed," he railed. "It's the least I can do."

"Don't bother."

The door slammed behind her.

The moment Skye walked into the newsroom she knew all hell had broken loose. Frenzied reporters scurried from desk to desk, conversing in low tones. There was a scoop in the making, she sensed. Whatever scandal was about to break, was a hot one.

She'd taken a taxi from the airport, chucked her suitcase into the Bronco, and raced into the building. Work, she hoped, would numb her ability to think and help her get over the pain of being used and discarded.

"What's going on, guys?" she asked, placing her new Coach portfolio on the desk, and trying desperately to ignore her overflowing in-box. A juicy story might keep her occupied—take her mind off the humiliation she'd just experienced.

It was as if no one heard her. All her colleagues suddenly seemed busy, immersed in urgent tasks. She sensed someone behind her and looked back to find Quinn. His fingers manipulated her aching shoulders, but he wouldn't meet her eyes.

"Pete wants to see you in his office when you get settled," he mumbled. "I'll be here when you get back . . . to offer moral support . . ."

"What's going on?" Skye looked in the direction of her boss's closed door. "Am I getting fired?" She managed a weak smile. "My buddy would tell me, wouldn't he?"

"Yes, he would. Now go." He pushed her in the direction of Pete's office.

Skye had called Pete from the airport to let him know she was back early. His assistant had taken the message. Now a sinking feeling invaded her stomach as she stood before his door. She took a deep breath and knocked.

"I'm not to be disturbed. What's with you people?" he growled.

"It's me, Skye."

"Why didn't you say so? Come in, gal."

She entered to find him on the phone, cigarette clamped between his teeth, head wreathed in smoke. He motioned for her to sit.

"You think they'll make an arrest?" he said to the person on the other end. For a brief moment their gazes met and held. She had the funniest feeling that this conversation was about Creed. Her trepidation built.

When the phone call ended, Pete's meaty fingers drummed the scarred mahogany desk. Without uttering a single word, he rose to pace the room. Noxious fumes trailed behind him.

"We've got big problems, gal," he said, at last. "I

have it on good authority Creed Bennett's about to be arrested."

"No!"

The worst had happened. Forget that she was angry with Creed—that he'd treated her abominably—that she hated his guts. Deep down, she knew he wasn't a killer.

"Have you been listening to the news?" Pete asked, carefully.

"I heard Jamie Washington's body was found."

Pete clamped down on his cigarette. "Your man's jacket was found in the woods close to her remains."

"That's hardly enough to implicate him." *God, let this be a huge mistake.*

Why was she defending a man who'd treated her poorly? Why had the news of his impending arrest sent her into a tailspin? They'd been getting along just fine, achieving a level of intimacy she'd only dreamed of, until that phone call from Rick. Then, in the blink of an eye, he'd turned into this callous monster, spewing hateful words at her, telling her he wanted her gone and purposefully driving her away. On reflection, maybe that had been his intent. Maybe Rick's call had been to alert him that an arrest might be imminent. Maybe he'd wanted to spare her.

"There's more," Pete growled. "Jamie's face and arms were scratched. There was blood on her clothes. Forensics says she must have put up a good fight."

"That's awful."

"It gets worse."

"How could it?" She pressed fingers to her aching temples and began a slow massage.

Pete rested calloused hands on her nape and applied pressure. "I've always believed in the man's innocence. I admire what he's done for the community. He's made enormous donations to the Boys and Girls Club. He's even paying that kid Malcolm's way through college. This whole thing makes me sick, Skye. But how do you explain Jamie's blood in his vehicle, splattered all over his trunk?"

"What?" It was worse than she thought. Far worse. A potential nightmare in the making. The room reeled around her. She suddenly needed air. "Pete, I spent time with Creed. We were together for the holidays. I don't believe he committed murder."

Smoke spewed from the ghastly cigarette, making her gag.

"That's not going to be a good enough alibi. Jamie's been dead a couple of months. She was probably murdered on the same night of Creed's benefit."

The room came into focus then receded again. She gulped in a breath.

"Hon," Pete said, "everyone in this town knows you and Creed have been spending time together," he chuckled, though there was little mirth to the sound. "Take an extended leave. Consider it a mini-vacation. Go visit your mother in California or, better yet, the Parisian boyfriend who keeps calling. My advice is to get lost till this thing blows over."

Now wasn't the time to explain to Pete that she and Creed no longer existed. They weren't even friends. By right, the story breaking should be hers. It was certainly newsworthy enough to catapult her to the top and to ensure the title of Senior Staff writer was hers. But her editor had already made the decision that she could no longer be objective. Nothing she said would make him think differently.

"Switch me to research," she pleaded. "It's back of the house." Busy work would help validate her existence and keep her from dwelling on how much she hurt.

"And if I did? It still wouldn't be enough. I know you, Skye," Pete said. "You'd find some way to become involved. I'm giving the story to Quinn. If you really want to help Creed, turn your back on this one."

She couldn't. She couldn't just walk away from him—no matter how poorly he'd treated her. "Please, Pete. I need to keep working," she argued, hating the fact her eyes glistened and her nose was moist. She'd always been a strong person. But how much could one person take? "What would it hurt to put me in research? It's not like I would be writing copy."

When he wavered, she moved in for the kill. "You said you were fond of Creed. You kept insisting he was innocent. Please give me this chance. I wouldn't involve myself needlessly. Help me to help him."

Exhaling on his awful cigarette, Pete seemed to contemplate her proposition.

"It's against my better judgment, gal," he eventually said. "But if it's the only way I can keep an eye on you, so be it. You've got to promise me you won't run off and play detective. You're not to be interviewing anyone or hanging around exotic clubs. If that Altarboy surfaces, you're to call the police right away. Do you understand me?"

"Perfectly."

* * *

Creed popped on sunglasses before getting off the plane. He still couldn't shake the feeling that something bad was about to happen to him. Even watching the Steve Martin movie had done nothing to lighten his mood. An eternal funk had settled over him ever since speaking to Rick. It weighted him down even now as he walked briskly through the airport. Where was his assistant? he wondered. Why wasn't he here to meet him?

He'd finally gotten in touch with Lydia just moments before leaving Fort Lauderdale. She'd warned him that he'd made front-page news in some of the more prominent papers. The paparazzi had dredged up ancient tales, painting him as an international playboy with no scruples. His motto was supposedly, "love them and leave them." *"A real lady killer,"* one article even said.

His jacket, complete with identification in the pocket, had been found near the Washington woman's remains. That had spurred the police into action. In his absence they'd obtained a search warrant and swarmed his property. When bloodstains were found in the Jag, his car had been immediately impounded.

Who would do this to him? The only ones with access to his vehicle were Rick and the handyman he employed to wash his car, reputedly Jed's buddy. Several months ago, Rick had lent the Jag to someone. He'd have to ask him who.

Creed claimed his luggage. As he exited the baggage area, he spotted Doreen, flanked by two gray-suited men. Intuition kicked in and he braced himself for the worst. His lawyer approached, eyes silently signaling him to stay quiet. Two men cut her off. One of them wore outdated gold-rimmed aviator glasses. The other sported a crew cut. Mr. Aviator Glasses placed a hand on his shoulder. The other cuffed him.

"You have the right to remain silent," he said, in a practiced monotone. "Anything you say, can, and will be used against you . . ."

Flashbulbs went off. The unthinkable had happened.

Twenty

One week later, the phone rang. Skye tore herself away from the T.V., hit the volume on the remote control, and reluctantly rose to answer.

A man's deep voice boomed, "Hey, girlfriend, you drop off the face of the earth?"

"Who is this?" Her tone was purposefully hostile, designed to turn off whoever it was. She'd been subjected to a series of crank calls lately. They'd escalated after the news of Creed's arrest and subsequent release on bail. None of those people had identified themselves as Altarboy.

"How soon we forget. It's Don Washington."

"Hi, Don." How did he get her number at home? she wondered. She longed to ask, but thought better of it. He'd just lost a sister. She should be more compassionate and tolerant of him. "How are you doing?" she asked, carefully.

"I rely on my Catholic faith to keep me strong. We need to talk."

"Has there been some new development?"

There was something about his answer that bothered her. She dismissed her unease. Most everything

about Don Washington made her wary. He came
with a hidden agenda, she sensed.

"Meet me at the Pony in an hour. I'll tell you then.
Maybe I'll even show you."

"Why can't we discuss whatever it is now?"

The silence on the other end stretched out.

"Kristina Brown's back. I have it on good authority
she'll be at the Pony with her new husband," he said.

Elation took the place of despair. "Kris is in town
with a new husband? Why didn't you say that right
off? I'll meet you in an hour." Skye hung up the
phone.

Creed snapped the paper shut. "Dammit!" His
muttered oath was followed by several creative expletives.

Rick, seated beside Creed in the upstairs living
room, didn't seem particularly perturbed. "Yes?" He
reluctantly pulled himself away from his game of solitaire.

Outside, three feet of snow lay on the ground, but
that didn't stop the reporters. Huddled into sports
utility vehicles, they kept vigil in front of his gates,
snapping photos at the first sign of movement. Each
was bent on out-scooping the other. Each hoped for
a picture of an angry Creed, the goal to vilify him
further.

This obsession with him had escalated from the
moment he'd been arrested. It had become more
intense when he'd posted an exorbitant amount of
bail, and, accompanied by his attorney, managed to
make it home. The mayor and Miguel Santiago were
to be thanked for his release. Both had come for-

ward, vouching for him. He would never be able to repay them, regardless of the fact that now he was a prisoner in his own house—a man with no peace.

"Read this article." Creed tossed the newspaper at Rick.

His assistant effortlessly caught the crumpled mess. He swiftly perused it and raised flashing eyes to meet Creed's. "Who do you think's behind it?"

"Skye Walker, of course."

It bothered him to think of Skye contributing to such an exposé. But some of the information only she could know. Subtly woven in were little bits and pieces of conversation they'd shared.

"The staff writer is Quinn somebody or other."

"Right."

Déjà vu all over again. Shades of Chantal. Although he'd treated Skye poorly and been an utter cad, he'd never considered she would want to get even. Or stoop this low. He'd spouted off about his troubled teenage years, the problems with his father, his irrational attachment to his mother. And it was all there. Skye Walker had violated his trust. He could never forgive her.

"You know what they say about a woman spurned?" Rick added, rattling the newspaper and wiggling both eyebrows, fertilizing the seed he'd planted.

Creed glowered. Rick's flippant attitude was beginning to get on his nerves. What did he know about his and Skye's relationship? *There is no relationship,* he reminded himself. *You killed it.*

The cell phone rang. They exchanged looks. Few people had this number.

Without another word, Rick punched the 'on' button. "Yes?" After a moment, he said, "It's for you," and held out the phone.

"Who is it?"

"You'll want to take it." Rick thrust the receiver into his hand.

Creed grunted something unintelligible into the mouthpiece and glared at him. He heard the feminine giggle on the other end and was afraid to hope.

"Creed, baby cakes, you okay?"

He was on a high again. A smile broke. Kris was back.

"Where are you?" Their's had always been a zany relationship.

"In town. Healthy. Whole. Married."

"Married? Did you say, married?"

"That's right."

"But how? When?"

"How about I give you the details in person?"

Their friendship had spanned more than a decade. From the beginning, they'd been two misfits drawn together. Creative people understood each other. Kristina had always been fiercely proud of her body and determined to do with it what she would. Creed desperately needed to be noticed. He understood why she welcomed the attention of drooling men, why she needed to be put on a pedestal and adored. They were both alike. Both wanted to be loved.

"You've called your family, I hope?" Creed asked.

There was a drawn out pause. He pictured her rolling those huge hazel eyes—eyes that reminded him of Skye's. "Not yet."

"When?"

"Soon. Look, I need space. Time to figure out how to break the news about Jason."

On cue, a man's voice yelled in the background. "You're holding up progress, woman. Tell Creed to meet us at the club and we'll talk."

"How about it? Say you'll meet us at the Pony in an hour."

He was about to refuse. Battling the reporters at the main gate was definitely not worth the effort. Yet the more he thought about Kristina's invitation, the more tempted he became. For a short time, he could get lost in her world of make believe. Few people at the Pony would recognize him if he dressed down.

"Okay."

He hung up, conscious of Rick watching him.

"You meeting Kristina at the Pony?" his assistant asked.

"Yes. Soon as I shower and change. Want to come?"

"Not tonight. I have other plans."

Without further explanation, Rick returned to his game of solitaire.

Skye stepped out of the Bronco, grimacing. The raunchy old pony and its blousy rider brayed from the top of the roof. She caught a lightning flash glimpse at the mannequin's boobs before the halter snapped into place. Deliberately ignoring the inebriated men getting their equilibrium, she slammed the door of the vehicle and strode purposefully across the lot. Minus the blond wig, Micky wouldn't recognize her, she hoped.

Huddled into his black leather jacket, Don waited

under the awning. A red knit hat warmed his head, and a small gold hoop swung from his right ear. He hurried to meet her, then ducked down and kissed her. She cringed.

"Glad you could make it." His hand lingered a moment too long around her waist.

Skye managed a smile and walked alongside him. They passed a bouncer she didn't recognize.

Inside, Don asked, "How's this?" He held out a chair and waited for her to be seated.

"It's fine."

Near them, a copper-colored beauty lap-danced over a stringy-haired, emaciated type. The woman wore stockings, a garter belt, and not much else. The man visibly drooled while tucking dollar bills into her garter.

"The feature," Don said, by way of explanation.

Skye wondered why a woman who looked like that was content to make money this way. The dancer was tall and elegant with an arresting face. Thick mahogany hair swung back and forth, skimming breasts that sported nipple rings. The blond man seemed awed. He appeared ready and willing to devour the stripper, given the least bit of encouragement.

Don ordered them drinks. "I was really sorry to hear about Jamie," Skye said, after the waitress departed.

"Yeah. It's been difficult for us."

His attention diverted to the gyrating woman. Skye touched his hand. Each person coped in their own way, she decided. "You were saying Kris is back?"

Don reluctantly tore his eyes from the bobbing woman. "Yes. She called me."

"What did she say?"

"Not much. Something about needing time to evaluate her life."

The waitress set down the Scotch and club soda they'd ordered. Don tossed back his drink. Skye sipped her soda. She needed a clear head.

"Kristina called looking for Jamie."

"She didn't know?"

"No."

"Did you tell her?"

Don shook his head. "I couldn't bring myself to."

"How about the fact that her family's been worried sick, and that the police are looking for her? We all thought she was dead." Skye knew that her pitch had escalated, yet she was powerless to stop it. Much as she loved Kris, her cousin had always been self-absorbed.

"She's *your* cousin. You tell her. She's heading our way."

The subject of their conversation dragged a handsome beige-complexioned man with her. She waved at them as if they'd seen each other only yesterday. Skye wanted to strangle her for the pain she'd caused. She stood up abruptly, sending the chair toppling.

"Kris."

Within seconds, they were in each others' arms. Laughing. Crying. Babbling. Not caring who saw or heard them.

Don remained at the table, giving them time.

"Skye, when I heard you were back in town, I wanted to contact you so badly," Kris hiccupped between hugs.

"Then why didn't you? It would have saved the family a whole lot of grief."

"Tell her," the same beige-colored man urged. He placed his arms around them, as if to shield them from curious stares.

"I was pregnant when I left. Probably about four months along. Jason and I didn't know if we wanted to marry. I decided to take time out and make my decision. I didn't want the family to know. You know what prudes they are. Jason ran an exotic club and I . . . well . . . I . . ."

"Danced? I know your secret, hon. Now tell me about the baby. Boy or girl? Why did you choose to do this alone?"

"She wasn't alone. She was with me." The man, whose arms encircled them, spoke up. "What Kris can't quite bring herself to say, is we lost our little boy in her seventh month. It was a rough time. We're both still trying to cope."

Skye couldn't imagine their pain. She tried to find words to express her sympathy, but anything she would say might seem inadequate. She stared at them, blinking back tears.

She noticed a man with the same build as Creed, dressed in a baseball cap. The bill was pulled low over his forehead, a newly sprouted moustache and beard making him look menacing. His coat was too large and had seen better days. Creed would never venture out looking like that.

Kristina's gaze followed hers. Her cousin's eyes were riveted on the man. She was off like a shot, shouting, "Creed."

Skye's stomach clenched. She forgot about Don Washington abandoned at the table. She hadn't seen Creed since the day he'd put her on that plane, making it crystal clear he wanted nothing to do with her.

* * *

"You have no idea how happy I am to see you," Kristina said, hugging Creed tightly. "I missed you so much. I missed having your shoulder to lean on."

He held her away from him, giving her the once-over. She looked thinner than he remembered, and seemed to have aged a decade. He put his own worries aside and placed his arms around her. "Honey, not as much as I've missed you."

"That's debatable."

He handed her a handkerchief. She blew her nose.

"Obviously not enough to let me know where you were. I could have helped," he said, putting her away from him.

"Don't start, okay? I've had my share of troubles. So, for that matter have you. I'm sorry about Ona, Creed. In a way I feel responsible. If I hadn't introduced her to exotic dancing, maybe she would still be alive." She stepped back, hazel eyes roaming his face. "Creed, why do I have the feeling someone set you up."

"Let's not talk about me. Where's Jason?" he asked.

"Over there with my cousin."

He looked in the direction she pointed. "Skye Walker's your cousin?"

"She's been my cousin these last twenty-seven years. We've never made a secret of it."

A crude expletive rolled off his tongue. His worst fears were realized. Skye had simply been after a story.

Twenty-one

"Shall we sit?" Kris asked, taking her new husband's arm and leading them to a table with a sign marked, "reserved." "If it's too noisy we'll go into the back. We have a lot of catching up to do."

Skye kept a careful distance from Creed, reluctantly following.

When she caught up with Kris, she said, "Look, maybe tonight's not a good time. Let's talk when it's more private."

She was about to walk away, when Creed grasped her elbow. Despite her resolve not to react, she trembled. It was anger, she decided—anger and outrage causing her to act this way.

"Get your hands off me," she hissed.

"How soon we forget. There was a time when you welcomed my hands all over you."

Though his voice was low, he'd deliberately set out to embarrass her.

"I was a fool."

"Uh, uh." Kris's voice came from somewhere behind them. "Maybe you two need to go off alone and work out your issues."

Both looked at her as if she were crazy.

"I know," Kris confirmed, "I got the goods on you two."

"There is *no* 'you two'," Skye practically shouted.

"Keep your voice down," Creed said, propelling her toward the exit and out to the deserted parking lot. "Kristina was right. We need to talk."

"You look ridiculous," she said, eyeing the get-up he'd chosen as a disguise. "Must be nice to have the kind of money needed to post bail. Most poor slobs would still be in jail, unable to buy their way out."

She wasn't being fair. But she wanted to hurt him as much as he'd hurt her.

"Your true colors are showing," he said, keeping a death grip on her arm.

That stopped her short. She was the aggrieved, the one who'd been cast aside, the person he'd thrown out of his house, shagged and discarded.

"What's that supposed to mean?" she challenged, eyeballing him.

His fingers tightened around her arm. Skye's breathing came in little spurts. It was bitterly cold out, and spiraling smoke flew from their mouths when either spoke. Despite the rough beard, moustache, and ridiculous sunglasses, Creed was still the sexiest man she knew. Deep down, and despite all that had gone bad between them, she loved him and actually believed in his innocence.

"I'm not the one who lied, Skye," Creed said, whipping off his sunglasses.

"No?"

"You were so busy obsessing over the disappearance of Kris, you forgot to mention you were related?"

What could she say? Any excuse would sound lame.

"Why didn't you tell me she was your cousin?" he persisted.

It was out on the table. She had nothing to lose. Skye faced him. "Would that have made a difference?"

His fingertips dug into her forearm. Hostility flashed from his eyes. "I hate liars. In fact, I despise them. You fooled me into thinking you were attracted to me. And idiot that I am, I entertained the thought that you and I had something special. I had mixed feelings about involving myself with a reporter, yet I fell—hook, line, and sinker. I convinced myself you were the real deal."

She heard the agony in his voice and gaped at him. She meant something to him, after all. She thought about the scandal surrounding him, the fact that most believed he was a killer. She thought about her position at the newspaper and the job still waiting in Paris. She thought about Jacques, who'd resurfaced, wanting to marry her. She didn't want Jacques. She wanted the man standing in front of her—moth-eaten winter coat and all.

"Let me explain," Skye began. "Initially, there was no need to tell you Kris was my cousin. I was sent to interview you, not divulge my personal life. I've always believed the less said, the more you find out."

"Spoken like a true reporter."

"That's my job." She bristled. He let go of her arm. Massaging her aching flesh, she waited for him to continue.

Moving into her space, he brought the frigid night air, and his heat, with him. "If I hurt you, I didn't mean to," he said, his mood changing swiftly. "Let's take a ride and sort things out."

"I don't think I should be going any place with you."

"You have no choice." His hand was already on the small of her back, ushering her past the rows of cars, and toward his car parked on the far end of the lane.

They never noticed the person behind them, following.

"Where are we heading?" Skye asked, ignoring her fluttering stomach.

"Home."

"Yours or mine?"

"Yours."

Creed had been driving in circles, trying to decide on a place where they could talk. Nowhere was safe. Any place public would leave them susceptible to pesky reporters infiltrating the town.

"What about my car?"

"Pick it up tomorrow."

Since the Jag had been impounded, he steered the vehicle he'd been forced to rent up the steep mountain roads. He owed Skye an explanation for his erratic behavior. Come hell or high water, she would hear him out. He parked under a willow tree in front of her chalet.

"I'm not inviting you in," Skye said, rudely. She leapt out and slammed the door behind her.

"I'm not sitting in the cold."

She blew on her ungloved hands. "You can freeze in hell for all I care. You're not coming in."

He followed her up the steep incline.

Arms folded, she waited, body blocking the door.

"Come on, Skye, give a little. I drove you home; the least you can do is invite me in."

"Why should I?"

On the other side of the door, her feisty dog, picking up the scent of a stranger, barked like crazy.

"Sssh, Hogan." Skye nudged Creed aside and inserted her key. She squeezed through the minuscule opening. He was right behind her.

The Jack Russell assumed a protective stance in front of his mistress. The dog's annoying barking ceased. He sniffed Creed's ankles. He'd won one battle. Would he win the war?

"I owe you an apology," Creed said, flopping down on her couch and patting the space beside him.

She ignored his invitation. "For?"

"My behavior in Fort Lauderdale. It was unforgivable."

"Unforgivable and uncalled for."

She glared at him. Hazel eyes flashed smoke and fire. Excitement coursed through him. He wanted to kiss that hateful look off her face and have her squirm beneath him.

"I said I was sorry. What can I do to make it up?" He removed his cap, tossed it on the seat, and ran a hand through hair that needed a trim. He'd have to remind Rick to get someone in.

"I'm not in a forgiving mood."

"Sit," he pleaded. "Let's talk this thing through."

She placed a buttock on the arm of the couch, carefully maintaining space between them.

"I didn't mean to hurt you, Skye." Creed captured her hand.

"You did."

The right words wouldn't come. It was important

he not screw up this apology. Their time together was precious and few. He could be sent to jail for a long, long time.

"I couldn't risk involving you in my mess," Creed continued. "I knew there was a possibility I might be arrested."

"So you made a conscious decision to drive me away."

She was talking. Summoning up the nerve, he laid his head in her lap. "I couldn't risk jeopardizing your career."

"Admirable of you. I'm an adult. I make my own decisions."

She was softening, willing to at least listen. Even her distrustful dog, Hogan, sensed it. He flopped down at Creed's feet.

Creed kissed her fabric-covered arm. She still hadn't removed her coat. "Am I forgiven, then?"

The scent of woman and the cold wet taste of wool hung between them.

He tried again. "I can't say I completely trust you, Skye. But I love you, like I've loved no other woman before. Let me spend the night."

His declaration seemed to shake her to the core. Distracted, she stroked his hair before giving a brief nod. He was up like a flash, taking her with him, dancing around the room, holding her close to a heart that pounded loudly. So loudly, he was certain it would bound from his chest and roll across the floor.

She'd agreed to let him spend the night. He would get to hold her, love her. This one night would sustain him through the difficult weeks ahead and through his farce of a hearing. Alleluia, Skye believed in him. The high-powered attorneys he'd retained,

despite their brilliance, could not take the place of
a warm body in his bed, or the fact she trusted him.
She would never betray him.

A vehicle crunched up the graveled driveway.
Hogan went instantly on alert. Skye shot him a bewildered look.

"Are you expecting visitors?" He followed her to
the door as she shook her head.

A car door slammed.

"Wait here," Creed said, stepping in front of her,
and yanking the front door open.

Strobe lights exploded in his face.

Creed balled up his fist. The man grunted an ob-
scenity. In his hurry to escape, his camera and equip-
ment fell.

"Get back inside," Skye screamed. "He's baiting
you. You're falling in with his plans. Please, Creed,
please. Don't let him goad you."

Sanity returned as flashbulbs popped again. The
driver of the van revved his engine. A member of
the T.V. crew called to his pushy colleague to hurry.
A streak of greased lightning almost knocked Creed
over. Hogan attached himself to the reporter's pant
leg. The man yelped.

"Heel, Hogan, heel," Skye shouted.

"Call your dog off. Oooouch!" the reporter
screamed. A string of obscenities followed.

"Hogan, get in here. Now," Creed shouted.

Amazingly enough, the dog listened. Turning tail,
it raced back to join them.

In an effort to find a more comfortable position
on the queen-sized bed, Skye twisted and turned.

Her mind was all over the place and she couldn't fall asleep. Creed snored softly beside her. Wrapping herself in the covers, she sat up. Creed's sleek, naked body lay tantalizingly beside her. His smooth caramel skin drew her like a moth to a flame. She needed to touch him and make sure that the person beside her was real.

Giving in to the urge, she ran a hand across his bare back then moved down to cup his buttocks. He moaned in his sleep. Their love making had been exhilarating. Wonderful. Simply out of this world. All the better for them not having been together in weeks. Now he lay sleeping the sleep of the exhausted. At peace for the moment.

A myriad of thoughts flew through Skye's mind. Marla St. James's decomposed body was found in an Everglades swamp only weeks after Creed returned to town. Tamara Linley's body had shown up on a Florida beach. Ona Di Santis had been discovered in a dumpster in Fort Lauderdale. Now this recent victim, a local girl, was found here, in the woods. Thankfully Kris had turned out to be alive, well, and married. Only Barbara Conway had yet to be accounted for.

Creed had known all of the victims. According to the coroner's report, he would have been in Fort Lauderdale when the women were killed. When Jamie Washington had come home for the weekend, he'd been in Mills Creek. He'd even picked the coed out of an audience and used her as a volunteer on stage. The finger and evidence pointed to him. How then could she be so certain he had nothing to do with the violation of these women, or their subsequent deaths?

Skye crossed her legs Native American style and focused. Maybe someone in Creed's entourage . . . maybe Rick. Rick would have been in Fort Lauderdale at the same time as Creed. He was here with him in the Poconos now. He'd been seen talking to Jamie Washington shortly before her death. And his business relationship with Creed had spanned a short time. How well did Creed even know him?

Creed stirred and muttered something in his sleep. "It's okay, honey," Skye said, rubbing the spot between his shoulder blades and trailing her tongue down his spine. The gold chain was back around his neck. It glinted, contrasting nicely with his skin. Again she noticed the ring hanging on the end of it, and wondered about its significance.

Why would Rick want these women dead, anyway? What in his past would prompt him to commit this massacre? If it was the last thing she did, she meant to find out all about him. She'd pump Creed, then she would do her own investigating. Freddy Newton, her cop buddy, might be able to help. His colleagues could run a background check on Rick Morales, and see if he turned out to be who he said he was.

Meanwhile, she couldn't just lie here. The laptop on her desk beckoned. She crawled out of bed, grabbed the computer, and flipped it on. She meant to check her e-mails and maybe send a message or two. Composing her thoughts, her fingers flew across the keyboard. She hit the "send" button before she could change her mind. She would call in a few favors and get her colleagues down south to help her out.

Afterward, she cursored through her messages. She scanned the sender's name, then the respective subject. None seemed terribly important. She got to the end and immediately became alert. Altarboy had surfaced again.

Twenty-two

"There's a man on the phone for you, sir," Vilma said. "He wouldn't give his name."

Rick reluctantly tore his eyes from the newspapers. "Probably another pain in the butt reporter. Give him to me. I'll handle him."

Creed's housekeeper turned the phone over, but didn't move away.

"Rick Morales," Rick said, in his smooth assistant's voice. Then, after a moment, he said, "Let me check." He whispered to Creed, "Your father," and held the receiver out. "He claims it's important."

Creed sighed but didn't attempt to lower his voice. "I can't imagine what's so important that he'd con the operator into getting my new number and calling me here. He must need money."

Vilma remained rooted to the spot, still staring at both of them. She'd either gone into shock or was feeling as trapped as he. With reporters invading every square inch of the property, they'd been restricted to the house. Tempers were stretched as taut as the proverbial wire. A telltale sign of cabin fever.

By the grace of God, he'd gotten back from Skye's without mishap. Actually, it had more to do with careful planning. He'd left at daybreak, idled the car out of the complex, and taken the back way home. The handful of reporters that kept vigil at the rear of his property were fast asleep when he'd driven by.

Tamping down on his annoyance now, he accepted the phone from Rick, and queried with some trepidation, "What can I do for you, Jed?"

"Is that any way to greet your father?"

The old man's speech was clear—clearer than he'd heard it in a long time. Could it be that he was turning over a new leaf?

"What is it, Jed?"

"I've got stuff to tell you that might help your case. Heard it on good authority."

"Go ahead."

"I don't want to talk on the phone. Meet me at the boardinghouse on South Street in an hour."

Creed pressed the receiver against his ear, balancing the instrument on his shoulder. He pinched the skin between his brows. Meeting Jed meant disguising himself, leaving the house, and dodging reporters. For all he knew, he was probably being led on a goose chase.

"That's not possible," he said, after a long while.

"Make it possible. It's important."

What if the old man really knew something? He'd be shooting himself in the foot not to hear what he had to say. His attorneys had already told him he didn't have a snowball's chance in hell of getting off scot free. Most likely they'd have to plea bargain the case. Not only was his jacket found at the scene, but Jamie Washington's blood had been discovered in his vehicle. The prosecution's case was incredibly strong.

With all this bad press, his reputation had taken a beating. His career was in serious jeopardy. According to Lydia, several of his engagements had already been canceled, and many hotels and resorts were attempting to get out of their contracts. Prominent women's groups were making life miserable with their threats of boycotts.

Rick claimed his fan mail had dwindled to almost nonexistent. What little mail there was held death threats, or were from people voicing negative opinions. Through it all, his ego had been seriously bruised. On the positive side, this nightmare had been a reality check, humbling him.

"Creed, are you there?" His father's voice penetrated.

"I'm here.

Rick was watching. Listening. He seemed to be taking an abnormal interest in the conversation.

"See you in an hour, then?"

"Right."

"Let me borrow your car," Creed said to Rick, the moment he hung up.

Rick's latest vehicle was one in a long chain of rentals. The zippy Sebring convertible was more suitable to Florida than the mountainous Pocono terrain. But his assistant had taken great pleasure in sampling every car Hertz had to offer. Creed doubted the reporters had been able to keep up with the changes. A plus for him. He had a better chance of not being followed if he drove Rick's leased car.

"Sure." Rick tossed him the keys. "You're going out?" He raised an eyebrow.

"Just for a moment."

"Meeting your father?"

"Yes."

"Be careful," Rick warned. "He could be leading you into a trap."

He hadn't thought of that.

When he headed upstairs to change, Rick called after him. "I ran into Kareem the other night. His car was in the shop, so I gave him a ride. He wanted to know how you were doing."

"If Kareem wants to know how I'm doing, all he has to do is call, or stop by the house. He's done neither."

Rick shrugged and returned to his newspaper. "What can I say? People are funny."

For the first time, Creed noticed the newspaper's front page. A wild-eyed photo of himself practically jumped out. The photographer had captured Skye's bewildered face, peering over his shoulder.

Despite all his efforts to protect her identity, he'd still managed to drag her into this mess. He hoped she still had a job.

"So what's the word on Rick Morales?" Skye asked her colleague at the Florida paper.

"He's sort of a mysterious type. Appeared out of nowhere when Tammy Linley went missing. As far as I know, he's dedicated to Creed."

Pamela Townsend took a noisy bite of whatever she was eating. The sound echoed across the long-distance wires.

"Has he always been a personal assistant? It's an odd field for a man."

"Let me think. There was an article written when

he first went to work for Creed. If I find it, I'll call
you."

"I'd appreciate that."

Skye hung up no more knowledgeable than she'd
been before. Now what to do?

Pete entered the room in a cloud of smoke. He
rattled the competition's paper at her. "Didn't I tell
you not to come in today? Your face is plastered all
over the front page of this rag. Reporters are camped
in the parking lot, waiting to take a gander at you."

Despite her heavy heart and seething emotions,
Skye managed to smile at him. "Imagine me making
news instead of writing it."

"It's not funny. I told you to separate yourself from
this thing. Get lost. Disappear. Instead, what do you
do? You go off cohabitating with the subject."

"We aren't living together."

"Tell that to a jury." He chuckled. "Sorry. Poor
choice of words. This excuse for an article puts
Creed at your home some time around one. He
wasn't there for tea at that hour."

"God, Pete, not you, too. Next the hacks will have
us married. They'll do anything to pep up a story."

Pete jabbed a stubby finger at the newspaper article. "A photo's worth a thousand words, my friend.
Go home while you can. Come back when this thing
blows over."

"You're not serious," Skye cried.

"Oh, yeah, I am. I got a paper to run. I love you
to death, but you're killing my business. You're dis-
tracting my employees. They all want to gab. Produc-
tivity's way down."

"What am I supposed to do at home? You know I
can't sit idle."

Using the butt of his cigarette, Pete scratched his head. "As of today, you're officially off payroll. You no longer work for me."

Skye tossed him a startled look. "You're firing me . . ."

"I wouldn't quite say that. You're on hiatus. If you repeat what I'm about to tell you, I'm going to deny it, understand? Call this private eye." He dug a dog-eared card out of his pocket and thrust it at her. "Dustin Goldberg owes me a few favors."

"I don't understand."

"Let me spell it out. Goldberg's well connected. Knows the dirt on most everyone in this town. Creed can well afford his fee. Let him do some digging. He'd unearth any enemies your man might have. Working in conjunction with him would keep you occupied, and out of trouble."

"Is he good?"

"The best."

Skye shot up and threw her arms around Pete. "I owe you big time. I'll never forget this."

Embarrassed, Pete warded off her kiss. His face reddened. "Don't go getting all emotional on me, gal. Just stay safe and watch your back. I got a bad feeling about that Altarboy."

Skye had told him about the red scarf and her latest e-mail message. It had been five words long— *"I tried to warn you."* She'd also gotten in touch with Freddy Newton, her cop friend, and brought him up to speed. He'd promised to check it out and get back to her.

"I'll be careful," she promised.

"Please."

Pete exited in the same cloud of smoke in which he'd arrived.

Creed headed the Sebring past row after row of broken-down houses. The neighborhood was made even more depressing by the bare winter landscaping. Even with the radio on, he could hear the wind whistling through the limbs of naked trees. The dried out boughs reminded him of skeletons' fingers raised to the sky in supplication, pleading for the Lord's help. It would take more than a miracle to save this neighborhood.

A feeling of shame overtook Creed. He had so much, yet he'd allowed his father to live like this. What could he really have done, anyway? Besides pick Jed up and physically move him. After his mother died, he'd offered to pay off the house. Jed had accepted. But the money he'd sent was drunk up or perhaps gambled away. Gambling was another of Jed's nasty vices. In the end, they'd lost the place and its contents. The only tangible memory of his mother was the gold ring he wore on a chain around his neck.

Creed turned onto South Street where a row of Victorians, in various stages of disrepair, had been converted into rooming houses. A handful of pedestrians pulled grocery carts, chock full of bags from the local Mr. Z's. At one time the area had been upscale, housing only the elite. Now it attracted the poor, elderly, and infirm. Forgotten people.

He parked the car in front of the turreted green Victorian Jed had described. At the last minute, he thought to put Rick's leather jacket, tossed across the passenger seat, in the trunk. Why tempt fate?

He pushed a button to pop the rear compartment, grabbed the expensive jacket, and jammed on the felt hat that was part of his disguise. He must look like a pimp, he thought, stepping out of the car. As he was about to toss the coat into the trunk, he spotted a gym bag. The words, *Gold's Gym*, were emblazoned across the front. It made him pause. Why would Rick join a health club when there were state of the art machines available at the house, where he could exercise in private?

Creed picked the tote up by the handles. It was surprisingly light. A tiny splotch of crimson marred the white canvas fabric, looking suspiciously like blood. After debating whether to open the bag, he gave in to his curiosity. He unzippered it and withdrew a pair of gloves and a red silk scarf. He didn't like what he was thinking. Not Rick, his assistant and trusted friend.

"Hey, boy, glad you could make it." Creed turned to see Jed picking his way around the rusting appliances on the scrap of brown lawn. Hastily, he shoved the bag back in place and slammed the trunk.

"What's so important you needed me to come down here?" he said rudely.

"Not hello? Not how are you? Just get to the point." Jed sounded amazingly lucid.

"I'm sorry. Good morning."

"Let's go inside," Jed said, already turning away.

Creed hadn't expected an invitation in. He hesitated, visualizing that the interior of the building must be even more rundown than the outside, and probably a lot less sanitary.

"Okay."

He followed his father up the crumbling concrete steps and onto a sagging porch. Two ancient rocking chairs, devoid of cushions, sat like sentinels. A strong odor of frying fish lingered in the hallways and followed them up the uncarpeted wooden stairs. The place was deserted except for another boarder, who eyed Creed curiously. Mercifully, his father had the good sense not to make introductions.

The small cubicle Jed called home was sparse but surprisingly neat. To make up for the lack of furnishings, framed pictures covered every inch of wall space. Creed averted his eyes from his mother's kindly face beaming down at him. It had been a mistake to come. Being here only made him more maudlin and made his memories crystal clear.

He could almost feel Nina's ample arms around him. He could smell her one indulgence—Chloe—a fragrance she diluted so that it would last longer. He could hear the sound of her sweet voice telling him and Tyler how much she loved them—that one day they would grow up to be somebody. They would do things that she'd only dreamed of.

Tyler was no more. But he'd fulfilled her expectations. He'd risen to the top. She hadn't lived to share in his achievements, or express her pride. He held the man seated at the tiny dinette across from him responsible. Jed's drinking and general irresponsibility had killed his mother. She had died of breast cancer, brought on by stress. There is no link, the rational side of his brain reasoned.

"Well?" Creed sat expectantly, waiting.

"How about I pour us a drink?"

Jed didn't wait for an answer. He was already up,

rummaging through the back of a closet. The boardinghouse probably had a no-alcohol-on-the-premises
policy. To think he'd fooled himself into believing
Jed had given up drinking.

His father slapped two glasses on the table.

"Nothing for me," Creed said, shoving his tumbler
away.

"Too good to drink with me?" Jed baited.

"It's not even noon." Creed bit back the insulting
names he wanted to hurl at his father. Might as well
hear the old man out, then make a speedy retreat.

The bottle Jed poured from had no label. The contents were clear as water. Vodka, Creed surmised,
watching him gulp down the liquid.

"It's like this," Jed said, hiccupping. "Remember
the man we passed in the hallway?"

Creed nodded. He'd kept on his sunglasses and
stared straight ahead. Even so, he'd managed to
catch a glimpse of red-rimmed eyes, broken capillar-
ies, and an enormous gut.

"Doug hangs out at the Pony. Hears a thing or
two."

"Go on."

"He says some guy comes down there most every
night. Always has a wad of money on him. Throws
your name around since it gives him entry to the
dancers. His latest squeeze is this dancer called
Veronique."

Rick. He ignored the sinking feeling in his stomach. "What's the significance of what you're telling
me?"

"Doug says there's something about him that don't
seem right. It's as if he's got it in for you. He's been

shooting off his mouth telling anyone who would listen that you did it."

"Did it?"

"Yes. Killed those girls."

"What's he look like?"

As if he didn't already know.

"I didn't think to ask Doug."

"Do that."

Creed rose, withdrew a handful of bills, and tossed them on the table. "I'm sure you could use this."

A scrap of paper came out with the money. He picked it up and glanced at it. *Try to have a Merry Christmas if you can.* The message was unsigned. He was wearing the same slacks as Christmas Eve. The note had fallen from Skye's gift and he'd pocketed it.

It was clear to him the woman he loved was in danger. No way would he sit idly by and watch a serial killer add her to his list.

Twenty-three

"Did you know Kareem Davis was back in town?" Kris asked, setting her cup on the kitchen counter.

The women were having dinner in Aunt Tonia's kitchen. Mariah, Kris's younger sister, sat hunched over a pile of fashion magazines at a far table.

"Actually, I did. We became reacquainted at a party Creed gave during Thanksgiving. Kareem's mother's not well. He took a leave of absence to put her affairs in order."

Kris made a wry face. "Is that what he told you? The truth is, the slime bucket's been fired. He's been blackballed by every television station in Florida."

"Why?" Skye's interest was piqued. She wondered if Kareem's mother was even sick.

Mariah had lost interest in her magazines and appeared enthralled by their conversation. "Kris, didn't you go out with him a couple of times?" she interjected.

"Much to my regret." She dismissed her sister and lowered her voice. "You were in Paris when the scandal broke. Word probably never got this far north anyway. Kareem's a regular at the gentlemen's clubs in Fort Lauderdale. He has this thing for exotic dancers. He was real tight with a friend of mind. When she dumped him, he went ballistic. Called her all sorts of names. Beat her so badly she was hospitalized. The doctor attending her in the emergency room reported her injuries to the police, but she was scared to press charges."

"Why was that?"

"It would be her word against his. Who would believe a stripper over a prominent sportscaster?"

"Did Kareem ever hit you?"

Kris averted her eyes. "He tried, but the bouncers at the clubs were all friends of mine. I broke up with him before it got bad."

Skye remembered how smooth Kareem was. Yet, she'd found him funny, upbeat, and personable. She'd forgiven him for the dirty prank he'd played eons ago. By telling her the truth, he'd freed her to embark on the most wonderful friendship of her life. A relationship that would be short-circuited if Creed went to jail.

"How did Kareem end up getting fired?"

"Word got out. Several dancers came forward reciting similar experiences. The owner of the club complained to the station manager. The station didn't want a scandal. They gave Kareem a hefty severance package and sent him on his way."

"Really?" Mariah's pouty red lips hung open. She'd crept up behind them.

"Don't go gabbing to your little friends," Kristina hastily added. "Keep your mouth shut."

"You return from wherever you've been, and you start bossing me around," Mariah huffed.

"You've got to promise, tall stuff," Skye interjected. "Nothing you've heard today will be repeated, or the photography shoot I promised is off."

"Fine. I promise. Just stop treating me like a child."

"You are a child. You're my baby," Aunt Tonia said, entering the kitchen and taking a seat next to Mariah. "It's good to have all my girls together."

Aunt Tonia's smile radiated across the room. She hugged Mariah before turning to Kris. "Although I can't say I approve of this one's chosen career."

"Mother, puhleese." Kris pushed back her stool and stood up. "I gotta go. My husband is waiting."

"Looks like dinner's over," Skye said, lightly, picking up her leftover salad and dumping it in the trash. "I'm leaving too. I have an appointment at Eve's."

"I thought you weren't working," Aunt Tonia challenged, eyeing her skeptically.

"I'm not."

"You're not meeting that awful Creed Bennett. Child, you need to separate yourself from that man before you end up massacred like the rest."

"Creed didn't kill anyone," Kristina said, saving Skye from coming to his rescue. "He's been a wonderful friend and confidante. He helped me more times than I care to remember, both emotionally and financially. He's one of the few people I trust with my life."

"You're a poor judge of men," Aunt Tonia mumbled under her breath, loud enough for them to hear. "Now you're hooked up with another winner. Humph. The owner of a strip joint. I must not have raised you right."

Stoney-faced, Kristina pushed past her mother.

"I'm meeting my husband at the club. Skye, you coming?"

Mariah shouted behind them. "Am I the only one whose boyfriend isn't shady?"

They ignored her.

It took two full days before Creed could bring himself to confront Rick. During that time, he'd managed to keep conversation basic. Now he stood in the solarium, drumming his fingers against the back of a chair, waiting for his assistant to show up. The white canvas gym bag had been stowed on the seat in front of him.

All smiles, Rick ambled in. "Hey, guy. How you holding up?"

"Is this yours?" Creed pointed to the bag.

"Can't say it is." Rick tossed a cursory glance at the tote again. He shook his head. "Most definitely not mine. Where did you find it?"

Creed reached over, and using his handkerchief, he picked up the bag by its straps. He removed black leather gloves and held them out. "What about these? Are these yours?"

Rick threw both hands in the air, palms up. "What's this? The third degree?"

"Answer me."

Rick's smile faltered. "I've never seen those gloves in my life."

"What about this?" Creed withdrew the red silk scarf. He waved it at him.

Rick's expression was priceless. Realization finally dawned as to what Creed was getting at. He looked like a man encountering his own ghost. He took a few steps forward and licked his lips. "Creed, you've got to believe me. I know nothing about that bag . . . its contents . . . nothing."

"I found it in your car," Creed said, relentlessly. "In the trunk, to be exact. You were prepared to let me take the rap for you. To go to jail for life. I could get the death penalty. How could you, man? I gave you a chance. Gave you the biggest break of your life. I counted on your loyalty."

Rick had totally lost his composure. His voice wobbled when he spoke. "Creed, you know I've done some things in my life I'm not proud of. But my days of dealing drugs were long over before I met you. I straightened myself out, went back to school, got my degree. I came to you with credentials, man. Credentials and excellent references. I've never hurt a woman in my life. I'm a lover, not a killer."

Creed wanted to believe him but the evidence was strong. He knew he should call his attorneys and get the bag to the police. Too late, he realized his fingerprints were probably all over the tote and its contents. When he'd pulled the bag from the trunk, he'd never expected to find those items inside.

"You were the only one driving that car up until you lent it to me. Isn't that right?" Creed asked.

"That's right. Unless . . ."

"Unless, what?"

"Unless the bag was left behind . . . forgotten maybe."

"By whom?"

"By the real killer. Someone I gave a ride."

Creed wanted desperately to believe him.

* * *

"Dustin Goldberg," the burly redhead said, extending his hand.

"Skye Walker," Skye whispered, shaking the beefy paw the private eye extended. She was taking a big chance coming to Eve's dressed like this. Given the lateness of the hour, she'd counted on the patrons being different.

A handful of people sat at the counter—taxi drivers, night workers, and women who looked like they might sell their bodies for a living. Women dressed like her, who shed coats to reveal too-short skirts and plunging necklines.

"Even in that ash-blonde wig and heavy make up, you're every bit as lovely as Pete said." Dustin eyed Skye appreciatively.

She chose to believe he was not coming on to her. "Thanks. I've heard a lot about you. Shall we find a seat?"

He signaled to the plump blonde in the micro-mini, clutching a bunch of menus. The woman tottered over in too-high vinyl heels.

"Ready to be seated, hon?"

"We're ready." Dustin took Skye's elbow.

They were lucky to get a banquette at the back. After a moment, T.T., the waitress, undulated over. The cones of her padded bra almost poked Skye in the eye. She hoped T.T didn't recognize her in her working-girl get-up.

"I like your color," the waitress said, pointing to Skye's hair.

"Thanks." Skye buried her head in the menu. She had no interest in food; she'd eaten more than her fill at Aunt Tonia's house. She wished Creed would get here soon.

"We'll have some of that coffee now," Dustin ordered. "I'd like you to come back when our friend shows up." He removed a notepad from his pocket and waited for T.T. to pour. After she left, he started in. "Let's begin with what we know. Six women went missing. Four of them turned up dead. One's back in town. Only Barbara Conway, the intern, is unaccounted for."

"Four of the women were definitely exotic dancers," Skye offered. "I suspect Ona Di Santi was as well."

Dustin scribbled. "Must be some connection there. And they were all associated with Creed Bennett in some way. Anyone else you can think of?"

"Probably Rick Morales, Creed's administrative assistant."

"I'll run a background check on him."

"We know the murderer's calling card's a red scarf," Skye added.

"Too bad we can't find out where the scarves were purchased." He tapped his pencil against slightly yellow front teeth. "I suppose the police are already on top of that."

"I have one," Skye said, excitedly.

"One of what?" Dustin shot her a glance that clearly said he thought she'd gone berserk.

"A red scarf. An anonymous somebody sent it to me for Christmas."

Dustin's tapping intensified. "You didn't turn it over to the police?"

"Well, not exactly. But I did call my friend, Freddy Newton. He's a cop. I told him all about it and the strange calls and e-mails I'm getting."

"And *he* said?"

"He'd look into it. I haven't heard back."

"Hmmm. I'll need that scarf," Dustin said, scribbling furiously.

The tip-tap of the plump hostess's heels got their attention. Creed, dressed in urban attire, trailed her. He wore a floor-length leather coat and a cap on backward. A tiny hoop earring circled one lobe. He toted a Tommy Hilfiger bag. His shiny, golden smile, revealed a mouthful of capped teeth. Skye almost giggled. She'd have to ask him later how he'd managed the gold.

"Nice get-up," he said, sliding in next to her. "You must have had a little help." He stared at her chest. Thanks to balled up athletic socks, it didn't quite rival T.T.'s, but came pretty close. On further inspection, she realized he'd used foil to create the illusion of gold teeth. Clever.

She came back with, "You're not in the position to talk."

"Touché. I look like your pimp."

"You said it."

"Children." Dustin looked mildly amused. "Can we get to business?"

Skye made the introductions. "What's in the bag?" she asked. "I know you weren't out shopping."

T.T. returned to pour Creed's coffee and refresh their cups. She blinked a couple of times but didn't acknowledge him.

When she left, Creed withdrew an athletic bag from the interior of the larger one he carried. He set it on the Formica table. "I found this in my assistant's car. Maybe it's best not to look at the contents here."

"You're thinking what I'm thinking."

"You've lost me," Dustin interrupted, "Fill me in."
Creed updated him. Dustin scribbled.

"Could Rick possibly be telling the truth? Did yo
check to see if there was an I.D in the tote?" Sky
asked.

"Yes, I took everything out. There was nothing."

"How about in here?" Skye reached over an
unzippered a tiny front compartment. She withdrev
a white laminated card with red lettering, an
flashed it at them. "Gold's Gym." Turning the car
over, she examined the bar coding at the back. "Jus
what I thought."

Creed picked up on her excitement. "Elucidat
for those slower than you."

"It's a gym pass," Skye cried, her voice rising i
excitement. "A lot of the clubs now have their mem
bers' photos and profiles on computer. It prevent
people from sharing passes. You swipe on entry. You
photo pops up. Presto, you're in."

"I'll take that," the detective said, pocketing th
laminated card, shaped like a key. "Hold on to tha
bag for a while longer. I'm heading down to Gold'
right now and see who owns that pass. Lucky for us
it's open twenty-four hours. Find the owner and it'
likely we've found our man. Now talk to me abou
this Altarboy."

"Hey, I almost forgot," Creed interjected, tossing
a scrap of paper on the table. "This message fel
from Skye's gift at Christmas time. I picked it up and
stuffed it in my pocket. I didn't want to upset her."

Dustin palmed the note.

"Anything else you two want to tell me?"

Skye covered her mouth as realization dawned. "I
know who Altarboy is."

"Who?" both men said in unison.

"Don Washington. After Jamie's body was discovered, I asked him how he was holding up. He told me he was relying on his Catholic faith to get him through. I bet you anything he's been an altar boy."

"Could well be. That doesn't mean he's our man. What would be his motive for killing his sister?"

Skye shrugged. "Beats me."

Creed placed his arm around her shoulders. "The man is deranged. Crazy people don't discriminate."

After Dustin left them, Creed and Skye faced each other in the parking lot.

"It's late," Skye yawned.

"Is that a hint?"

"Not really. But there's no place to go. We can't go to my house. Reporters are camped on my front lawn, and your home is out of the question."

Creed chuckled. "No after-hours club would have us dressed like this. We'd be arrested."

"Unless we went to the Pony," Skye said. "No one would recognize us there, and if they did, I doubt they'd care. We might even run into Don Washington. Rick's also been known to show up, and Kareem has this thing for exotic dancers. Who knows? We might run into the entire crew."

"Kareem—a stripper groupie?"

"I take it you're surprised." Skye told him what she'd heard, adding, "This might be a good time to do some sleuthing. All three men are suspect. Rick's been in the same places you've been. The bag was found in his car. Don keeps showing up in the most unexpected places. And from the very beginning he's acted strange, as if he had something on his mind. Kareem's hot for exotic dancers. He has a history of dating them and beating them up. He's also been in the same geographic area as you."

"An interesting cast of characters. If we go, we'll have to take your car."

Skye threw him a quizzical look. "What happened to yours? How did you get here?"

"Taxi. Rick needed the Sebring and I didn't want to chance using my rental car. I walked to the main road and had the driver pick me up at a superette."

Skye shifted gears and backed the car out of the lot. "Just think, depending on what Dustin finds tomorrow, your life might return to normal again."

"My life will never be the same," he said, taking her hand. "Unless, of course, you're in it."

The emotion in his voice surprised her. Their gazes held. She had a devil of a time looking away.

"I mean that," he said, curling his fingers around hers.

"Do you?"

"With all my heart."

No point in getting her hopes up. Short of a miracle, Creed Bennett might never go free.

Twenty-four

"Mind if I join you?"

Skye looked up from the drink she hadn't touched. A man from the bar beamed down at her.

"Sorry," she said, "I'm expecting someone."

"No problem." He ambled off.

By agreement, she and Creed had split up. That way they had a better chance of working the room and checking out the patrons. The stripper on stage, dressed in full western gear, undulated her hips. The crowd hooted and cheered. A second glance revealed her to be Veronique, the friendly woman Skye had met weeks ago when she'd come to audition.

Tonight, the nipples of Veronique's more than sizable attributes were covered by metallic stars. When she humped and bucked, salivating men stuffed crisp dollar bills into her g-string. She rewarded them with a smile and a jiggle.

Skye spotted Don at a table up front. He was seated with two men. She prayed he didn't recognize her. She looked over to see Creed on the far side of the room, lounging against the wall. His presence reassured her. He had an eye on the customers, scoping them out. But his body language said he was acutely aware of where she sat.

Even in his ridiculous disguise, he was by far the best-looking man in the place. She knew she was being partial, but another cursory glance at the patrons didn't change her mind. Across the bar, she met Rick's unrelenting gaze. He winked. She smiled back, raising her glass of soda in bold salute. He needed no further invitation. He was up like a shot, heading her way.

"Hey, good looking," he said, taking the stool next to hers.

She kept the smile fixed on her face but said nothing.

"You alone?"

"Not anymore."

"That's good." He moved his seat closer. "So what's a good looking girl like you doing in a place like this?"

She didn't trust herself to answer.

The third drink served to dull his anxiety. The missing bag no longer seemed important. It would turn up, he was sure. He found the music soothing, and the smell of warm bodies and cold beer was enticing. Through narrowed eyes he watched the dancer on stage gyrate. The stars on her nipples rotated in circles. Her flat stomach and shapely legs drew him to the pot of gold between her thighs. He let his fantasies take him away. Sex with her wouldn't be as good as with Skye Walker, he thought. Skye, of the cool demeanor, but underneath it all an alley cat. He'd seen her with Creed Bennett. Her Parisian chic didn't fool him one bit.

It would be up to him to unleash those uninhibited emotions. He would make her scream, then beg him for mercy. Then he would leave her a panting, writhing mess under him. And when she called out his name, he'd tie the red scarf around her neck, silencing her forever. Until then, he'd make do with the woman across the bar—alone and obviously looking.

"Come here often?"

Skye smiled but didn't acknowledge the comment. Kareem Davis sidled in to the vacant seat beside her. He ignored Rick.

"How come I haven't seen you around?" he persisted, while stirring his drink with his index finger.

"I'm new in town."

"You must be a dancer."

"I am."

"I'm the welcome wagon." He trailed the tip of his frigid finger against her inner arm. "The best man to show you around. How about we start with a tour of the parking lot?"

Next to her, Rick cleared his throat. Skye ignored him. There was no mistaking Kareem's invitation. She ventured a look in Creed's direction. He stood on alert, ready to come to her rescue at the slightest hint of trouble. Her savior. Her love.

In all their wildest imaginings, they'd never thought she'd be faced with this. Two of the suspects were hemming her in on both sides. The decision as to what to do was in her hands. Skye picked up her purse. "Okay. Let's go."

As she turned to leave, she ran smack into Don.

"Excuse me," he said, reaching his hands out to steady her.

Jed took a healthy swig of vodka from the bottle then passed it to Doug. They'd driven to the Pony in his friend's beat up K car, and parked in a remote section of the lot. If they worked up a good buzz, there would be no need to spend much money inside. Maybe they would buy one drink.

"I say that Mike Tyson's the best darn fighter this century's seen." Doug hiccupped.

"That young pup doesn't hold a candle to those old boys. Mohammed's my man. Though Foreman was a force to be reckoned with."

"Aaah, what do you know?" Doug swiped a mottled fist across his mouth before taking another swallow. "You ready?"

"In a minute."

They were the only people in the parking lot from what they could tell. A brisk January breeze whistled through the barren trees. The muted sound of music and raucous cheering came from inside the building. Two figures appeared out of nowhere, heading their way.

Instinctively, Jed placed a finger to his lips. "Sssssh." Both men, conditioned to becoming invisible, hunkered down. A man and a woman passed the car and proceeded down the row.

"Looks like that hooker's got herself a John," Doug whispered.

Jed squinted into the night, the poor lighting in the lot making it difficult to see. The woman's white-blonde wig stood out against her darker complexion. Something about the way she walked sparked a memory. A larger, furtive figure dodged and bobbed amongst the parked vehicles.

"See that," Jed whispered. "Something's up. Call me paranoid, but since that Washington girl's been murdered, this town just ain't safe anymore."

"According to dem pigs, your son's what's making it unsafe."

"Them pigs are wrong."

Appearing to be in deep negotiation, the hooker and her John faced each other. The man following them crouched down.

"Uh oh. I got a not-so-good feeling about this." Doug gulped another mouthful of vodka and passed the bottle to Jed.

Jed screwed the cap on tight. "So do I. If something bad goes down, you and I are the only witnesses." He nudged his buddy. "Get out of the car. We're moving in closer."

"How about you and I take a ride?"

What would be Skye's answer? Creed wondered. His thigh muscles ached from hunkering down behind the late-model Camry. He resolved to start working out again. An easy promise to keep with a long jail sentence ahead.

"Not a good idea," Skye said.

Creed released the breath he didn't realize he'd been holding.

"Why not?" Her companion's tone was low. Oily. Persuasive. "What will it take?"

Creed heard the sound of clothing rustling—of bills being counted.

"Fifty. One hundred. A couple of hundred. Name your price."

"I beg your pardon."

"Let's not play games."

Skye's companion's voice rose. Creed wanted to deck him. How dare he insult his woman? He reminded himself it was important to stay hidden. The scene needed to be played out.

"Don't blow it, Skye," he muttered.

"What's with you?" Skye's companion said. "You knew why you were coming out here."

"Did I?"

"Okay, you're holding out for a hotel—a bed. Is that it?"

"That's it."

Creed thudded his palm against his forehead. If Skye got into that car there wasn't much he could do to protect her.

"So how long have you been dancing?" he asked.

His change of mood threw Skye. "A couple of years."

"Like it?"

"Love it."

"My mother used to strip," he said, taking her by the elbow and moving her toward a black Porsche.

"Awesome. Your mother was an exotic dancer?"

He stopped dead in his tracks. Skye stumbled against him. "There's nothing awesome about a whore."

"If you feel that way, why are you at the Pony?"

He took the car keys from his pants pocket. "It keeps me on track. Reminds me of my mission. Get in."

His face had hardened, and even in the dim parking lot, she saw the steel glinting from his eyes. Skye refused to budge.

"You wanted a bed. I'm getting you a bed," he said.

She couldn't think quickly enough. His face loomed above hers. Ugly. Uncompromising. Menacing.

"Get in, bitch."

"Hey, who are you calling names?"

His hand moved so fast, she didn't see it coming. The blow from his balled fist threw her off balance. She bit down. The metallic taste of rust filled her mouth. Too frightened to utter a sound, she stared at him. God spare her, where was Creed?

He had her by the nape now, tugging on her hair. The wig fell off. A gust of wind rolled it across the pavement. Their eyes met for one electric moment, recognition dawning. He threw back his head and roared, maniacal laughter echoing across the lot.

"Skye Walker? I couldn't have planned it better myself."

"Run, Skye. Run." A man's voice came out of the blackness.

In those few important seconds, she processed the information. Kareem Davis, demented animal that he was, had killed those women.

Adrenaline finally kicked in. Arms pumping, she screamed and charged blindly across the lot.

* * *

A fist connected with flesh. Creed was up like a shot, the need to stay hidden forgotten.

High heels skidded across the pavement. A string of profanities and the thud-thud of chasing feet galvanized him to action. The commotion came from some place to the left of him. Discarding the heavy coat weighing him down, Creed charged toward the sounds.

Men seemed to be running from all angles, chasing after the couple. Two of them blew by him like the wind; another came from the opposite direction. A voice he recognized as Rick's shouted, "Call the police."

"I got the son of a bitch," another man's voice wheezed.

Bodies hit pavement.

"Hey, Doug, help me."

"I'm right here, man."

Creed lost his glasses in his race to assist. A tangle of clothing he recognized as people lay sprawled on the ground. Kareem writhed under two men. A string of colorful oaths poured from his lips. Creed recognized one of the men seated atop him. It was his father.

Don held a hysterical Skye in his arms. He soothed her. "I'm Altarboy, Skye," Creed heard him say. "I suspected Kareem and tried warning you."

Rick assisted the struggling men holding Kareem down. Dustin Goldberg was among them. All the while, people poured out of the building, coming at him from everywhere.

The sound of sirens pierced the night.

The urge to kill Kareem was strong and real. An even more powerful urge came over him. He had

the most incredible desire to hold Skye in his arms
and make sure she wasn't hurt. If that animal had
done permanent damage to her face, or her psyche,
he'd pay. He made his way over to where Skye stood
clinging to Don.

"Skye," he said.

He didn't think she'd heard him.

"Don't bother her," Don Washington snapped.

He remembered he was still partially disguised. He
plucked the gold foil from his teeth and tossed his
cap on the ground.

"Creed Bennett, is that you?"

"Creed," Skye repeated, as if awakening. She
pushed out of Don's arms.

Suddenly they were holding each other. Swaying.
Crying. Oblivious to the police, who'd come on the
scene. Of screaming people. Of his father asking
them if they were okay. Of the fact that it had begun
to snow.

He couldn't let Skye Walker get away. He needed
her as much as the air he breathed. God, how he
needed her.

Twenty-five

Serial Killer is Magician's Best Friend

Kareem Davis, a prominent sportscaster, has confessed to killing five women. Barbara Conway's body has yet to be found. Kareem's own mother moonlighted as an exotic dancer. A sexual deviant, Kareem could only be aroused when establishing a position of dominance . . .

"Looks like we've been scooped again," Skye said, snapping the tabloid shut.

Pete made an ugly sound. "Psssh. Who pays attention to that rag?"

"Plenty of people. Two out of three shoppers read it in line at the grocery stores."

"But do they buy it?"

Skye threw the paper in the backseat while Pete parked. He stubbed out his cigarette, came around, and opened her door.

"Do I look okay?" she asked. "No lipstick on my teeth? Smudge on my nose."

"Except for your swollen cheek, you're perfect." He kissed her on the forehead.

Skye touched the tender spot where Kareem had punched her. It smarted. To celebrate Creed's innocence, a select group of people had been invited to the mayor's home for cocktails and dinner.

Skye was suddenly nervous. Neither had seen each other since last night, when real conversation was impossible. After Kareem's arrest, a doctor had tended her face, and she'd been given a sedative. Answering the police's relentless questions had taken hours. Then she'd spent the rest of the time dodging her reporter buddies. Somehow in that process, she'd managed to lose Creed. Later, a stranger had taken her to Aunt Tonia's home, where she'd slept the sleep of the exhausted.

Pete squeezed her shoulder. Reality intruded. "I'll be needing your decision soon. I can't hold the position indefinitely."

"I know."

He'd offered her a Senior Staff Writer's job, a post that only a few months ago she'd coveted. Now she wasn't sure. Mills Creek would never hold the same memories for her. Creed, now that his name was clear, would most likely head off for parts unknown. What did she really have left in this town? Her own mother had moved. Le Monde and Paris were starting to look better and better. Even Jacques.

"I've been waiting for you to arrive."

Oblivious to the cold, Creed was standing on the front steps, dressed in a double-breasted jacket and beige turtleneck. His presence made her quiver.

"How do you feel?" he asked, taking the steps two at a time.

When he was next to her, gentle fingers explored

her face, touching the spot where she hurt, soothing her pain.

Pete cleared his throat. "I'll leave you two love-birds alone." He sidled past them.

"We need to talk," Creed said, putting his arms around her.

"Maybe I should tell the mayor not to hold dinner," Pete muttered, shuffling off.

"Creed's the guest of honor," Skye stalled.

Creed tugged her in the direction of his Jaguar that had been released back to him. "My father's inside holding court, entertaining everyone with stories about me. We had a long talk last evening. Eventually, we'll work our issues out. Rick will cover for me."

They drove around several snowy blocks in silence. The tips of Creed's fingers drummed the steering wheel.

"What is it you wanted to say to me?" Skye eventually asked.

Creed pulled the car up to the curb. They came full stop in front of a huge colonial home. Smoke billowed from the brick chimney.

"I'm leaving Mills Creek, Skye," Creed said.

Surprise, surprise. She'd known the moment his name was cleared he'd be off on a gig, signed up for another international engagement, their brief interlude forgotten.

"I'll miss you," she said, quietly. "It's been fun."

"You're coming with me."

"What?"

He'd lost his mind. She couldn't just pick up and run off with him. She had a career to think of—a life.

"You can freelance, can't you?" he said, answering her unspoken question. "Or you can join forces with Lydia and take care of P.R. If that isn't challenging enough, we can collaborate on a book. I've agreed to write an autobiography. Just think, Skye, we would live in some of the most exotic parts of the world. We could make Fort Lauderdale our home base. Paris, if you prefer . . ."

"Hold it." She brought a finger to his lips, silencing him. "You've forgotten something."

"I did, didn't I?"

"I'm waiting."

He took her in his arms and kissed her soundly. "I love you, Skye Walker," he said, when they finally came up for air. "I want you in my life."

He tugged at the chain around his neck and removed the ring that served as a pendant. "This was my mother's. I'd planned on giving it to you at Christmas. It's my way of saying that I love you more than life itself. Will it do until I can get you a real engagement ring?"

"It'll do." Arguments forgotten, Skye held out her left hand. In a daze, she watched him slip the ring on.

Magic wasn't the only thing that had brought them together. It seemed it was fate.

Dear Reader:

I can hardly believe that ILLUSIONS OF LOVE is my fourth Arabesque/BET book. It seems that only yesterday I penned REMEMBRANCE . . . my first Arabesque novel.

ILLUSIONS OF LOVE came to me on a chilly November morning as I lay recuperating from surgery in my little Pocono's home. As I looked out my window at the mountains, I realized that Skye and Creed's story needed to be told. I also felt compelled to share my love for an area that still remains virtually unspoiled. If you have never experienced the Poconos, I urge you to visit.

I want to thank you from the bottom of my heart for all the wonderful and uplifting mail you have sent me. You have touched my heart in so many ways. I hope I have touched yours. May we enjoy many more years of pleasure together.

My next BET novel will feature a heroine you have met before. Stay tuned for Onika (Niki) Hamilton's story. She was described in REMEMBRANCE as the half-African/half-British combination of classic good looks and subtle sex appeal.

Please keep your letters and e-mails coming. You can e-mail me at:

Mkinggambl@aol.com

Or you may write me at:
P.O. Box 25143, Tamarac, FL. 33310.

My Web site can be viewed at:
http:\\Marciaking-Gamble.webjump.com

Warm Wishes
Marcia King-Gamble

ABOUT THE AUTHOR

This cruise line executive was born on the island of St. Vincent in the West Indies. At age fifteen she relocated to the United States and has since lived in New York, New Jersey and Seattle. Currently, she resides in Florida. Marcia is a graduate of Elmira College and holds a degree in psychology and theater.

A world traveler, Marcia has spent time in the Far East and in exotic parts like Saudi Arabia and Istanbul. She has a menagerie of animals, four cats and three dogs to be exact. She destresses by attending step aerobics classes and is on the board of the Society Of Consumer Affairs Professionals In Business.

Marcia is the Author of four novels and a novella.

Coming in June from
Arabesque Books . . .

NEVER TOO LATE FOR LOVE
by Monica Jackson
    1-58314-107-3 $5.99US/$7.99CAN
When Tiffany Eastman is offered a temporary place to stay by her friend'
father, successful surgeon Jason Cates, she never bargains on the sudden
attraction that puts her heart at risk. As the simmering passion between
them grows, the two must confront their fears in order to find true love . .

MAD ABOUT YOU by Roberta Gayle
    1-58314-108-1 $5.99US/$7.99CAN
Public relations whiz Regina Primm jumps at the chance to work with
one of Hollywood's biggest stars, Langston Downs. But their sudden
fiery desire can hide their deepest insecurities for only so long and the
couple learns that they must trust in each other to find a real life happy
ending.

WHAT THE HEART KNOWS by Geri Guillaume
    1-58314-109-X $5.99US/$7.99CAN
When Meleah Harmon starts receiving threats, she turns to her sexy new
employee, Tarrant Cole, for help. But Tarrant is convinced that Meleah
wronged his family and is working only to gather evidence against her
Now both must deal with emotions they weren't expecting . . . in order
to develop a love to claim forever.

TRUST IN LOVE by Mildred Riley
    1-58314-110-3 $5.99US/$7.99CAN
Against her better judgement, attorney Aleesa Haskins falls hard for pilot
Miles Kittridge. In her heart, Aleesa knows they can be happy together
but there's a part of her life that remains a mystery—and, until she solves
it, she must rely on the forces of fate to decide if their love is true.

Please Use the Coupon on the Next Page to Order

Enjoy the Summer With Arabesque Books